To: Betty

THE GUARDIANS

Catherine Elizabeth Bell

27 May 2014

CATHERIN ELIZABET BELLE

THE GUARDIANS

TATE PUBLISHING
AND ENTERPRISES, LLC

The Guardians

Published by Tate Publishing & Enterprises, LLC
127 E. Trade Center Terrace | Mustang, Oklahoma 73064 USA
1.888.361.9473 | www.tatepublishing.com

Tate Publishing is committed to excellence in the publishing industry. The company reflects the philosophy established by the founders, based on Psalm 68:11,
"The Lord gave the word and great was the company of those who published it."

Cover design by Nino Carlo Suico
Interior design by Richell Balansag

Published in the United States of America

ISBN: 978-1-63367-613-8
1. Fiction / Action & Adventure
2. Fiction / Native American & Aboriginal
15.06.03

This book is dedicated to Carter L. Davis, my friend, my mentor, and my colleague. Carter challenges me to broaden my knowledge, stretch my imagination, and reach for greater achievements in the literary world.

And to my spouse of many years who accepts my penchant for acting or reacting contrary to established rules of society; rules "they" say are the norm, yet no one can authenticate who "they" are or how "they" came to be the authority of social conduct—a conduct that stifles individuality.

While the Jicarilla lore is authentic, the history real, and the location in Northern New Mexico exists, the story and characters are fictitious, a figment of my wild imagination.

Contents

Prologue 9

Part 1: Life on the Res 13
Part 2: Attempted Murder 159
Part 3: Apache Medicine Woman 232
Part 4: Gozhish [Time Passes] 255
Part 5: It's a Good Day to Die 263
Part 6: The Request 266
Part 7: The Angelic Flight 279

Epilogue 283
Reference Materials 287
Glossary of Jicarilla Apache Terms 289

Prologue

She had done it; her life's dream had come true, and now all she desired was coming to pass. She had just come out of the Jicarilla Apache Reservation Council meeting and now held in her hand a ninety-nine-year lease agreement for a small section of land on their reservation.

She stood there, feeling the heat from the blazing sun beat down on her and the dry desert wind blowing across the land, whipping through her hair like wind in the trees. A peace had come over her as she looked over the vast expanse of desert and the huge rock mesas that dotted the land. The peace in her slowly turned to exhilaration as a smile spread across her face.

It had been a long hard struggle for her to reach this point, achieving this dream of hers. Her husband had died after forty years of marriage, leaving her alone and her income reduced by half. Now all she had left was her writing and her dream.

The hardest part was convincing the head of the council, the Respected Elder who was aged and wise due to his long life in the desert. They traveled together to an obscure canyon located in a remote area southeast of La Jara Lake. This is where Sarah hoped she could have her new home, isolated from all contact with the white man's world.

While they were in the canyon, Sarah knew that the chances were slim of getting her dream, unless a miracle happened to change the Respected Elder's mind. Then it happened—a lone eagle landed on a rocky out crop about fifteen feet above their heads and looked at them. The Respected Elder froze in his tracks as he watched the eagle, who in turn stared directly into his eyes. Moments seemed like hours as they watched each other, and time seemed to stand still. Then as the eagle spread its great wings and screamed toward the heavens, a lone feather fell out of its wing and drifted down, landing at Sarah's feet. The Respected Elder spoke not a word as he slowly bent over, picking up the feather.

As he held it in his gnarled hand, his mind drifted back to a time when he sat around the fires listening to the Apache lore of the great medicine men of the Jicarilla Apache. How his parents and the grandfathers rebelled against living on the reservation enslaved by the white man's chief in that faraway place called Washington. Recalling in his lifetime, the Apache had been denied the use of Peyote in their rituals and the use of the eagle feather in their healing and ceremonials. In spite of adopting the White Eyes ways in aspects of the Apache life, his aged soul still adheres to the customs of old. Remembering words of the wise elders now in the happy hunting ground, he speaks, "What you wish shall be. The Great Spirit has spoken, and no one shall go against it."

With that, they left. All that she had hoped for was provided. The council provided the building contractors to build the home in the cliff face, which would be entirely self-contained and have all she needed to live and take care of the needs of her animals. But there was a price to pay for what she wanted.

She would be considered a ghost by the Apache tribe and have no contact with any of them, unless it was deemed necessary by the tribal elders or by special request from her. The other part of the price that Sarah would have to pay was that she could never bring another white person to her location, nor tell them where she was. In short, she would disappear from the world and only be known or alive on paper.

Her only contact with the outside world would be through her computer and nothing else as long as she lived there.

This was all done with the help of her lawyer and friend John Wheaton who lived out of state. He handled the liquidation of her assets as well as covered her trail so no one could find her. To the rest of the world, she no longer existed.

She would hold true to her word as the council requested. Sarah was at peace with her animals and her solitude.

PART I

LIFE ON THE RES

The early morning sun glistens through the tinted glass, warming the cave. Sipping her morning coffee, Sarah enjoys the quiet solitude of the Jicarilla. Listening to the rustle of the breeze through the pines and the lonesome howl of the coyote echoing across the sagebrush covered valley warms Sarah's heart.

Saddling Mesquite, she rides toward the wooded countryside. As Rusty bounces along beside the pair, they turn to the south. The crisp morning air and bright sunshine are a sharp contrast. Sarah languishes in the quiet of the canyon, catching a glimpse now and then of a rabbit searching for food and the feisty roadrunner darting through the sagebrush. Off in the distance, a trail of dust drifts up toward the pale blue sky. The old red truck with wooden sideboards is Pete Tsosie heading toward the country store near Dulce; she chats with Pete at the feed store on occasion. Mesquite ambles on through the fragrant sagebrush as the dust from the old truck fades in the distance.

The clear blue sky blends in elegant contrast to the dark skyline, meshing with the blur of dark green pines. High overhead, the bald eagle soars through the air, searching for his morning meal. Watching his path through the sky, Sarah remembers the lone eagle feather that proclaimed her destiny to the Respected Elder and pays tribute to the magnificent bird. The aroma of the olive green pines seeps through, and tiny nodules peek out along the limbs of the scrub oak heralding an early spring. The warm sun, the intoxicating scent of pine, and the soaring eagle cast a web of mystery around Sarah as she rides across the valley.

Time has no significance in her isolated world and passes unnoticed as the trio of friends travel south. The noisy call of the crows snaps Sarah from her daydream. Looking at the terrain, Sarah realizes she has traveled further south than usual. Turning Mesquite toward home, she watches Rusty dart here and there, chasing a squirrel up a tree and flittering after the native roadrunner. No human sound intrudes on the quiet solitude of the canyon she calls home.

Reaching the barn, Sarah unsaddles Mesquite, rubbing him down until his coat shines with a mahogany luster. Dumping a serving of oats in the feed bin, she puts down fresh hay in the corral. Mesquite nuzzles Sarah's hand, looking for the juicy red apple that he's come to expect. She quickly produces the sweet treat. Mesquite devours it then bumps her between the shoulders, begging for a second. Sarah turns, wrapping her arms around his neck, burying her face in his long, silky mane. Oh, how she loves this beautiful stud.

Rusty lays at the edge of the barn enjoying the warm sun. Calling him to her side, they proceed into the sanctity of her cave. The hands on the clock point to high noon, and she wonders where the time goes.

Always thrilled by the expanse of her canyon and the wind rushing through her hair, she feels sated with life. Rusty's adoring eyes touch Sarah's heart with warmth, pulling at the very depth of her heart. She sits on the hardwood floor, stroking his black and gold coat as he gently lays his muzzle in her lap. Time stands still as the two friends lavish in the warmth of their love. Soon, Sarah rises to heat a cup of coffee left from breakfast then runs warm water in a bowl of dry dog food. While Rusty chows down, she fixes herself a small salad and a hot bowl of soup. Sitting in the kitchen, Sarah feels a transcending peace in the echoing silence.

The glistening sun sends a kaleidoscope of rays dancing across the vast room. Sitting at her computer totally engrossed in her current manuscript, time, that ever elusive commodity, drifts away. As the light dims in the cave, Sarah slips out of the world of rhyme and meter. Stretching her stiff muscles, she thinks about her aging body and quickly puts these unsettling thoughts out of her mind as she begins her evening chores.

The radiant sun dips behind the western ridge as Sarah puts Mesquite in the barn for the night while Rusty enjoys his evening run. When he returns, she punches the magical button that closes out the world. No light escapes the shield, and no evidence of human occupation exists to the naked eye. She is secure in the mountain cave as sounds of the lonesome coyote calling for his mate echo through the dark canyon.

Entering through the garage, Sarah ambles into the main area of the house, Rusty right on her heels. She pauses to turn on the stereo, filling the room with strains of Irish music where earlier peace had echoed through the silence. He sits nuzzling her hand with his cold, wet nose waiting patiently for his mistress to offer him jerky. As she stands to go to the kitchen, he dances excitedly around her, just barely containing himself so he does not trip her. The antics of Rusty, her beloved companion, bring laughter resounding through the mountain cave. Rustling the bag, holding his treats, she dips her hand into the beloved jerky while Rusty sits at her feet, his black eyes glittering with excitement and his tail pounding a delightful rhythm in high anticipation. As the final stains of an Irish ballad comes to a finale, Sarah goes to her computer; the *tap*, *tap*, *tap* of the keys echo through the night.

Days pass into years and still Sarah is content in her isolation. She rides Mesquite almost every morning with Rusty bounding along, always managing to stay out from under Mesquites hoofs. To no one in particular, the words are spoken, "Oh, I how I love this life, riding through the wild mountain country, the solitude, the quiet. There is no place on earth like the Res." Every rattlesnake trail, every arroyo is familiar to them.

And true to the Apache's word, they keep their distance. Sarah's only contact with the Apache is when she goes into town to buy supplies, which she usually orders in quantities to last several months. Only once in the past five years has she met with the Jicarilla Apache Council. Sarah asked the council for permission to set up a firing range near her cave, promising that it is only to practice her skill with her pistol—no rifles.

Permission was granted, conditional to their review at the end of sixty days. Sarah chose a small recess in the mountain just north and a little to the west of her cave. The council approved the location. When they made their unannounced visit, they found that she had picked up all her brass. Finding no visible trace of the area being used for target practice, they granted the use of said location to continue in conjunction with the ninety-nine-year lease. That was some three years back.

Sarah spies Apaches passing close enough to see but never coming near enough for her to hail them or for them to greet her, but for either to do so would be a violation of her lease. She greets numerous Apaches at the trading post. Most of the conversations have been in relationship to her order of supplies or the weather. Once or twice an Apache woman chats with Sarah, but that is rare. She enjoys these times, as she has great respect for the tribe.

No one associates the blue jean–clad gun-toting white woman seen riding through the countryside with the polished author, Louise O'Hara. That is the way Sarah wants it. Her agent, Joan, handles the sale of her books. From time to time, Louise agrees to a book signing. But on those rare occasions, she drives into Farmington where she rents a room as the eccentric woman Sarah O'Hara from nowhere. Waiting for her will be a note from her attorney, with a key to another room rented for Louise O'Hara. Sarah keeps her two worlds separated. It really is not that difficult; she likes the mystery of being the eccentric white woman, Sarah O'Hara, and Louise O'Hara is someone she pretends to be on occasion. Even the Jicarilla Apache Council Members do not know about her writing or her dual personality. When she returns from her book signing, Louise goes to her reserved room, checks out, and has her luggage sent to the airport where the contents are shipped to her attorney's address. Then Sarah, the eccentric white woman, checks out and drives back to her cave deep inside the Jicarilla Reservation. Ah, the subterfuge appeals as much to her as the solitude.

She returns late one afternoon after being gone for over a week. As always, when she has been gone for a while Mesquite is restless, neighing as she pulls the SUV into the garage. Rusty bounds all around, knocking Sarah to the ground where she sits as he bathes her face in loving, excited, slurping tongue licks. Not taking time to unload the truck, she saddles Mesquite, and the three friends ride out for some much-needed exercise and solitude. Traveling their usual route through the trees along the eastern slope, Sarah notices deer tracks, a doe and her fawn. Further on, as they head toward the west, she sees tracks where a rattler has slithered through the soft soil. All these signs of nature are a welcome sight after a week in the hustle and bustle of city life.

They ride several miles when, whispering on the wind, Sarah hears a small voice calling. Halting Mesquite, she strains to hear the voice. Riding into the wind, she pushes forward her ears, cocked, intently listening. Not another sound does she hear as she continues her search. Just as she is about to turn back, the sun sinks below the horizon, casting gray shadows across the land; she reaches an escarpment. Looking over the edge, she can barely discern a small boy lying in a heap at the bottom of the cliff. Sarah's heart throbs with dread as she ties her rope to Mesquite's saddle horn; cautiously slipping over the edge, Mesquite holds her weight. Reaching the small boy, she finds him unconscious and unresponsive. Running her hands over his wee body, she discovers his leg is broken. Looking around the area for small limbs, she pulls off her coat and removes her shirt tears it in strips, which she uses to bind branches into a makeshift splint. Replacing her coat, she ties the rope around her waist, and picking up the small Apache boy, she throws him across her shoulder, calling to Mesquite, "Back, back, boy."

Slowly, Mesquite backs away from the edge of the cliff, pulling Sarah slowly up the rugged face of the arroyo dirt and rocks, pounding her head and shoulders as she tries to protect the boy and hang on to the rope. Time is endless as Sarah's arms strain with the weight of the small boy. Tightening her grip on the lariat, she calls encouraging words to her horse, "Back, Mesquite. Back, boy!"

At last, Sarah reaches the edge of the cliff where she immediately feels Rusty's fangs dig into her coat as he drags her all the way on top. Sarah lies very still on the ground as the cool desert air dries the perspiration; night slips across the land. Taking deep breaths, she calms the racing of her pulse, then slowly, so as not to hurt the young lad, she crawls a safe distance from the edge of the escarpment. He groans with the movement but doesn't awaken. Sarah gathers the rope, attaching it to her saddle, then lays the small boy across the saddle while she mounts. He is shivering, but is it from the night air or shock? She wonders how long he has lain at the foot of the cliff. Opening her coat, she wraps him inside it for warmth.

Knowing Mesquite will go home, Sarah gives him his head and concentrates on holding the lad so as not to jostle him too much with the movement. Nearing the cave, the boy begins to squirm but soon relaxes as she whispers softly to him. Reaching the corral, she lays the lad on a bale of hay, hastily unsaddling Mesquite.

Carrying the boy into the kitchen, she bathes his face and wraps him in several blankets then places him on the floor in the back of the SUV. Not intending to be left, Rusty leaps upon the passenger seat beside her. Feeling the urgency, Sarah shifts gears in the vehicle and pulls out on the poor semblance of a road. The pot-holed road between the cave and NM 537 is a treacherous journey, and she hears the boy groan with each bump of the SUV. Driving cautiously, she watches lightning dance across the ebony night. The ten miles to NM 537 seem endless; she is anxious to reach the blacktop where the road is smoother and she can make better time.

Not a drop of moisture has fallen. "Guess the lightning heralds the usual dry electrical storm familiar to the arid land, Rusty."

Time hangs suspended as she drives the lonely stretch of highway. Relief lightens her heart when she sees the clinic up ahead on the right. Parking at the emergency entrance, she quickly picks up the small boy, rushing into the clinic. Taking him from her, the staff rushes him into an examining room as Sarah explains to them how she found the boy.

The Apache police are called, and Sarah once again tells of finding the boy below the twenty-foot drop, of splinting his leg, scaling the cliff, and the drive into Dulce.

The police asks, "Who is he?'

Sarah replies, "I don't know." She explains who she is and suggests the tribal police call the President of the Council. Sarah never once left the clinic. With an outward calm she does not feel, she watches the clock on the wall that never moves as she waits for the doctor's evaluation.

As he rounds the corner of the hall, Sarah is instantly on her feet. "The boy has regained consciousness, his leg is broken in two places, and he has a mild concussion." He could see the anxiety in her face. "You did well with your makeshift splint, preventing further damage to his leg. He should heal nicely."

Giving an audible sigh, "Thank you, Doctor. That is very good news."

"The young boy told us who he is and how he fell. However, he remembers nothing about his rescue or the trip to town. The boy was following a trail like his grandfather told him the warriors did a long time ago. The boy lost his way and began to run. He stumbled and fell over the cliff."

As the doctor concludes his remarks, the tribal police and the council president arrive. "Chief, the young lad is Jimmy Begay. Will you notify his family? I would like to keep him overnight. He took a nasty fall."

Now that the boy is safe, Sarah wonders how this will affect her lease. The tribal council president is not too happy with her having brought the boy to the clinic. His black eyes glisten with reproach.

Glancing at him, she straightens her shoulders, and in a firm authoritative voice, she asks, "Should I have left him there to die?"

Watching his reaction to her words, she wonders how he and the officer will explain about the "off limits, nonexisting, eccentric white woman" rescuing their son? And according to the doctors saved his life? She knows it will take time to notify the family of little Jimmy's accident and how he arrived at the clinic. Like so many of the families on the Jicarilla, they have no phone.

As the police are preparing to drive out to Begay's *kogha* (home), Sarah asks, "Please, I would like to go with the officer."

With the charcoal orbs glowing in a stoic face, the council president reluctantly agrees. The officer opens the backdoor of the cruiser for Sarah to climb in. Sliding into the driver's seat, the officer pulls out of the parking lot and heads for the Begays. The family lives about ten miles southwest of Sarah's cave as the crow flies, but by the roads, it is closer to twenty miles. Once they turn off NM 537, the ride is dusty and rough. There is no designated road, just a sheep trail. Sitting in the back of the cruiser is worse than sitting atop a bucking horse, and Sarah is jostled in spite of the restrain of the seatbelt.

It has been five hours since Sarah hauled the young boy from the bottom of the cliff. And it's well past midnight when they reach the *kogha* of the Begays. The Apache president tells Sarah, "Remain in the vehicle. Do not leave the car unless you are invited to do so."

After the officer relates to Jimmy's parents the events of the night, they ask to speak with Sarah. Inviting Sarah to share the hospitality of their *kogha*, coffee is served along with mutton stew and fry bread. It pleases Sarah that she is treated with respect for the rescue of their young son.

This is her first contact with anyone other than the council or people at the trading post since she was granted residence on the reservation six years ago. She feels privileged, and at the same time, a deep concern creeps through her body, chilling her to the bone.

As the three intruders leave the *kogha* of the Begay family, they are preparing to drive into Dulce to see their son. The trip back is a silent one; Sarah does not ask how the rescue of the small boy will affect her lease. She is too tired to deal with that right now. The officer follows the rattle trap of an old truck the Begays are driving, pulling in behind them at the clinic.

Upon arriving back at the clinic, the officer opens the door for Sarah to exit. Before she can enter the emergency room to check on the boy, the council President says, "Sarah leave, you have done enough."

She is not surprised, but it hurts nonetheless. *Guess I'm not as tough as I think I am.* His cryptic response is tempered by the kind words of the officer: "Thank you, ma'am, for bringing the boy to the clinic. He is going to be okay."

Sarah nods, and turning, she climbs into the cab of her truck. Tired from her exertion but relieved that the boy is safe, she feels a deep concern about her future. With her mind a whirlwind of thoughts of the night's events and the ramification, she sits staring into the pitch-black night.

Rusty nuzzles her hand, breaking the reverie holding her immobile. He can contain himself not one minute more as he greets his mistress with yips and slobbery kisses. She absently responds to his greeting. As he settles down beside her, she turns on the ignition and pulls on to the highway. The return trip is interrupted only by the flashes of dry lightning piercing the ebony night. Only the owls and mountain lions are prowling the Res in the early morning hours. Sarah has time to think on the drive, and her thoughts again wander back to the events of the evening. Like the lightning bolt shattering the sky, it dawns on her that she could not have heard the boy calling; he was unconscious! What did she hear? Who did she hear?

Parking the vehicle in the garage, she climbs wearily out of it. Sitting on a bale of hay, she listens to early morning sounds of the waking mountain—the call of the meadowlark, the owl's ruffling feathers as he settles himself after his nocturnal ramblings, and the roadrunner darting here and there in search of his first meal of the day.

Rusty chases through the area a couple of times then comes back to sit near Sarah as she begins her ritual of brushing Mesquite. She gives him a bucket of oats, puts down fresh hay, and offers him a juicy red apple. Her horse cared for, Sarah takes Rusty into the kitchen. Putting on a pot of coffee, she places a heaping bowl of food down for him. Sarah pours a cup of the fresh brew and walks slowly to the bathroom where she runs a tub full of hot water sweetened with lavender bath oil. Stripping off the dirty, sweat-soaked clothing, she slips silently into the waiting luxury. Sarah sips the hot liquid as exhaustion creeps through her aged body. All she can think of is sleep. Rising from the cooling water, she slowly dries her aching body then massages a lavender-rich fragrance into her aging skin. Slipping into a silvery silk gown, she crawls into the warm, satin covers of her king-sized bed. Hardly aware when Rusty crawls up next to her, she drifts into an exhausted sleep. Her last thoughts are of the call for help that a small unconscious boy could not have made.

Awakening about mid-afternoon, laughter escapes her as she feels the warm nuzzle of Rusty's nose to her bare back. This prompts a romp with his favorite toy, which just happens to be a Christmas bell given to him many seasons ago. As Sarah tosses the bell across the room, Rusty has it in his mouth in one strong leap and, with gusto, lays it in her lap as she sits cross-legged on the bed, repeating the play until both are tired. She wraps her arms filled with love around her beautiful German shepherd—her friend, her confidante, her protector.

Rising, Sarah selects silk long johns, faded jeans and shirt, and her time-worn boots. It is mid-September, fall is in the air, and a blanket of snow will soon cover the beautiful forest of piñon, juniper, and aspen.

Quickly, Sarah runs a brush through her hair that hangs to her waist, twisting it on top of her head. She is hungry, and no wonder, since she has not eaten since noon yesterday when she stopped at Aztec for lunch. Sarah opts for a tuna salad with fresh grapes and hot cranberry tea. She had better enjoy the fresh fruits and vegetables, because when the snow comes, her trips to Dulce will be less frequent. She will be eating basic staples: pintos and tortillas alternating with frozen dinners from the large walk-in freezer housed in the pantry.

Enjoying her breakfast, she wonders if little Jimmy Begay has been allowed to go home, or how his leg is healing? Fat chance of her getting answers to her questions, but she can't stop wondering. The Apache is off limits to her—that is part of the agreement in the lease. Sarah doesn't miss companionship; she has Rusty and Mesquite and isn't one to trust the human species. Past experiences have taught her none are worthy of her trust. However, she does have a special interest in the young Apache boy, Jimmy Begay.

Rested, her hunger sated, it's time to unload the truck she left packed from her trip to Farmington. Carrying her two small bags into the bedroom, she gradually sorts the contents to be put away, then she returns for non-perishables she purchased while in the city: coffee, tea, stone ground flour, pintos, lard, and bags of dog food for Rusty and sacks of oats for Mesquite—things she will need to make the winter. In a day or two, she will drive to Dulce, stop by the feed store, and order hay delivered.

With everything put away, it is time to exercise Mesquite. Sarah grabs her old coat as she goes out the side door to the barn. Mesquite meets her halfway across the corral, anxious for one of their sojourns into the valley and forest. While Sarah saddles Mesquite, Rusty bounces back and forth, urging her to hurry, but in spite of his urging, it's late afternoon before they ride out. Their ride will be a short one; she rarely rides past the dusk of evening shadows. Turning back toward her mountain, there is a straight stretch of valley where she gives Mesquite his head; he prances about waiting for Sarah to drop the reins over the saddle horn. As she leans forward, whispering words of endearment in his ear, he smoothly races through the sagebrush, riding like the wind for only a brief time. Oh, how refreshing to feel the wind glide over Mesquite's mane, flipping her hair against her head as rider and horse bask in the joy of being free. Sarah sits tall in the saddle; Mesquite's signal to slow to a cooling pace, and she smiles, enjoying nature's paintbrush coating the corral in hues of purple as the final rays of the sun drop behind the western slope.

With the sun behind the ridge, a chill spreads across the canyon; yes, the air smells of winter. It will soon drift across the northern border onto the Jicarilla. Rusty scatters doves and sage hens as he cuts through the arroyo, stopping at the corral fence just as Sarah reaches down from her perch on Mesquite to open the gate.

Laughing at his antics, Sarah unsaddles Mesquite, rubbing him until his coat shines like diamonds in the dim light of the evening shadows. Slipping him his sweet red apple, she checks to see that his supply of hay and water is ample as she passes through the barn into the kitchen with Rusty right on her heels.

Grabbing a cup of stale coffee, popping it into the microwave, she moves to her time-worn oak desk, glances through the tinted windows at the first flakes of snow, and sighs with contentment. *Freedom is a state of mind, but it is even more cherished when you can behold it in life, not just a place you go in your thoughts.*

"Ah, I must get to work. My agent is pushing for an early deadline." Sarah works into the wee hours of the morning. Rusty, laying in front of the electric logs, curls up on the old braided rug he favors. As Sarah slowly pushes her chair away from the computer, Rusty opens his eyes following her every move, sees her stretch, and starts toward the kitchen. *Ah, his signal to race me to the cabinet that holds his treats.*

Laughing, she reaches for the glass canister filled with his treats. Yipping encouragement, letting his joy erupt, he tries without success to sit patiently at her feet. Smiling at his pleasure, she hands him his treat and picks up a snack bar and a small glass of chocolate soy milk for herself. Returning to the big room, she turns the stereo on as she makes her way to her favorite recliner. With Rusty lying at her feet, Sarah relaxes to the quiet refrains of classical music, dozing only to be awakened by the silence in the room as the CD comes to an end.

Crossing to the bedroom, she notices the clock on the wall reads 2:00 am. If she is to get back into a routine, which is very important both in self-discipline for her writing and for the care of her animals, she will have to set the alarm. Undressing in the early hours, she takes a quick bath and slips into a soft, billowy silk gown, the one indulgence in her hermit's life. Just before she slips between the lavender sheets, Sarah sets the alarm for 7:00 am. Drifting into the land of slumber, her thoughts are about how peaceful life is when a man is not a part of it.

When the clock sings its morning tune, Sarah realizes that, once again, Rusty has slept beside her. Reaching over, she gives him a big hug, resolving to share her bed with the devoted friend. Sarah dresses as usual in her silk long johns, followed by her usual jeans and boots. Putting the coffee on, she fills Rusty's food and water bowls. Sitting at the table, she eats a breakfast bar as coffee perfumes the air.

Filling a thermos with the rich elixir, she and Rusty head to the barn. Mesquite whinnies his greeting, trotting to Sarah, nuzzling her shoulder.

Cinching the saddle tight, she adds a few first-aid supplies to the saddlebags. Planning to visit the place where she rescued little Jimmy, she rides through the winding arroyos, occasionally seeing a rabbit dart through the sagebrush or a roadrunner stretching his long legs as he runs across the valley seeking his breakfast. She searches the azure skies for the beautiful bald eagle that is always soaring aloft when she is out riding. She admires the stately bird and is grateful for the deposit of his beautiful feather at her feet, which seemed to be the deciding point for the Respected Elder who reported the incident to the council. Rusty runs along the edge of the arroyo, keeping pace with Mesquite. Climbing out of the arroyo, Sarah admires the wide expanse of the valley floor heading southeast where she found the boy. It isn't long before she stands at the exact location where she dropped down the steep embankment to rescue the young boy. However, in her exploration, she discovers that just fifty yards further east is an easy access to where the boy lay, not visible in the late evening shadows. *Oh well, that's life.* Sarah feels good that at seventy-five, she still has the stamina the rescue demanded of her.

Sarah watches the speck of dust rising from a vehicle headed toward the paved road leading to Dulce. Immediately turning Mesquite around, she calls Rusty to her and turns towards home. She is too happy here on the Jicarilla, she will not jeopardize her world. She and her trusted companions amble through the pines and scrub oaks savoring the aroma of the fresh scent and the sagebrush permeating the breeze, whispering across the prairie.

Mesquite is anxious to run and prances restlessly; Sarah lays the reins over the saddle horn and, bending forward, whispers in his ear. He leaps forward…he is free sailing like the wind. Sarah, with her arms around his neck, feels as free as Mesquite. This is her lifelong dream come true. She is free—really truly free.

Off to the west, a lone rider watches the trio race toward the corral. He stands under a pine with the reins of his pinto tied loosely to the limb behind him. Crushing the stub of his cigar between his fingers, he places it in his shirt pocket. She is back in her cave, this eccentric white woman. He wonders about her, where is she from and why she chose to live the life of a recluse here on the Jicarilla.

Sarah, Mesquite, and Rusty race into the corral, glad to be home, unaware of being observed. Their race with the wind leaves Sarah totally entranced. She hums as she brushes Mesquite's coat to a lustrous mahogany. A laugh escapes her mouth as Mesquite uses his head, pushing her toward the apple bin; she will not be surprised if one of these days he just helps himself.

Sarah's laughter rings through the corral and into the night, but Rusty is not the only one to take note of his mistress's joy. The lone observer standing hidden in the pines wonders about her gaiety. He stands silent as the last refrains echo through the canyon. Patting his horse on the nose, he steps wearily into the saddle; he must be getting back before he is missed. In the cool night air, a chill singes his body as a sadness creeps across his weather-beaten face, and he shakes his head no. *There is no one to miss me. No one has missed me in years. What am I thinking?*

Sarah and Rusty playfully enter the kitchen, a warm and cozy room very inviting after the brisk air of the great outdoors. She stands silently in front of the cabinet wondering why she is not hungry. *Could it be that I am sated with the joy of living.* Putting coffee on, she walks into the quiet solitude of the big room. Sitting down in front of the cyber monster, she calls up her voicemail account. There is one from John telling her that her things have arrived and have been put away for the next trip. Sarah tells him that things went well, but she is glad to be back in her cave. She instructs him to tell her agent, Joan, that she will accept no personal appearances until late May of next year. Sarah thanks John, as she always does, for the protection of her privacy. Before sending the e-mail, she sits remembering how upset John had been at her proposal; insisting that she would be miserable alone, frozen in for months on end, with no physical contact of people. She smiles; after these six glorious years, John has come to understand that Sarah chose the perfect life for her. She has never been happier, and without hesitating, she clicks "Send." There is an e-mail from her agent, which she ignores.

Sarah returns to the kitchen for a steaming cup of coffee, noticing that the clock on the wall shows almost noon. Scrambling eggs with green chili and cheese, she folds the mixture in a warmed tortilla. She always makes a little extra, as Rusty, a good New Mexican, loves his breakfast burritos and stands drooling. When Sarah sits down at the table, he is right at her elbow. Leaning over, she gives him a big hug and places his plate on the floor. Silence is broken only by the noise of the two friends sharing a hearty lunch.

With the kitchen cleaned up and everything put away, it is a good time to order the hay that will be needed for the months ahead. When she picks up the keys to the truck, Rusty darts out the door and ignores her standing at the open tailgate sitting by the passenger side door waiting. "Oh, Rusty, you are so spoiled. Here you go, boy." A familiar game between the two friends brings joyous laughter echoing across the dale. *This kind of love and devotion comes only from four-legged friends.*

The trip to Dulce is a dusty bumpy ride until they reach NM 537. Arriving at the trading post early afternoon, she orders the hay making arrangements for it to be delivered the following week. She picks up a few things at the market to add to her pantry: fresh apples for Mesquite chocolate for her, and jerky for Rusty along with extra coffee. With the snow beginning to pile up on the northern slopes, travel will be more difficult than its worth.

As Sarah stops at the gas station to fill the tanks of her truck, she is unaware that she is being watched. A lone figure stands across the street near his SUV, chewing on a cigar that has gone out. With his hat pulled low over his eyes, he watches the eccentric white woman, who looks more like a small man. He again wonders why she is here, why she coerced the council to give her a ninety-nine-year lease. But most of all, he wonders why she consents to being isolated from her own people as well as the Apaches. Jake knew of her rescue of Jimmy Begay. He heard how she asks the council president, "Was I supposed to leave the boy to die?"

She has guts—maybe that is what festers my curiosity? Whatever it is, I cannot get this unusual woman out of my mind. He watches her drive away and head south on 537 toward her self-imposed isolation. Jake knows the rules set down by the council: no contact with the white woman.

What in the world am I thinking? This woman is off limits literally to everyone. Why? Jake shakes his head as he climbs into his SUV and heads out on patrol.

Jake is a retired member of the Apache Detective Bureau. Now and again, he fills in for off-duty officers or helps out when extra officers are needed. As a courtesy, the chief always offers Jake one of the SUV cruisers; this is one of those times. Jake lives alone and has been since his wife of many years died of cancer several years back. When he isn't helping out on patrol, Jake has a *kogha* over near La Jara Lake, some five miles northwest of the white woman's location.

Unknown to Jake, she is being observed by another member of the tribe. Behind the local tavern unseen, a lone Apache observes the movements of the woman the council allowed on the Res. He finishes relieving himself, zips his pants, and enters the tavern through the back door.

"What took you so long?"

He is a little tipsy from all the alcohol he's consumed. Slurring his words, he said, "That white woman the council allowed on the Res just left the feed store."

Joe looks up from his beer. "Why do you care? Taint nothing to us."

"Don't you think it's strange they let this weird woman live undisturbed on the Res. The council never did that before?"

"She has kept the rules set down by the council, what more does she need to do?"

Pausing to take a slug of whiskey, he continues, "Ah, shit, man, what if she hasn't?"

This conversation is making Joe a little uncomfortable. Hesitating, he asks, "What the hell are you talking about, Pete?"

The bartender watches the two in their loud conversation and wonders why the white woman is the subject of discussion—she bothers no one. *What is their interest in the woman? They seem to be all heated up over something. Well, I'm paid to tend bar, aint' none of my business. Let the council deal with them.*

Sarah arrives back at her cave unaware of the interest her presence sparked in Dulce today. The sun is just setting over the mountains, leaving her just enough time to unload the things she bought in town before the sky turns to ebony.

Off in the distance, wolves prowl and coyotes howl in the night. She has seen tracks of the bears foraging in preparation for their hibernation this winter. *Ah yes, then there is the mountain lion whose tracks I see trailing a deer.* All these creatures that live in her forest are special to her and while she enjoys then, putting Mesquite in the barn will keep the predators from the temptation of feasting on him.

At last, it is time to relax and enjoy the solitude of her cave. Sarah rinses out the residue of coffee from that morning and puts on a fresh pot. Rusty has plenty of food and water as they have been out and about most of the day. While the coffee is brewing, she goes to the living area and turns on the stereo; tonight, she chooses a CD featuring cowboy songs. Sarah relaxes in her recliner, lost in the sounds of the old west. When the CD finishes an hour or so later, Sarah saunters into the kitchen and pours a cup of coffee. Rusty, not about to let her forget, races to the counter where he knows the jar holding his favorite treats sits. Sarah nuzzles the back of his neck with kisses of her own as she reaches for the canister containing Rusty's beloved jerky. Picking up a meal bar to go with her coffee, she returns to the living area being sure to bring extra jerky or Rusty. Sarah puts in another CD of the cowboy songs and relaxes in her recliner.

This is the perfect time of day; her companions are safe within the confines of the cave. Her remote hideaway is obscure from the outside world. Perhaps for the first time in her life, Sarah feels safe; here on the Jicarilla, she has found peace.

Sarah knows she must stay active or her seventy-plus years will catch up with her. *Gosh, it is hard to believe that I acknowledged my birthday just a few days ago.* She had stopped celebrating in 2001 when the twin towers were destroyed along with portions of the Pentagon and the plane that went down in Pennsylvania. Sarah could find no joy in the many useless deaths of 9/11. Terrorists have taken many innocent lives around the world as governments try unsuccessfully to stop the slaughter. Maybe that's why she feels so safe here in the mountains of the Jicarilla. There's nothing here of interest, not even enough population to make an attack notable.

The CD finishes, and the silence reminds Sarah that she needs to clean up after the day out on the range. Putting her coffee cup away and setting up for morning, she heads for the bedroom with Rusty right behind her. Luxuriating in the warm sudsy water, she washes her hair, blowing it dry then snuggles between the warm sheets. Tonight, Rusty does not wait until Sarah is asleep; he crawls on the bed, lying down beside her and their eyes meet in a clear understanding of how it is to be.

Drifting into a peaceful sleep, she is unaware of the old Apache who is bound to protect her or of the storm brewing from the malcontent of a lone Apache fostered by resentment.

Rising, Sarah feels an unease that has become an unfamiliar emotion since she moved to the Res. Silently she says a prayer of gratitude for her obscure cave deep in the heart of the Jicarilla. Here no one reminds her of what she already knows that she is out of sync with the world. *Papa always told me it was okay to be different, but he didn't tell me that being different left one on the outside and at odds with the rest of civilization.* Here in her own private world, there is no one to tell her that she is crazy or paranoid because she has a different perspective from most of the human species. Rusty and Mesquite thinks she's wonderful. She never abuses them, cusses them, or neglects them. They are the best friends she will ever have.

With that thought bringing a smile to her time-worn face, she dresses and heads for the kitchen with Rusty right on her heels. It is just after seven as Sarah opens her cave to the outside world, and she sees the night has brought a couple of inches fresh snow. *Is it really the first of October? Why only yesterday the sagebrush was in bloom.* The smell of coffee seeps through the air, tempting her taste buds. "I'm glad I dressed warm for our ride today, Rusty."

The sun is just creeping over the eastern slopes but hasn't had time to warm the canyon. Finishing her coffee, she goes to the barn where she saddles Mesquite. The smell of winter is in the air…fresh and crisp bespeaking of the long cold days ahead. Today's ride is uneventful as most of them are; nothing is stirring. Rusty didn't even scare up a rabbit. Sure indication there's a change in the weather when even the animals have enough sense to stay safe in their burrows. Their pleasant ride ends in Mesquite's race across their half mile of fairly smooth ground. A special closeness has developed between horse and rider; one watching the fluid motion of the two would swear they are one.

Back at the cave, Sarah unsaddles Mesquite; brushing him after their long ride in the country is a true labor of love. As she puts the currycomb away, he pushes her with his nose demanding a special treat—a savory red apple. His antics always bring a smile to her lips and a glow to her face.

Sarah fills his oat bin, placing fresh hay out and filling the water trough while Rusty makes his usual surveillance. Then he scurries to reach the kitchen door arriving just as Sarah does. The invigorating brisk temperatures whet her appetite, and she sets about preparing lunch; thawing a package of ground beef, adding diced onions, green chili, oregano, and garlic powder she soon has a burrito topped with shredded cheddar cheese—a meal fit for a queen. Like a good ruler of her domain, Rusty also shares in the bounty.

While Sarah cleans up the kitchen, Rusty languishes by the door, licking his whiskers. As soon as she picks up a full cup of the warm elixir she so enjoys and heads for her computer, Rusty bounds ahead, lying down on his rug by the fireplace as she sits down at her desk. Several days have elapsed since she checked her messages, and as she boots up her computer, there is a note from John asking how she is fairing with the weather. She smiles; he knows she is all right, but after all these years, he still asks. He notified her agent, Joan, that she will not be doing any outside activity. There's an inquiry from Joan about the progress of Sarah's manuscript. She e-mails him that it is progressing nicely and should be ready for editing in another two or three months. There are no other correspondence of any significance, just advertisements, which she deletes.

Switching to her manuscript, she becomes so engrossed in her work the afternoon flies by. When she finally stands to stretch, she has been sitting at the computer over four hours. She needs a break, and a diet soda would taste good about now.

Rusty moves from his favorite rug in front of the electric logs bounding ahead of Sarah straight for the cabinet where his jerky is kept. After the game of "round and round the table we go," Sarah gives Rusty his treat and pushes the button plunging the outside world into obscurity.

Across the way behind a stand of scrub oak, Jake, an old Apache, stands watching the white woman as she closes down her cave. He learned to track from his grandfather and to remain hidden during his observations, skills honed during his years as a detective. He does not know why he feels the need to look after this crazy, eccentric white woman.

Jake sniffs the air. *There is a big storm coming. I might have to forego my surveillance. What the hell am I doing? I don't even know this woman. Why do I feel the urge to protect her? Or do I?* Jake climbs back on his old pinto, making his way toward La Jara Lake and his *kogha* on the other side of NM 537; he looks forward to a hot cup of coffee and the warmth of his fireplace.

Unaware of the interest of the lone rider sitting in the trees, Sarah goes back to her manuscript working until the world outside is hidden in ebony shades of night. Arching her back to relieve the stiffness from sitting hours in one position, she is pleased with the afternoon's work. Ah, yes, it merits some quiet relaxation with the soothing sounds of classical music. As the music drifts through the warm, cozy cave, Sarah moves to her recliner. "Rusty, it has been a productive day." Peace at last has come to a life that has known mostly strife and sorrow. With Rusty curled at her feet, she slips into a restful slumber a false sense of being safe surrounds her.

It is early morning when Sarah wakes to the gentle nuzzle of Rusty's cold nose as he reminds her that he needs to go outdoors. "Well, Rusty, that old recliner sure was comfy."

She sees the golden orb rising to warm the brisk morning as she opens the cave to the outside world. While Rusty makes his early morning rounds, Sarah brews a pot. When he returns to the cave, she takes her coffee into the bathroom where she strips while filling the tub with hot water and lavender-scented bubble bath. Slipping slowly into the satiny moisture basking in the relaxation of the intoxicating scent, Sarah sips her coffee.

"Ah, what will we do today, Rusty? The barn and corral needs mucking out. By the time the manure is scattered a mile from the cave, it will be warm enough for our morning excursion." Sarah dresses in layers of warm clothes; as she works, she will need to shed some of them. Raking and cleaning the barn and corral she loads the manure onto the trailer. With the ground frozen, the truck never hesitates to pull the trailer through the new snow. *The pasture will be greener in the spring because of the fertilizer with more sagebrush and mountain flowers dotting the landscape.*

Upon her return to the cave, Sarah saddles Mesquite and grabs beef jerky and a canteen of water; she is as anxious as Mesquite to be out in the valley. The ground is covered with a good six inches of fresh snow; Sarah's first concern is for Mesquite and loops the reins on the saddle horn as he has an uncanny knack of missing gopher holes. Nothing deters Rusty in his jaunt about the countryside with his boundless energy; he is tireless. This morning, they stick to the tree line riding in a southerly direction; less snow will have accumulated under the trees than in the open valley.

Having ridden for about an hour, Sarah sees evidence of another rider, a small pony. The tracks are headed in the direction of the cliff where she found Jimmy Begay. *Is it the boy? If so, why is he wandering around in the cold weather and on a school day?* Sarah wonders if he is playing hooky. She parallels the tracks for about twenty minutes when it dawns on Sarah this would be Thanksgiving break for the kids. *Ah, the boy is on holiday, so he is not playing hooky.* For some reason, Sarah feels relief. *Why do I care? He is nothing to me. That is not true. I cannot rescue someone and not have an interest in their welfare. Maybe it is the mother's instinct, or even animal instinct.*

As the distance narrows between her and the other rider, Sarah sees that it is the small boy. Slowing her pace, she veers slightly west to avoid contact, watching the boy ride to the place where he had taken his tumble. She decides to keep an eye on him until he starts to retrace his tracks. When he dismounts to look around, Sarah sees that his leg has healed. *That's good.*

Soon he mounts his pony and heads back the way he came. When he has gone about a half mile, he sees the tracks paralleling his trail. There is one rider and a set of smaller tracks that seem to be together. *It could be a wolf, but wolves usually run in packs and this is one lone set beside a horse.* He wonders about the rider. He has not seen anyone else on his rides. Then he remembers the strange white woman who is more man than woman that rescued him. *Could she be the one came upon my trail?* It is getting late, he must return home. *Another day when I get an earlier start, I will follow the trail to see where it leads.*

When Sarah is satisfied that the young boy is returning the way he came, she turns Mesquite back north, praying the boy will reach home safely. They have been riding for over an hour and have an hour's ride back to the cave. As they ride north, she watches the buildup of clouds. "Mesquite, we can expect a heavy snowfall within the next twenty-four hours. That will mean good crops of grass and feed in the spring and summer. And plenty of berries for the birds, with lots of pinons for the squirrels—it will be a good year."

Snowflakes begin to drift through the evening sky as they arrive back at the cave. Sarah unsaddles Mesquite, brushing his coat paying special attention to his mane. There is something magical in brushing his mane and coat; she feels a quiet peace in the ritualistic movements—oneness with her special friend. Putting the currycomb away, she picks up a burlap bag to wipe the snow from Rusty's coat;

deciding it is more fun to play than to get dry, he challenges his mistress to a tug-of-war with the burlap bag. Laughter fills the air as Sarah and Rusty roll over and over in the hay. Before long, Rusty stands a ways off, looking at her with his tongue hanging out seeming to say, "Boy! That was fun."

Sarah sits in the hay, pulling pieces of straw from her hair and clothes watching Rusty shake all the hay from his lustrous coat. Slowly standing, she brushes the straw from her old Levi's, then reaching into the bin, Sarah hands Mesquite the sweet red apple he has come to expect.

Entering the kitchen with Rusty on her heels, stimulated with the joy of living, a smile spreads across her weather-worn visage as she closes the veil to the canyon and the world beyond. After a day of shoveling manure and the long ride, she is tired but refreshed. Standing inside, looking out the transparent screen, she marvels at the technology that leaves the area looking just like the side of the mountain to an outside observer.

Just as Sarah turns from the awesomeness of man's ability to create, she notes the heavy flakes of snow falling on her valley. A shiver spreads across her body as she thinks of the cold that comes with the blanket now coating the earth.

Sighing, she said, "Ah yes, a hot bubble bath is the perfect relaxation for the end of a very enjoyable day." Strangely enough, her tiredness slowly drifts away in the lavender-scented aroma of the steam rising from the tub. Sarah slips into an ice blue silk gown and robe; she loves the feminine touch of silk.

Now that she has indulged herself, it is time for a snack and review of her e-mail. Choosing a soda from the fridge, Sarah refills Rusty's dish with food and gives him fresh water. Taking her drink with her, she pulls up her messages. There's a nice note from John asking about the weather and inquiring about the progress of her book. He had a note from Joan saying she is anxious about the deadline. Sarah replies that the weather is usual for this time of year and the book will be ready for the editor in another couple months—mid-January or at least by the end of February.

Checking the satellite weather she sees the experts predict about a foot new snow, she states, "Who cares? Mesquite is warm and snug in the barn. Rusty and I are in the cave. All is well with the world." She thinks about her words, *Well, old girl, I see you have taken to talking to yourself.* Laughing out loud, "Who cares, I live alone and I like my own company."

The blizzard-like conditions over the next several days keep Sarah and her companions indoors. She spends the time working on her manuscript; it won't be long until she can send it for editing, and then the rewrites; there are always a few things the editors want changed. That's the life of a writer. "Aaahhh."

As Sarah works away inside her cave, she is unaware of the interest of the retired tribal detective or of the times he has trailed her on her rides. Would she feel her solitude and serenity threatened by his presence?

Seven years have passed since she first came to live on the Res, and with each passing year, her solitude becomes more precious. She relishes her solitary life and looks forward to the dawn of each new day.

She celebrates the birth of Christ by reading the Stations of the Cross, a ritual she started many years ago. She basks in the relaxation of her free time since her manuscript is now at the editors.

As usual, the New Year brought more snow. Sarah debates whether she wants to clear a path down the center of her valley or not but decides against getting out the plow. Mesquite can handle a couple of feet if they stay at the tree line. Saddling Mesquite with Rusty at her side, they ride near the trees, letting Mesquite set the pace and the trail.

The sun, though shining bright, is not warming, and nothing is stirring for miles around. Tracks are visible in the snow—a coyote tracking a rabbit; further down are the tracks of a deer with the paw prints of a puma following behind. Such is the nature of things on the Res.

The trio ambles for about a half mile then turns back the way they came, not wishing to exhaust her two faithful companions. After all, they didn't have to be out in this weather; it is a choice that they make to enjoy the brisk, exhilarating air. Rusty running circles around the horse and rider stirs up the snow, leaving the valley looking as if a herd of buffalo trampled through as they make their way back to the cave. Never tiring of the antics of her faithful companion, she smiles as Rusty plays tug-of-war with the burlap bag she is using to clean the snow from his fur. Back in the warmth of the cave after the exhilarating ride, her animals cared for she relaxes with a hot cup of coffee.

The cold wintry months pass into spring as patches of earth begin to show through where the warm spring sun beats down on the chilled ground. In the shadows on the slopes and among the trees, mounds of snow still climb up the trunks of the pines and oaks that dot the landscape; bare Aspen scattered through the pines will soon be showing some hints of green. There have already been signs of tiny green spouts in the valley, and soon it will be time for her spring trip to the trading post in Dulce where she will replace staples used over the long winter.

Nodding off in her chair, she said, "I must be getting old, Rusty. Let's go to bed." He bounds for the bedroom, leaping on the bed as Sarah enters the room. Her joyous laughter rings though out the warm cave as the two companions drift off into the land of the sandman's slumber.

Rising to a cold, crisp morning, Sarah and her companions take their usual ride, staying near the base of the mountains on the east side of her valley where the ground is still frozen then cross toward the west ridge, traveling along it until they near the cave. Along the southern stretch, she sees where a horse and rider angled a little to the east, probably one of the older Apache who lives in the area. Riding only a short distance this morning, they enjoy the exercise and fresh air.

Spattered with mud, they return to the cave, and Sarah curries Mesquite, trying to remove the mud from his coat, cleaning his hooves, placing him in the barn. Trying to get Rusty clean is quite a chore as he decides it's playtime the minute she picks up the burlap bag, darting just out of her reach, teasing her as she grabs for him and misses. Thirty minutes later, Rusty is somewhat cleaner, but Sarah is covered with mud and hay. With her loyal companions now clean and fed, Sarah washes the mud from herself and settles down to work on her newest book.

Over the next few weeks, the wind and sun take their toll on the mud-mired valley. It is a warm day in late April when Sarah rides out with Rusty prancing at her side. They head south along the eastern edge of the mountains. The larks are singing high in the trees while the crows loudly scold the intruders. "You thieves! What do you plan to steal today? I'll bet it will be bright and shiny." Sarah is accustomed to leaving a shiny button in a tree or on the ground near her cave; she loves watching them as they slyly check out the surroundings before stealing the gleaming object. Their caws almost drown out the lovely warble of the larks in the early morning of nature's music. "The sounds of nature—that is why I live in this paradise."

These three carefree companions relax and enjoy their ride through the forest. They never tire of being outdoors; fresh air, warm sunshine, and wide open spaces give a sense of oneness with the creator.

Veering toward the west, she is aware of another rider a little further south paralleling the trio. Signaling Mesquite to halt, she watches the rider change course to intercept them. It is unusual for a rider to approach her as they usually turn away just as did she. Today, Sarah can't explain even to herself why she stays there. As the horse and rider draw near, Sarah recognizes the young Begay boy she rescued and starts to turn Mesquite back to the North when Jimmy calls to her, "Wait, I must talk with you."

Sarah turns back and waits. "Hello, Jimmy, I see your leg is healed."

"Yes, I wish to thank you for rescuing me, but I do not know who you are. My people call you the white woman."

"Jimmy that is all you need to know."

"I know that you do not exist to the Apache people, I think that is wrong. You bother no one! But I know I would be dead if it had not been for you. Please be my friend."

"Jimmy, I must follow the rules they gave me."

Sarah sits in silence for a minute before she replies, "I am Sarah. This is Mesquite. And that is Rusty."

"I will tell no one of our talk. How often do you ride?

She hesitates only briefly. "We ride most every day."

"If you ride on Saturday, will you ride near the cliff where I fell?"

Looking at the young face that glistens with anxiety, she asked, "Should I?"

The young man's eyes shine with delight. "I would like it very much."

Sarah turns Mesquite without saying a word, heading back north to her cave. Rusty is fascinated by the presence of the young lad and does not immediately respond when Sarah calls. It takes her calling a couple of times in an insistent voice before he runs after her in leaps and bounds.

As they continue toward home, Sarah ponders the situation: *Will I go to the cliff on Saturday? What grandmother could resist the plea of a young child, a child she knows in her heart she saved? How will the council respond? Will they evict me after seven years? Am I willing to risk everything I value—my home, my solitude, my peace?*

Lost in thought, she does not see the lone rider partially hidden by the cedar on the western hills. As Jake observes her encounter with the young boy, he wonders about the short conversation, but in his wisdom of seventy-plus years he knows exactly what was said and what the agreement is. He just doesn't know when. *When?*

He'll just have to ride over every day. It is a good thing the department does not need him now, and his time is his own. There are times like this he is glad he is retired. Soon, they will not let him help out. He will soon be eighty. He pinches out his cigar, places it in his pocket, and mounts his old pinto. "Life is good. And this is just enough mystery to whet my interest."

As Sarah approaches the cave, Jake rides back west toward La Jara Lake, a couple of hours ride before he reaches his *kogha*.

Riding into the corral, unaware that Jake has been watching her; she unsaddles Mesquite brushing his coat to a shining luster as Rusty lays in the warm sunshine. It has been a good ride, but troubling especially when she knows she will risk meeting Jimmy. *What does my future hold? Am I really willing to risk my way of life for a small boy's plea?* She had when she rescued Jimmy, but that was different; his life was in danger. *What will I tell myself to convince me it is worth the risk I run?*

She finishes currying Mesquite, giving him his favorite treat and enters the cave with Rusty darting ahead of her. She places a cup of the cold coffee in the microwave to heat. As she stands waiting for the coffee to heat, she hears her stomach growl and remembers skipping breakfast. *That's what I need...food.* Sarah heats some leftover pinto beans, adding some green chili and cheddar cheese. "Now that's a meal fit for royalty." Rusty waits but not too patiently for his share. "Woof, hamburger! Woof! Woof!"

Sarah finishes her meal, and after washing up the dishes, she enters the main room, sitting at her computer to check her e-mails. Her book went to her editor in February, and she expects there will be a request for rewrites any day now.

There is nothing from her editor, just a brief note from John stating that he will be retiring in June. He is recommending a young attorney, Jack Green, to handle her affairs. It is hard to believe that John is retiring; he has been in the same office for fifty years or more, ever since he got out of law school. "I don't want a new attorney." John has been the family attorney for all these many years and a long-time friend. "What will I do without John handling my affairs? Well, I trust John, so I will just have to accept his recommendation." She asks John if Mr. Green understands the importance of her "disappearance" then hits Send.

Sarah sits facing her computer staring at the wall. *So many things are going on in my quiet world—life-changing things. Am I prepared for these changes*?

It is a fair afternoon with the weather man reporting clear and sunny skies for the next few days; Sarah decides it's a good time to order hay. The delivery trucks should be able to get in to the area; there are still a few bales in the barn and running low especially this time of year could mean doing without.

Sarah grabs her old hat and coat as she starts out the door with Rusty right on her heels. She puts Mesquite in the barn then backs the truck out of the garage. When she lowers the tailgate, Rusty hops in the back; he likes riding in the truck almost as much as their treks through the countryside.

The trail to NM 537 is little more than a cow trail, and the snow has left soft spots not yet dried by the wind and sun; mud splatters the sides of the truck like raindrops falling in the parched desert. By the time they reach the highway and head north to Dulce, the sun is high overhead. As the warm sun shines through the windshield, touching Sarah's weathered face, she feels a peace engulf her, confirming her long-standing belief that the sun has soul-healing qualities.

The ride into town goes quickly, and Dulce, like all the reservation, is mud-splattered and weather-worn, but beautiful to the beholder. Stopping at the feed store, she orders fifty bales of hay, discovering that the price is about fifty cents higher than last season's; with winter spreading across the land, the higher prices are expected.

At the post office, she checks general delivery, finding tons of catalogues from companies that she orders from on line. Sometimes when she doesn't pick up her mail for several months and the box will hold no more, they toss the fourth-class stuff. That suits her just fine, most of it she pitches before walking out the door.

The postmistress asks, "How's the snow out your way?"

Sarah responds quietly, "There's about two feet in the valley." The few words spoken is typical of the conversation—giving very little information and receiving none.

After filling the truck with gas, she stops by the café for a cup of coffee and a piece of pie.

The waitress is friendly, asking, "You're the one who rescued little Jimmy Begay last year."

Sarah nods ascent.

The waitress sticks out her hand. "Mary Begay, Jimmy's my nephew. Been hoping to meet you. I want to thank you for bringing Jimmy to the clinic in Dulce."

Sarah takes her hand but does not respond verbally.

"I know what your agreement with the council is. If you are questioned, I will tell them I started the conversation. You have never bothered anyone and have kept your agreement. How long have you lived on the Res?"

Sarah hesitates then answers, "Starting the eighth year."

"That is long enough for the council to realize you will not bring trouble to the Jicarilla or abuse the land."

"I could never do that. I have never known such peace and happiness as I have found here."

Sarah finishes her coffee; saying good-bye to Mary Begay, she crawls into the cab of her truck and heads home. *Home, what a good sound that is!*

Jake stands outside the sheriff's office, watching the interaction in the restaurant between the two women. Seeing Sarah leave, he ambles across the street. *Might as well have lunch before I head out. Besides I wanna talk to Mary.*

As he enters the café, Jake greets her, "*Da nzho*" (*It is good*), making his way to a booth.

"*Aoo, da nzho* [Yes, it is good]. What will you have, Jake?"

"A bowl of mutton stew, coffee, and cherry pie."

When she brings him his meal, Jake asks, "Have you met the eccentric white woman?"

Leary of the question, Mary asks, "Why do you want to know?"

Jake understands the question. "I mean no harm to either of you. I am not inquiring in an official capacity. I saw you talking to her through the window. I guess I'm as curious as anyone."

"I wanted to thank her for saving my nephew, Jimmy." Mary relates the rest of her conversation with Sarah to Jake. "She doesn't talk much."

"If she is as happy as she says she is, she would not want the council to have any reason to break her lease."

Her black eyes flash with emotion. "Are you going to tell the council that I talked to the 'white woman'?"

Jake looked at Mary for a minute. "Mary, I know nothing of any conversation taking place. Do you?"

Mary smiles. "No, Jake, I don't recall a conversation with anyone of that description."

Jake eats the rest of his meal in silence. Learning nothing except that the white woman's name is Sarah and that she is happy living on the Res, he pays for his meal and walks out of the café, resolving to do all in his power to protect her right to live on the reservation—even if he has to oppose the council.

As he walks to his truck, a special glow emanates from his eyes. *I have a name. I no longer have to refer to her as that white woman—she is Sarah.* He feels good knowing her name, but for some reason, it does not fit the image he has of her. *I will think on her name, she needs an Apache name.*

Saturday morning arrives warm and clear. Dressing in her usual jeans and boots, she picks up her old Stetson hat as she leaves the bedroom. Rusty is at her heels, following her into the kitchen where she will have coffee and breakfast. While the coffee perks, she scrambles eggs, adding green chili and cheese, and since she hasn't made tortillas or fry bread, she eats without either.

Rusty scarfs down his plate of eggs then sits wagging his tail in anticipation as she cleans up their breakfast dishes. Standing quietly, sipping the last dregs of coffee, as though in a trance, she ponders her rendezvous with Jimmy Begay.

Without giving thought to what she is doing, she prepares a picnic lunch consisting of a thermos of coffee, peanut butter sandwiches, and jerky packing extra, even more than she would normally take for her and Rusty; a sweet red apple for Mesquite is added to the fixings as she goes though the barn. Giving Mesquite a hug, she steps into the saddle, and with Rusty running ahead through the sagebrush, stirring the creatures nesting at their roots, Sarah heads toward a rendezvous she might live to regret, compelled by a force within, she neither understands nor can she ignore.

The sun rising over the eastern slopes is warming and reminds her of how much she enjoys riding. What a beautiful day! Realizing she is holding the reins so tight her knuckles are white and painful, she rides though the quiet valley, yet she is surprised at how calm she feels as she nears the site. The solitude with nature always has a soothing effect; the sounds and smell of the outdoors is a symphony of serenity.

As Sarah approaches the meeting sight, she is unaware of a third party standing closer than he has ever ventured before. Jake stands quietly with his ever-present cigar in his mouth, watching this "white woman" who he is drawn to by an unknown entity, noting that Jimmy has yet to arrive.

She rides a little further west then back east to see if she has missed Jimmy. Wanting to stay in the area, she dismounts, tying Mesquite's reins to a small scrub oak then sitting down in the shade of the tree watching Rusty as he bounds here and there frolicking in the new grass just beginning to peak through Mother Earth.

While waiting, she sips her coffee, leaning against the tree listening to the breeze rustle the sage, creating a soft melody of sound. Time passes, and her body is aching from sitting so long; she rises and stretches to limber her old bones easing the stiffness. Putting her cup back in her saddlebag, she reaches for the saddle horn preparing to ride out, but at that precise moment, she hears the approach of a rider. For a brief moment, anxiety touches her soul, dismissing it when she sees the approaching rider is Jimmy.

Jimmy hails her, "You came."

Watching his face for a reaction, she says, "You asked me to."

A big grin spreads across his young face. "I didn't think you would."

"I almost didn't, I have a lot to lose by meeting with you."

"The council has to know of our meeting before they can make you leave, and I will never tell."

The worry lines across her brow ease. "I believe you when you say you will not tell. You seem a young man of honor."

Swelling with pride, he says, "I am an Apache brave, my word is sacred."

Smiling at his declaration, she notices the sun high overhead. "Dismount, Jimmy, why did you want to see me?"

"I want to know the woman who rescued me. And I am especially curious why the council forbids contact with you."

"That is the agreement I made with the council in order to live on the reservation. She pauses before continuing, "I don't know why they made the rule, but until now, I have lived by it." Remaining silent for a time, she asks, "I want to know about the boy I rescued." Why were you out here alone? How did you fall?"

"With the dignity of a young warrior," he says, "I often go off by myself. I like to pretend I am living as the grandfathers lived in the olden days where tracking was necessary to live and counting coup was important to a young warrior. I pretend I am that warrior. That's what I was doing when I lost my footing and fell off the cliff." Jimmy grins. "I am familiar with the area, so my parents do not worry about me. My grandfather told them I was a wise boy, that I would be okay. In the morning, they would have searched for me. They told me that when the police arrived, they did not know what to think."

Both the "forbidden white woman" and the young Apache boy sit listening to the wind rustling the pine needles, gazing across the arroyo, each lost in their own thoughts.

Looking at her with the intensity of a young lad, he quietly says, "They wanted to know about you, too, but the council said they were to have no contact with you. You are forbidden."

"The council spoke the truth that is our agreement."

Sarah learns that Jimmy is a good student, that he studies hard, but he would rather be outdoors riding through the countryside.

After a while, Sarah speaks, "Jimmy, I'm rather hungry. It has been a long time since breakfast. Would you like to share a snack with me?"

Like the youngster of ten summers that he is, he asks eagerly, "Yes, what do you have to eat?"

Sarah went to Mesquite, bringing back her saddlebags laying a small blanket on the ground placing the thermos and two cups on it, she opens the sandwiches and jerky, placing them in the center.

Rusty bounds from under the scrub oak near Mesquite, racing to see what his mistress will offer.

Jimmy, being a bright young student, notices a shiny red apple still in the saddlebags but does not ask its purpose; that would be impolite.

Sarah pours two cups of coffee; she hands one to Jimmy along with a peanut butter sandwich and a handful of jerky. Just as she does, Rusty nudges his mistress, invoking a laugh as she hands him a strip. They sit in silence, eating the picnic she prepared.

Jake moves closer. He hopes to hear part of the conversation between Jimmy and Sarah. Being concerned his presence might alert her dog and the horses if he gets too close, he is content to observe from back in the trees. His experience at surveillance tells him the meeting is pleasant for both parties.

No one says anything as Sarah puts the thermos and other stuff back into her saddlebags, leaving a couple pieces of jerky out for Rusty. Jimmy, with the keen interest of the young, watches her remove the apple and hears Mesquite, whiny, taking the apple from Sarah's hand, chewing the juicy treat with gusto. He smiles at the trio of companions that he now considers his friends and moves toward his own pony mounting.

Sarah mounts as the secret meeting comes to an end, turning north as Jimmy turns south.

Jimmy halts, calling out, "White woman, will you come back next Saturday?"

Sarah halts Mesquite, turns in the saddle without speaking, pauses a moment to consider her response, then nods her ascent.

Off to the east, Jake hears the question asked by Jimmy and sees her affirmative nod. He knows she is playing with dynamite by meeting the boy; he also knows he will be there before they arrive on Saturday, hopefully near enough to hear. When he is sure neither Jimmy nor Sarah will see him ride away, he steps upon his *lii* (horse) and heads northwest to his *kogha*.

As Sarah rides slowly back to the cave there is much to consider. She is drawn to this young Apache boy as a mother to a stray, yet she is concerned about asking too many questions. She does not wish to seem nosey and resolves to let Jimmy set the pattern for conversation.

What? Am I out of my mind? I have met him once. How stupid it is to commit to a second meeting, but that is exactly what I have done. She has promised to meet Jimmy next Saturday, and in her heart, she knows she will keep that promise.

Time passes quickly especially with her thoughts elsewhere. Suddenly, her thoughts turn to the present; there, just a few yards away is her cave. Approaching the corral, she opens the gate from the saddle, and as they enter the corral, Rusty bounds in right on their heels. Their rides are always enjoyable; being in the great outdoors with the smell of pinon and sage rising on the breeze is a passion she nurtures. Brushing Mesquite, her thoughts returned to her visit with Jimmy. She likes this young Apache and looks forward to their next meeting. *What a careless old fool I am becoming. What on earth am I thinking?* But despite this, she cannot resist the temptation.

Sensing his mistress's preoccupation, Rusty sits waiting his turn for attention as Mesquite very happily receives his second tasty apple of the day, pushing Sarah with his nose to show his pleasure. As she puts the currycomb away, Rusty races through the garage into the kitchen ahead of her.

It is early afternoon of a very pleasant day as Sarah puts on a pot of coffee, making sure Rusty has food and water; she waits to see if he will ask for jerky. Sitting at the table, she smiles as he edges closer until he lays his head against her leg. Sarah grins; she could never refuse him and reaches for the canister that holds his jerky. No longer able to contain himself, he starts bouncing all around with enthusiasm that belies his age. Handing him the much-desired jerky she pours a second cup and heads for her computer.

There's a note from Jack Green, her new attorney, more or less introducing himself and letting her know he is up to date on her affairs. Her agent, Joan, has contacted him regarding the manuscript, which is at the editors; she will be sending a list of recommended rewrites in a day or two. He relays that John is officially retired and is spending time in his garden. He also tells her what John failed to mentioned, that he has terminal cancer and has been given only a few months to live. Sarah sits numb in her chair. John is a long-time family friend who she met through her father and the only lawyer her father ever liked or trusted. To her, that is the best endorsement she could have. *John is a dear and trusted friend.* She e-mails Jack the acknowledgement of the pending rewrite of her manuscript, instructing him to keep her up to date on John's condition.

Her father died in 1998! *My goodness where has the time gone? Has it really been eighteen years since my father passed away*? That is hard to believe; in many ways, it's like only yesterday. She misses him as much today as she did the day he died. She and John are the same age, and here they are, telling her that her best friend is dying. *"How can that be? I feel so young."*

For just a brief moment, she allows a sadness to creep through her spirit. *Pooh, I live in paradise with my animals and my solitude—that is enough for me. That and my writing.* And with that thought, she is again in her private world of peace and contentment. lost in the manuscript she is currently creating.

Well, when God closes one door, he always opens another. She knows there will be something ahead just as pleasant as the past has been. Will she be open to the changes that are coming faster than she would like. Of course, she will. Has she not always flowed with the ups and downs life throws at one! She will be ready.

Sarah shuts down the Internet and sits idly in front of her computer, staring out into the wide open spaces in front of her cave. She finds peace and serenity in the vast valley before her thinking about how wonderful it is to be hidden in the deep mountains of the Jicarilla, south of Cordova Canyon.

Reality surges through her reverie. *What have I done, agreeing to meet Jimmy Begay, again?* Now she is beginning to question her sanity in even talking to him today.

There are so many thoughts running through her mind; she cannot get a good prospective. Pushing back from her computer, she walks to the kitchen and pours another cup of coffee, sitting there deep in thought for what passes like only a minute or two but has really been over an hour. When her faithful Rusty brings his worn-out Christmas toy, placing it in her lap, she does not respond, letting it fall to the floor. He picks it up, placing it back in her lap, nudging her leg as he does. Absently she places her hand on Rusty's head, but he is having none of it and again places the toy in her lap, nudging her leg, breaking into her revere. Unable to resist her loyal companion, she picks up the beloved toy, tossing it toward the great room. Rusty bounds after it, returning it to her lap. Sarah's laughter roars through the cave; Rusty wins. His distraction is the perfect solution to her ponderous thoughts. They play continuously for the next thirty minutes. By the time both are exhausted, Sarah is in her normal happy state. She says a silent prayer for the love of her devoted canine.

Returning to the big room, she places a CD in the stereo, and as the music filters through the cave, she runs a tub of hot water laced with the aromatic lavender bubble bath and slips slowly down in the luxurious warmth. The heat of the water brings a soothing aura of relaxation as the events of the day seem to come in to perspective.

She will continue to see Jimmy Begay and trust the Gods it will work out, smiling 'cause deep in her heart, she knows things will be all right.

Jimmy wakes bathed in sweat, shaking; this is the third night he's had the same nightmare. He wipes his face with the sheet as he looks over at the clock, which reads 3:00 a.m. Staring out the window, looking into the darkness, he freezes; fear grips his young mind when he sees glaring at him a pair of blazing golden eyes—orbs unmoving, showing no sign of life. In the eerie darkness of the room, he hears a voice haunting yet soft: "Come to the Sacred Mountain, a choice to make." Then the piercing eyes disappear into the night.

Shaking violently, he wraps his arms around his legs, remaining thus for the rest of the night, afraid to move from his bed or to sleep. *In the morning, I will visit the Ancient One who believes in the traditions and can explain the meaning of my dreams and the voice speaking to me out of the darkness. He is wise, all seeing and all knowing. He is Grandfather!*

As the sun blazes high overhead and the shadows of the night are gone, he dresses, going outside the house around to the side that holds the window of his room. On the ground below is a set of coyote tracks—only two, not four, and no mud on the window sill. No tracks can be seen leading to his window or away from it, only at the base of the window. Trembling with the eeriness of what he sees and doesn't see, he touches the pouch he carries around his neck, asking the Gods' protection. Then saddling his pony, he heads for the *kogha* of the Ancient One. *I must seek the answers.*

Two hours later, he reaches his destination, finding the ancient one sitting outside his *kogha*, eyes closed, slowly rocking back and forth as he chants. Suddenly he stops, and opening his eyes, he stares at the young warrior. "I have been waiting for three days and nights for you. Enter!"

The Ancient One steps inside, motioning for Jimmy to sit on the other side of a small fire that illuminates the interior. Sitting in the traditional way, the Ancient One tosses a bit of powder on the fire, causing it to flare, sending a wisp of smoke curling upward. Looking at the lad, he says, "Tell me of your dreams, leaving nothing out. You are safe here."

The trembling subsides, and after a few minutes, he takes a deep breath and begins, "In my dream, I am standing on a high mountain overlooking the land when I see the white woman riding hard, looking over her shoulder as if something is after her. Following the direction of her gaze, I see a dark shadow trailing her, growing larger with each passing moment, covering the land with a gray evil. Suddenly, a large eagle dives from out of the gray mist, attacking the shadow, driving it back, allowing the white woman to escape.

"The ebony glob suddenly appears in front of me. I am paralyzed by the evil emitting from the mist as death comes for me. Before the evil creature touches me, the eagle swoops down, landing between me and the evil squawking a warning. Words are being said, but I cannot understand them. It is a language I have never heard.

"Standing there in a trance, unmoving, I watch as they turn toward me and speak as one, 'You must choose your path, time is running out.'"

Starring into the fire, he continues, "They disappear as if they never were, and that's when I wake! What's the meaning, Grandfather?"

Nodding his head, looking at the young man, he replies, "Tell me what was said to you last night in your dream, omitting not one word."

The young one stares in disbelief. *I have always been told that the medicine man knew all, but how does the Ancient One know all? How? How does he know? The voice said to trust the wisdom of the Ancient One.*

Jimmy takes a deep breath and begins again as he comes to the end, "The last thing I saw looking out my window was a pair of golden eyes with a blaze so intense they burned right through me. I hear a voice say, 'Go to the Sacred Mountain. There to choose your path.' When I blinked, the eyes were gone, that's when I woke from the dream." Pausing, he relates to the Ancient One what he found when he went outside and looked on the ground.

During this whole time, the ancient one just sits, looking and listening, not moving or making a gesture. Thus it is impossible to guess what he is thinking. Finally speaking, he says, "You have met the one we call Brother Coyote. He is the strongest of our Gods and also known as a trickster. He has summoned you—for what reason, I do not know. As for the Eagle and the Dark One, they are good and evil, both claiming your soul. I know that there is and has been a great battle going on among the Gods. Now the battle is coming to our lands and to us. The outcome, I do not know, but you're destined to play a major role in this battle."

With eyes closed, he pauses briefly then continues, "You will stay with me this day, and tonight we will go to the Sacred Mountain where you will find the answers you seek. Now, though, we must prepare for the journey and what lies ahead."

The rest of the day, the Ancient One prepares his bag with herbs, totems, and charms to protect them, as well as instructing the young one on how to act in front of the Gods and what he might expect. But in his heart, Grandfather knows that this young one is on his own; there is nothing he can do to protect him once he is with the Gods on Sacred Mountain.

Turbulent clouds have been gathering in the sky most of the day, and as they reach the Sacred Mountain late in the evening, the skies open up and lightning flashes across the heavens, and thunder shakes the land as rain pours from the heavens.

The Ancient One looks at the young lad. "This is one of many ways the Gods will test you for courage and determination. You will climb the Sacred Mountain to the top to meet with them. What will happen and what you will see, I do not know, nor can I go with you. From here, you must go alone. I shall wait here, protecting you as I can. Now go! Find your answers." With that, he sat on the ground, chanting the ancient prayer for guidance and protection as the rain runs down his weathered, old countenance.

The young man cranes his neck, looking up the face of the mountain as rain and wind rips at him; taking a deep breath, he begins his ascent with nothing to assist him. Setting his feet firmly, inching his way up the mountain, he claws the ground for something to grasp hold of, finally getting a toe hold with first one foot and then the other. For hours he climbs, only pausing to catch his breath now and then, the wind whipping and rain pounding him every step of the way. Nature's violence rips at him from every direction, trying to dislodge him and send him falling to his death, but the young warrior perseveres. Lightning strikes the rock's face as he climbs, sending showers of rock and dirt down upon him, but still he climbs. He never looks down, only up, with astounding determination for one so young. A voice inside his head persistently drives him every step of the way until finally, reaching the top, he falls, hitting his face on the ground where he lays gasping for breath as the storm rages all around him.

Lying on the muddy ground, the first voice that he hears is the same one that compelled him ever onward. "You are strong, young one. You have passed the first test."

He looks up, startled; there in front of him is the coyote with the golden eyes. Sitting, watching! The young one notices how the storm rages all around him, but the coyote's fur is unruffled by the wind and not a drop of rain touches him.

There is a smirk on the face of the trickster as he looks at the boy. "Come, be at peace. You will not be harmed. We have much to talk about, and you have much to decide the fate of the tribe and the lands are now in your hands."

The young man gets to his feet and walks over to the coyote, dropping to his knees, bowing, speaking for the first time. "I am honored, Great One, but I am confused. Why have I been summoned?"

The coyote laughs. "Be not afraid, young one, your confusion will soon be gone. As for why you were chosen, because I so wish it! You are unsoiled by the ways of evil and still pure in heart, qualities it will take to complete your task."

With a calm that surprises the young warrior, he asks, "What do you wish of me, Great One? What must I do"?

The Coyote smiles as its golden eyes flash like the lightning ravishing the mountain. "There are two paths in front of you. You must choose. One path will lead your lands to ruin, and your tribe's heritage will disappear like sands in the wind. But your people will prosper and become wealthy over time. The white woman must die! The second path will save your lands, your heritage, and your people will prosper. But evil will fight you at every step, trying to destroy you. You will be feared and shunned by all, an outcast from your own people, except for two who will be there to help and support you. Now you must choose."

At that moment, twin bolts of lightning strike on either side of the Coyote, shaking the ground, sending dirt and rocks flying in all directions. Ducking his head to avoid the onslaught of debris, the lad slowly raises his eyes. Standing on either side of the great Coyote are two others; one is the great Eagle, protector of life and justice, and the other is the Dark One, a shapeless mass of darkness that pulses evil.

The young one trembles with fear; this is the evil he felt in his dream, standing before him, "Great One, how will I know which is the right path for me? I do not wish to choose. There is so much at stake."

The Coyote's eyes flash in anger as lighting strikes the ground all around the young man. "Choose, or all will be ravaged this night."

The young lad feels fear like in his dream—a fear of uncertainty. Taking a deep breath, he feels the greatest serenity he has ever known creep through his mind, his body relaxing. Standing straight like the young warrior he is, he simply nods to the coyote.

He responds, "So be it. The future of your people now rests in your hands."

With that, the Coyote places one of his paws on the young man's head; instantly, ancient knowledge and wisdom flood his mind. Locations of secret caves are revealed—places of power long forgotten and hidden though the ages.

He is overwhelmed by the images filling his head; visions of the past, the present, and the future race across his mind's eye. He collapses on the ground as Coyote speaks to him one last time. "You have all the knowledge and power that you will ever require to fulfill your path. Whether you succeed in your quest is your choice alone. The Ancient One below knows of your decision. He will be there to guide you on your journey. Go! You have much work to do."

The days slip by until it is Saturday, the day Sarah is once again to meet Jimmy. Sipping her early morning coffee, she plans the food for their picnic; placing fresh grapes in a plastic container she strips chicken for sandwiches, filling the thermos with hot coffee. She adds pieces of jerky for all of them, especially Rusty.

Stepping into the barn, she selects a couple of red, delicious apples, one for Mesquite and one for Jimmy. She had not missed his curiosity or his observation last Saturday when she gave Mesquite the apple.

Saddling Mesquite, she ties the saddlebags in place, riding with Rusty trotting by her side. Though she is anxious to see Jimmy, there is a nagging hint of concern; she knows that in doing so, she is risking everything she values about her life on the Jicarilla.

However, the morning is beautiful, and as always, she is captivated by the aroma of cedar, pinon, and pines; she marvels at the beauty of the emerald green leaves against the white bark of the aspen. The meadowlark chirps his greeting, butterflies flitter among the sage, adding flashes of color, and wild buttercups dot the landscape with bright circles of golden yellow. *Ah! The day is perfection.*

Sarah is happy in her solitude here on the Jicarilla. Once again, the thought crosses her mind. *What the hell am I doing?*

At the rendezvous point, Jimmy is waiting and hails her in the Apache way. "*Da nzho*" (It is good).

She does not know how to respond in the Apache and asks, "Jimmy, how should I answer you?"

Jimmy replies, "*Aoo, da nzho* " (Yes, it is good).

Sarah tries the response, clasping her hands over her ears, hearing how terrible she sounds and the snicker that escapes Jimmy's young mouth brings a smile that touches her green eyes with a hint of glee.

Jake smiles at Sarah's attempt to use the Apache response. He had arrived very early as he wanted to be close enough to hear the conversation between Jimmy and Sarah, but he did not want to be seen. He is settled into the forest not far from the pair, unaware that Rusty is venturing near him.

Sarah asks, "What do you like best about school, Jimmy?"

"I like working with the computer. I learned that engineers who build things can use the computer to design what they plan to build."

"Do you like to build things?"

"Yes, I want to be an engineer when I get older. Then I can travel the world and build lots of different things—not just buildings, but dams and bridges."

As she listens to Jimmy talk, she sees a dark shadow cross his eyes. It is so fleeting that she even questions whether it was really there. She shakes her head. "You will have to study very hard if you are to be an engineer. It won't be easy but if you want it bad enough you will be able to achieve your goal."

Jimmy ponders what she has said. "I will study very hard. I want to make my parents proud of me." Pausing in his thoughts, he says, "I want to be an asset to *diide* [the people]."

Smiling, she says, "I'm sure you will be."

Listening to the discourse, Jake knows better but is drawn closer to the pair as they sit in the cool shade of the scrub oak.

As Sarah goes to her saddlebags for their picnic, Rusty spots Jake, barking an alarm, and the more Jake tries to quiet him, the more insistent he becomes.

Sarah, immediately alert, lets her eyes follow the tree line until she spots Rusty and sees the stranger standing in the trees. Slowly removing the strap on her pistol, she walks toward Rusty and the stranger he is holding at bay.

Knowing he has been caught, he steps out into the sunlight, only to be greeted by a snarling German shepherd. Halting in his movement, he waits to see what the white woman will do. As she nears the intruder, she calls to Rusty who immediately goes to her side. "Who are you? Why are you here?"

"I am called Jake, Sarah. I ride this way often and have watched you ride many times. I live over by La Jara"

While on the surface she appears calm, her insides quiver with anxiety; slowly taking her hand from the top of her holster, she stands waiting, surprised he knows her name. "Why have I not seen you?"

Jake grins. "Thank you, I was not sure whether you would shoot me or not. And I know the rules the council gave you, *ligai isdzanii* white woman]."

Sarah laughs. "No, I would probably have let Rusty have you." Sighing, she says, "Well, you are here now, and I can't be punished for two any more than for one. Won't you join us? We are having a picnic."

"Yes, I will. Thank you."

When they approach Jimmy, he greets Jake. "*Ha annsi shiitsooyee?* [How are you, Grandfather?]"

Jake replies, "*Doo ansj* [I am fine]."

Walking over to Mesquite to retrieve the picnic from her saddlebags, a cold chill runs down her spine. Knowing that Jake is a tribal police officer, she realizes that it is only a matter of time before the council will be aware of her rendezvous with Jimmy. With a sinking feeling in her gut, she returns to the shade of the scrub oak where Jimmy and Jake have been in deep conversation.

Spreading the blanket on the ground, she proceeds to unpack the chicken sandwiches; pouring the coffee for Jake and Jimmy, she lays the jerky in the center of the cloth along with the two red apples. Rusty moves where he is position between Jake and his mistress, but he still keeps his eyes on his favorite treat lying in the middle of the cloth. The trio sit quietly eating, each occupied with their own thoughts.

Rusty surprises Sarah, accepting tidbits of chicken from Jake, even edging closer to him.

Finishing his sandwich in record time, Jimmy asks, "May I give Mesquite his apple?"

Sarah nods approval as Jimmy picks up the apple slowly, approaching Mesquite, who bobs his head, accepting the sweet treat offered. Jimmy brushes his hand along the long shiny mane then turns back to the others.

Impatience getting the best of him, Rusty prances around Sarah, begging for his jerky. As she hands him several of his favorite treats, her laughter echoes across the valley floor at his antics.

All this activity just confirms what Jake observed in the past; Sarah and her animals are loyal companions.

Jimmy grows more restless as sun rises higher in the clear sky. "Jake, can we tell her now? It's not fair to make her wait."

"Yes, Jimmy." Pausing, Jake with a serious tightening of his jaw, continues to speak, "Sarah, we know what the council rules are, and this meeting has not taken place. Do you understand?"

Sarah looks at him, a puzzled expression shadowing her eyes; she's not sure she understands this conspiracy. She sits without speaking or moving even an eyelash.

Jake continues, "We like you. You have lived here over seven years. Most people do not know you are here because you bother no one. We choose to be your friend. The council will not hear of our meeting with the 'white woman' who lives in the canyon."

Sarah did not know what to say. She remains stunned in absolute silence, unable to breathe at the words she is hearing and these words from a tribal officer of the law.

Jimmy, young and wise beyond his years, says, "Jake, it's okay if she doesn't answer us. She doesn't talk much anyway."

With a big grin spreading across his face, Jake winks at Jimmy. "That's good we like quiet squaws."

At this, Sarah roars with laughter, and the tension is broken. Jimmy and Jake join in the laughter, which roars even louder as Rusty pounces in the middle of his mistress. He is not going to be left out of the play.

She gathers her wits about herself and begins to put the picnic residue away. There is the one lone apple left. She hands it to Jimmy.

"May I give it to my pinto?"

"It is yours do with it as you wish."

Jimmy grins and takes the apple to his pinto. Giving it to him, he leaps upon his unshod pony, rides off a few feet, and turns back. "Next Saturday?"

Sarah nods, overwhelmed by the conspiracy the two Apache braves, one young and one a wise elder, devised.

Together they watch Jimmy ride off toward the mountains. Jake allows his eyes to glance at the woman beside him, asking quietly, almost in a whisper, "Me, too?"

She stands looking at this weather-marked old Apache whom by a conspiracy is a friend. "Yes." With everything back in the saddlebags and the bags back on Mesquite, Sarah mounts and rides slowly toward home.

Jake sitting astride his faithful pinto falls in beside Sarah's Mesquite as though they are guided by powers unexplained; they ride north in silence side by side. About a quarter of a mile from Sarah's cave, Jake turns west.

She calls Jake.

As he turns to the drawl of her voice, she says, "Thank you."

Jake raises his hand to signify acknowledgment, each riding in the direction of their homes, Jake to his near La Jara and Sarah toward her cave.

Jake's thoughts turn to the conspiracy he engineered with Jimmy; the boy was so distressed that he might report the meeting with Sarah to the council. He could not hurt the boy, so he agreed that they would tell no one of the friendship of the white woman and the boy whose life she saved. Besides, Jake admits, "I like the idea of seeing her myself." *Being captivated by this white squaw with or without Jimmy, I will protect her.*

It is late afternoon as the trio approach the corral where she unsaddles Mesquite brushing his coat until it shines like burnished mahogany. As she works. her thoughts turn to the day's events. *Will Jake keep his word? Or should I go to the council and confess to meeting with Jimmy? What is the right thing to do? Will Jimmy, an eleven-year-old, let it slip about our friendship? Will Jake be honor-bound to tell the council? He did say he would not. Can I trust him? Well, do I trust Rusty? Of course, I do! Rusty says he is okay; he sat next to him didn't he and took food from his hand? Rusty doesn't sit by anyone but her. I will have to trust Rusty's instinct…at least for now.*

Sarah puts the currycomb away; calling Rusty, she goes in to the kitchen where she brews a fresh pot of coffee. While it perks, she puts the things away from their picnic as Rusty lays content by the door.

When the coffee is ready, Sarah pours a cup, going to her computer. She checks her e-mail; there's a note from Jack. He writes to let her know that he has received a royalty check, which he deposited. Sarah acknowledges receipt, logging out. She is not going to work on her book this afternoon.

Ambling to the stereo, she turns it on as sounds of the cowboy classics filter through the cave. Sarah sits in her chair, listening to the age-old words, drifting to sleep with Rusty's head in her lap.

Not far from where Sarah sleeps, the clan's Ancient One's vision sees the *ligai isdzanii* sitting with two other figures whose identity is obscured in the mist—one is young, one is old. It is not the vision of the two Apache with her that bothers him it is the danger surrounding the white woman raising the hackles on his leathery neck.

As the three friends continue their weekly picnics, they move their location a little to the west back in the trees where it is cooler this time of year and they are less likely to be seen. These outings are very special to all of them, and although Sarah is unwilling to acknowledge how deeply she feels, the experiences give a sense of elation each time.

Jake insists he bring the picnic this time, and Sarah finds herself looking forward to his contribution. While she rarely cooks for their Saturday rendezvous, on this occasion, she bakes brownies. Filling the thermos with the usual coffee, she packs the brownies, jerky for Rusty and six red juicy apples, one for each of the mounts and one for each of them. As Rusty bounds into the corral, impatient to start, Sarah saddles Mesquite, attaching the saddlebags as the sun peaks over the eastern slopes. The aroma of sagebrush and pinon tickles her nose with their intoxicating scent as she rides through the corral gate. "Ah! Nature's perfume, so pleasing!"

Sure that Jake will be there waiting, Sarah can't remember how or when he became important to her; she is like a young filly with not a brain cell working on the day of their rendezvous. She dreams of what it would be like to sit by the fire in her cave with Jake sharing a cup of coffee listening to music. *Why am I even thinking this way? How stupid! Men always complicate my life! How asinine such a thought is!* Sarah scolds herself for being foolish; it has been a long time since she has even thought of sharing her life with any man even for a meal. Yet here she is sharing one day each week with Jake and Jimmy and finding great pleasure in the companionship.

Lost in her thoughts, the landscape slips past as she suddenly becomes aware that Jake is standing in front of her with his hand raised in greeting. Smiling, she raises her hand in acknowledgement as Rusty leaps all over Jake, bounding back to Sarah and Mesquite, urging them to hurry. Sarah's laughter echoes through the hills; her canine always brings a smile to her lips and joy to her life.

Reaching the edge of the trees, she dismounts, tying Mesquite to a scrub oak where there is plenty of grazing. Removing the saddlebags, she lays them near the quilt Jake spread on the ground.

Sitting cross-legged on the quilt, quietly chatting about the weather, Jake comments, "I know Jimmy has been helping you with the language. Would you like me to help?"

Sarah laughs. "Jake, do you really think I can get this southern drawl to form the Apache words?"

Jake grins. "Who knows, but we will have fun trying." Neither interested in idle conversation, they sit in silence, listening to the sounds of the forest lost in their own thoughts.

Time slips idly away as they become aware that Jimmy is late arriving. Looking at the sun, it appears to be about midday, and Sarah is a little concerned. It's not like Jimmy to miss one of their outings; he is always the first one to arrive. And since no one must ever know of their friendship or of their rendezvous, they can't seek his whereabouts. "I wonder what is keeping Jimmy this morning."

"He might be helping with the sheep, sometimes he does." Rising, Jake prepares their picnic, laying out a feast fit for a king: fry bread, chunks of barbecued goat, and slices of sharp cheddar. Sarah pulls her saddlebags to her laying the container of brownies on the blanket, noting they are the perfect compliment. Eating in silence, savoring the delicious repast, she pours coffee for them as Jake, leaning against the old oak, lights his cigar.

Sarah lies back on the quilt; her thoughts turn to the beauty surrounding them as she drifts to sleep, wondering how with such little conversation so much is being said.

Jake, deep in thought, watches Sarah sleep, pondering how to ask the question that's upper most in his mind, *Why does she choose to isolate herself on the Res like a hermit? None of my business, but I would like to know what draws her into such isolation. Do I dare ask her?*

Opening her green eyes shaded from the sun's rays by the tree, she finds herself staring into a pair of ebony orbs; ones that hold a puzzled glint disappearing as soon as Jake realizes she is watching him, leaving Sarah with the query, "What are you thinking, Jake?"

Knowing he was caught, he answers, "Sarah, Why have you chosen this life of isolation, not only from your own people but are considered a ghost to the Apache?"

Looking at the blue sky, she watches the small wisp of white clouds slowly move across the heavenly expanse. *How much do I tell him? Do I really want anyone to know why I chose this life?* As she ponders the questions Jake asked, a brilliance rivaling the golden sun ascending to its highest peak sends vibes rippling through her, and she is shocked to realize that she does want to share with this aged Apache befriending her in defiance of the tribal council.

Jake sits quietly, waiting for Sarah to speak, and just when he thinks she is not going to answer his question, he hears her soft voice. "It is not something I have spoken of in many years. It is not just one thing but a multitude of events, experiences, and heartache that urged me to seek a way of life that would offer me the peace and serenity I crave."

Jake says nothing but nods his head hoping she will continue.

Laughing, "Well, Jake, you want the long version or the condensed?"

"I would like to hear anything and everything you are comfortable in sharing, Sarah. Please continue."

Sarah ponders where to begin the saga she meant never to speak of. Then she says, "When my dad came back from the war, he adhered to the discipline and training he learned in the Navy. By the time I was ten, I had been through his version of basic training. He tolerated no sign of emotion or complaints. Whatever was going on well, that was the way of it. He never explained anything, only showing me once. I was then expected to know how to complete the task whether it was fixing a flat, overhauling an old pickup truck, herding cattle, sowing a field, or as he would say, woman's work.

"Raised by my dad alone, I spent most of my time on the farm and ranch with the hands. My dad talked very little but expected much. He had two mantras. 'Suck 'er up, get 'er done' and 'Sister, carry your own weight.' He taught pride and honesty in oneself and ones accomplishments.

"At the age of twelve, I was raped by a family member and never told anyone. I was too ashamed. After that, I kept everything bottled deep inside. I found running with the wind rippling through my hair gave a sort of release of pent-up emotions. So every chance I got, I ran and ran until I was exhausted gasping for breath, or I would go into the fields or the woods for hours upon hours alone with just the sounds of nature and precious solitude."

"When not in school, I worked on the farm or with the cattle on the ranch. I was more a tomboy than a girl. Finding comfort and renewed strength in solitude, I continued to spend time alone. Being more at home with the animals, I spent a lot of time with the livestock and hounds. The animals seemed to sense my needs and offered me comfort—even Papa's hounds protected me from humans, including him.

"He taught me it was okay to be different, but he never told me that being different was one of the most difficult roads I would ever travel.

"As I grew older and moved out on my own, I found I lacked the feminine skills to function comfortably with women, not knowing how to converse with them. I taught myself the necessary things to function in society but was never at ease around women or crowds.

"Spending thirty years in middle management, I enjoyed the many career fields I found myself in. Success to me was measured by the knowledge gained and the ability to use it in gainful employment. In spite of the accolades received, I never felt comfortable in the so-called upper society.

"Finding that most people had their own definition of honesty, and it never seemed quite real to me, closing my business and retiring, I decided that I would do what I liked. Dress the way I wanted in blue jeans, cowboy boots, and Western hats and live a quiet life unhampered by the rules of society. Mr. O'Hara was a city boy but respected my country antics and attitude at times, not really seeming to care what I did as long as I did not involve him."

Hesitating, Sarah continues, "I have never met a woman I could trust, the ones I dared to trust betrayed me. Growing older, I preferred the company of men and having been raised among the male population, I didn't understand the attitudes of both the males and females. The males assuming more than friendship, and the women sure I was after their man. Over the years, my best friends have been one or two men who accepted me as a friend, not a liaison, but it's always been a two-edge sword.

"All my life, I've been labeled by a society that did not accept anyone who saw things in a different way or lived by their own code, simply tagged for being different."

Sarah ponders Jake's response to what she is about to say but knows it is a part of who she is. After pausing, she continues, "Call it a gift or a curse, and I have done both over the years. Being sensitive to the auras of others, I pick up vibes of good and evil. Sometimes the auras are so strong that I feel bombarded, and it is necessary for me to leave to retain inner calm."

Silence permeates the air, then in a whisper, Sarah says, "Jake, I am at peace with nature, which can be calm and soothing or angry and raging, but in all my years, I have never found serenity among people." Gazing at the far off tree line she continues, "I like me and have no trouble being alone with me.

"When Mr. O'Hara passed away, I set out to fulfill a long-time dream, acquired when I lived in Farmington and Aztec, working side by side with Apache peers. Petitioning the counsel to live on the Res was something I had wanted to do since I first saw it in the early seventies. So here I am, jeopardizing everything I cherish about my life.

"It doesn't make sense even to me, but my own sense of right would not let me turn away from rescuing the boy or from responding when he hailed me. Jake, I have never been happier. Yet I have violated the lease by seeing Jimmy Begay and you. While I know what I risk, I could not turn away from the boy, and that makes me a big time fool." The look on Sarah's face indicates she will say no more.

Jake sits quietly processing what she has told him. He senses that she has only touched the surface of a troubled life that she has survived and how hard it must be for her to trust him enough to share even this much of her history. And he knows he could never betray her. "Sarah, you have nothing to fear from either of us. Thank you for sating my curiosity. You are quite a woman, Sarah Louise O'Hara."

Sarah is embarrassed by his comment and lowers her head at his words.

Raising his work-worn hand to her face and with the tips of his weather-beaten fingers, he lifts her chin until their eyes meet. "You are a brave woman worthy of an Apache name, so' I'll be thinking on it for our next meeting."

She is shocked at the tinkling sensation that races through her body at his touch; she can only nod her head. She dares not speak. Sarah sits gazing into Jake's eyes, as Rusty waits with patient indulgence, his head lying in his mistress's lap. But as Jake gets to his feet assisting her to stand, he begins to prance around, weaving in and out between their booted feet. As they stand immobile, gazing into each other's eyes, what passes between the glistening orbs is a mutual understanding.

Without words, the two friends pack their saddlebags mount their horses in silence, riding north along the western slope near the tree line. Jake finds himself not wanting to veer west to his *kogha*, yet he does. No words are spoken between this old Apache and the forbidden white woman; words would have been totally inadequate. About a mile from Sarah's cave, Jake turns his pinto west without saying a word.

Sarah halts Mesquite, gazing at the back of the Apache who has become so much a part of her life. She smiles as she sees Jake stop, look back, and raise his hand in salute. Raising her hand in reply, she turns the roan toward her cave.

The trio of friends is arriving earlier, staying later; many times Sarah arrives back at her cave just as the sun is sinking behind the western slopes and Jake travels an hour or more reaching his home after darkness spreads across the land. As she grooms her horse after their day's outing and prepares the cave for the night, she breathes a sorrowful sigh. *Next*

Saturday is so far away. Entering her home with Rusty on her heels, she can't help but wonder why Jimmy was not at their meeting, but knowing that, she will not ask.

With a cup of coffee, she retires to the main room, picks up her manuscript, and begins to read the last few pages she has written. As the clock chimes midnight, she lays the pages aside and, with her ever-faithful companion, seeks the comfort of her bed.

Jimmy returns to their rendezvous the next Saturday but offers no reason for his absence. How can he tell them he has been on a quest? Jake would ask questions and Sarah would want to know what a quest is. No, he can offer no explanation. He is relieved when they accept the silence regarding his absence. And so they continue their weekly outing, during the heat of July and August moving into the trees at the edge of the valley where it is cooler and less visible to passersby.

As the summer fades into fall, the three friends spend many Saturdays picnicking, chatting while the two Apache teach her to speak the language of the People. Her laughter echoes across the open valley as she tries to pronounce the words as Jimmy does.

"*Keesda* [feast]. Ah, Jimmy, I am hopeless when it comes to your beautiful language. You and Jake might know what

I am trying to say, but I doubt another Apache would. You are a good teacher. It is your pupil that is difficult."

Jake roars with laughter. "Jimmy, I am afraid she is right. Maybe in many moons, she might learn a little bit," winking at him. "But we won't give up, will we, pal?"

"No way, Jake, we are relentless."

Sarah ruffles his hair as she reaches for the apples to be given their ponies and hands them to Him. "Get on with you now."

The time for the feast is rapidly approaching, and while Sarah has gone to the feast before, she is undecided about this year as Jakes asks, "Sarah, the feast is just about a month away. You will be going, will you not?" Jake waits anxiously for her reply and hopes it does not show on his face.

She looks at him, trying to judge his meaning and sees no hint of his emotions. "Yes, Jake, I plan to attend."

Seeing a smile spread across his face as Jimmy returns from the horses, Sarah picks up the blanket and begins to roll it to go behind her saddle. She knows she has made the right decision in going to the feast.

The *Go-Jii-Yah* (feast) is held from September 14 to 15 at Stone Lake, about eighteen miles south of Dulce. The feast originated hundreds of years before when the clans of the Jicarilla—Red Clan and White Clan—were still nomadic hunters and gathers. The date was firmly established in the late 1800s when the Apache were moved to the Jicarilla. Tepees are set up while cooking is done outdoors hospitality comes first for everyone, and the feast is open to the white eyes as well. There will be a rodeo, native dances, foot races, and plenty of good food to sample.

Mounting their ponies, they ride off into the distance each returning to their *kogha*. As Jake makes his usual turn toward his, he finds it harder and harder to leave this white woman.

Riding in the opposite direction, Sarah's thoughts are melancholic. *These Saturdays never last long enough. With each passing rendezvous I crave more time, especially with Jake. How did this happen? How did he become so important to me? I must never let him know. Life would really be complicated then*. As she awakens from her deep thoughts, the corral is right in front of her. "Well, Mesquite, guess we don't get our run today. Tomorrow, I promise."

With all her chores done for the evening, she retires and settles down at her computer, getting serious about finishing her book; as her hands fly over the keys, time slips away. With back aching from sitting so long, Sarah stands and stretches to work out the kinks. *Wow, has it really been five hours?* Rusty dances around then, with a woof, heads for the kitchen.

Laughing, Sarah follows her devoted shepherd. "Okay, Rusty! Okay, boy! Its break time. How about a snack, fellow?" Placing his extra tidbits on the floor near his water bowl, she fixes herself a ham sandwich with a few blue corn tostadas and a soda. Sitting at the table eating, her thoughts once again turn to the old Apache. *How did he become so much a part of my Saturdays and my world?* Sighing, she puts her dishes away and retires for the evening with her devote shepherd stretched out beside her.

Sleep did not come easy as dreams haunt the remaining hours of the night. The essence emanating from the vision is dark and frightening, indistinguishable eerie shadows bombard her as the fear overwhelms her dream persona she chokes with emanate death. As the black evil's screeches reach a crescendo, she sees death hovering in the gray mist, when suddenly a large eagle appears and the pernicious darkness dissipates. Sarah, startled out of her dreamed-filled sleep, is drenched in perspiration, terror gripping her, she gasps for breath.

Rusty crawls to her, placing his head on her thigh. As he does, she wraps her arms around him, laying her head against his warm, comforting body. Looking at the clock whose hands seem suspended, she sees that it is two o'clock. Too disturbed by the nightmare to return to sleep, she slips from the bed, dons her robe, and with Rusty at her heels, goes to the kitchen makes coffee.

The hours pass with her still sitting at the kitchen table. Not being prone to dreams or nightmares, she wonders why now. Her childhood nightmares stopped their nightly ravages when she was in her fifties and that has been a long time. *What does it mean?* She has never had anything to fear on the Res. Pondering her years here, she remembers the deciding factor on her being awarded the privilege of living here. The eagle feather that swayed the Respected Elder to grant the ninety-nine-year lease, *When I ride across the Res I always see an eagle, and now, the eagle sent the evil from my dream. What is the connection? What does it mean?*

Jumping from her seat, she rushes to her computer, and the next several hours are spent researching the eagle in the Jicarilla Apache Lore. Only tribal members may possess eagle feathers and must acquire a permit from the US Fish and Wildlife Service. Permit applications must have their tribal certification enrollment from the BIA. She discovers that long waiting periods exist to receive one of the permits.

The Jicarilla Apache may wear the feathers and use them in their religious ceremonies or their cultural activities. But as a white woman, she cannot even pick up a feather, should she find one that has fallen from an eagle soaring in the skies.

Suddenly, her mind is jolted with harsh reality. "Oh, dear God in heaven, the Respected Elder gave me the feather that fell at my feet some seven-plus years ago. I could be fined for having the feather in the cave."

Sitting in shocked silence, she realizes that she could never give up that life changing eagle feather. *No one must ever know that I have it—no one!*

The sun rises above the Sangri de Cristo Mountains, spreading its golden haze across the crisp morning air as the meadow lark chirps his morning song. There is an air of excitement running through Sarah's cave; the feast days are here.

The Go-Jii-Yah Feast is held at Stone Lake, southeast of Dulce; the feast is open to visitors of all nationalities as long as they are respectful of the Apache culture. Seeing the snake as a bad omen, the Apache have no contact with this reptile and ask that no snakes or snake products be brought on the Reservation. Some Apache are comfortable with touching and displays of emotion while others are not. The body language of individuals will cue you to whether they will accept a show of affection. The owl is a night creature and is considered to be a bad omen, especially if he hoots near you. Oh yes, photography is not permitted.

All these things run through Sarah's mind as she prepares for her trip to Stone Lake. The eccentric white woman backs her truck out setting the screens that hide her mountain cave from prying eyes. Mesquite and Rusty have the run of a spacious barn attached to the inside corral with plenty of food and water and will be safe until her return.

Dressed in typical jeans, boots, and Western hat, Sarah arrives at Stone Lake parking where she is directed by the attendants. Leaving the vehicle, she is unaware her arrival is observed by Pete Sosa and his cousin Joe—two disgruntled Apache.

Frowning at her arrival and uttering an ugly snarl, he demands, "Hey, Joe, what's she doing here?"

Not giving the white woman a thought, Joe doesn't understand what Pete finds so offensive about her living on the Res. "Hell, Joe, the feast is open to the public. Why shouldn't she be here? What have you got against her? She does no harm. Hell one rarely sees her."

"Don't you find it strange that the council allows her to live on the Res?"

"From what I hear, Pete, she abides by the rules set down by the elders of the council. What's your beef?"

Pete stands there glowering as she walks into the crowd. "But what if she hasn't? A white woman on the Res should never have been allowed."

"Stop festering over something that is none of your business. It was a decision made by the council. We have no reason to question their wisdom. Besides, down through the ages, other whites have lived with the Apache."

"Maybe you do, but I don't like it. The Res is no place for white eyes, and I intend to find a way to get rid of her."

At Pete's declaration, Joe walks toward the rodeo grounds, shaking his head. *He is so full of hate. I wonder why?* The bull riding will be starting soon, and he signed up to compete this afternoon. *I need to stay away from Pete, he's trouble. We've been friends a long time, but he's gotten mean and ugly*. Aware that Pete did not follow, he glances back to see what is keeping him. Pete is walking around her truck, pausing by the driver's door. *Damn! My old friend is getting to be bad news. What the hell is he doing?* "Pete are you coming or not?"

"Yeah! Yeah! Be right there."

Sarah wanders through the grounds, stopping at the booths where some of the artisans have their jewelry on display. She loves the native jewelry and plans to indulge her fantasy before she leaves; she sees a bracelet and Concho belt that catches her fancy. Strolling on through the various food vendors, the smell of fry bread reminds her she did not take the time to eat breakfast; purchasing a small bowl of mutton stew and fry bread, she finds a quiet place to sit devouring the fresh cooked food.

Her eyes wander through the crowd of natives in their colorful costumes and visitors from all over the southwest searching for a glimpse of Jake or Jimmy. She can't help herself; she longs to see Jake even though they will not be able to converse. Glancing at her watch, she sees it's nearly time for the afternoon bull riding to begin. Putting the residue from her meal in the trash barrel, she heads toward the arena when, out of the corner of her eye, she sees Jake heading in the same direction. Slowing her pace so they will not meet, she feels a longing deep inside—an ache familiar but so strange. He is in uniform, which means he is helping out during the feast; even more of a reason not to encounter him. Sighing with resolve, she climbs into the stands for the afternoon events.

How strange it would be if others knew she cheered for the bull and not the rider. Her love of animals brings this odd emotion swelling to an aching cosmic eclipse as she watches rider after rider try to stay on the various bulls. One, a man the announcer called Joe Sosa, succeeds in staying seated for the eight seconds. One or two others manage to stay for the count, but most of the time, the bull dumps them. While the clowns distract him, the unseated cowboy dusts off his pants and climbs out of the arena. The sun is low on the horizon when the last bronc has been ridden for the day; tomorrow, finals will be held and winners announced.

Tonight, the dancers perform the rain dance for visitors. Knowing she has a little time before the evening festivities begin, Sarah wanders back to the booths and picks out the bracelet and Concho belt she couldn't resist. Completing her transaction, she walks back to her truck, placing the items in a locked box under the camper shell. As she turns to walk away, she is stunned to see scrawled in the dirt on the side of her truck, "Die, White Woman!" An icy chill rolls down her spine as she searches the area for anyone loitering there; she sees no one except a family heading to the food area. *Who would do this and why?* Puzzled emotion flits across her eyes as she searches the gray shadows, then taking a deep breath, she turns back toward the vendor's stalls.

Walking back through the vehicles, she sees Jimmy and his parents arrive and park a few rows over; the sight of familiar faces tempers the icy chill wrapping around her. He smiles, tilting his head slightly in greeting. Sarah eyes beam with pleasure, and like the young boy, she nods her head just a tad in salutation, continuing toward the area designated for the ritual dances to begin as the sun hovers on the horizon.

Sarah watches the sun slip slowly behind the mountains, setting the sky ablaze with radiant jewel tones shifting to vibrant colors of lavender deepening to purple. The gray shadows turning to ebony are again set afire with bonfires, giving an eerie glow to the night as those who are to perform the rain dance gather. Standing beneath the spreading limbs of the regal spruce, Sarah sips from a paper cup full of steaming coffee gazing into the night, watching the black velvet sky come alive with brilliant diamonds. Lost in the beauty of the night, she is unaware of an inebriated buck watching her from the shadow of a camper parked among the first row of vehicles.

"Pete, why did you scrawl on her truck? What if someone saw you? I've never seen you so angry?" *What fuels his anger? He has made me apart of whatever he is up to, and I don't' like it.*

Pete snarls. "She has no right on the Res. The council should never have granted her the lease." Pausing to take a slug from the bottle in his jacket pocket, he says, "I am going to prove to the council that she doesn't belong here."

Joe grows more concerned with his friend's ranting. "You keep saying that, but what do you mean? And how the hell are you going to do that? And why do you care?"

The two drunks continue to talk in low tones, finishing the bottle. Without answering his questions, Pete says, "Come on Joe, I need another bottle."

Trying to figure out how he is going to shake this terrible obsession of his friend, he follows Pete into the night.

As the drums beat out a cadence, the ritualistic performance of the rain dance begins. The spectators gather closer in order to see these magnificent dancers in traditional dress. Sarah chose an excellent spot, giving an unobstructed view of the colorfully attired Apache. She can't help herself as she keeps time with the beat of the drums, becoming lost in the ancient ritual oblivious to those standing around her.

Keeping the council's edict of no contact with the white woman and to keep the pact he made with Jimmy Begay and Sarah, Jake quietly comes up behind Sarah. His voice a mere whisper, he breaks into her reverie. "Sarah, don't turn around. Tilt your head forward for yes, left for no. Have you been to your truck recently?"

Understanding his reasoning for the instructions, Sarah moves her head forward in answer to his question.

Unable to see her face and her reaction, he takes a deep breath. "Did you see anyone around at the time you discover the writing?"

She tilts her head slightly to the left, wanting so much to reach out and touch him but not daring; she hardly dares to breathe, let alone move a muscle.

Realizing she is quite calm about the incident, he replies, "I'm going to have the forensic team see if they can get fingerprints. I'll see you officially soon. Don't worry, white woman." With those tender words, he fades into the darkness.

Sarah feels the air shift as Jake disappears into the shadows. He must have been making the rounds as he's working security for the feast. When he returns officially, she has several questions to ask him or the sheriff. At least it wasn't scratched into the truck, only written in the dirt covering it.

As Jake strides toward the command center behind the announcer's booth, he hears a young voice he recognizes as his little friend, Jimmy Begay, calling. "Jake! Jake."

Pausing, he waits for the lad to catch up to him, then as the lad skids to a stop in from of him, "Jimmy, what are you doing out at this hour, and where are your parents?"

"Oh, Jake! Have you seen her truck? Who would do such a mean thing? What can we do? How will we find out who did this?" There is anxiety and concern in this small lad, which Jake shares, but has no intention of letting him know.

"Whoa, Jimmy, we're not going to do anything. Yes, I have seen the truck. Yes, I am going now to call the forensic team to see if they can get fingerprints. Sarah knows about it, I spoke with her briefly a minute ago."

With tension in his voice, the young boy asks, "You didn't tell, Jake. You didn't tell, did you?"

In spite of all his efforts, a smile spreads across his face. "Of course not, nor would I ever do that, Jimmy. She is our friend. We will protect her secret…and ours."

Jimmy remembers his vision and his quest, and although he is not ready to share the responsibility, he has assumed his demeanor and his voice turns very serious. He stands straight as he believes a warrior would. "I promised to guard her and our secret with my life. I will not fail her."

Seeing the look on the young warrior, Jake realizes the depth his attachment to the white woman. Placing his hand on the lad's shoulder, he says, "Jimmy, we won't let anything happen to her, you can count on that. Now let me get about the business of trying to find out who would dare do this terrible thing. Go back to your parents. As soon as I know something, I will find a way to let you know." Jake moves off as Jimmy turns back, sprinting across the ground to where his family waits.

Using his radio, he advises, "Sheriff, we have a bit of graffiti on a vehicle in the parking lot near the corral. Ran the plates on the truck, it belongs to Sarah Louise O'Hara. Thought you might want to check it out yourself."

"Be right there, Jake, go ahead and call the forensic team."

"Roger that." Jake stays close as he waits for the sheriff he allows his eyes to search the area, looking for anything or anyone who might have seen the culprit in the act of the vandalism. Watching the sheriff's approach, he steps out of the shadows to greet him.

"Wouldn't have bothered you, Ben, but thought you would want to see this considering whose truck it is." Jake flashes his light on the side of the truck, observing the expression in the eyes of the sheriff as he reads, "Die, White Woman!"

"What the hell, Jake? Has she seen this?"

Jake knows he has to play it smart. "Don't know for sure, Ben. Last time I saw her, she was standing near the tall aspen by one of the fry bread booths watching the dancers. You want me to find her?"

"Yeah, but do it quietly. Have you seen any other graffiti this evening?"

"No." Walking toward the arena, he sees Sarah standing almost in the same place he had left her. "Sarah, the sheriff wants to see you over by your truck." Lowering his voice, he says, "He doesn't know you have already seen the graffiti or that I stopped by and told you earlier. I will take my lead from you."

"Jake, he will have to know that I have seen the scrawl and have some concern as to why such a thing happened."

Smiling in the shadows where no one can see, he replies, "You are an honorable woman, Sarah. And I am proud to call you friend. Ah, but we will keep that to ourselves, or Jimmy will have our hides all tanned out and hug on the wall."

In spite of her deep concern, Sarah laughs. Moving toward the truck with Jake at her side, it takes only a few minutes to reach the sheriff. "Howdy, Sheriff!"

"Ms. O'Hara, thought you might oughta see this. We called in the forensic team. They're just now arriving." Raising his hand for the team to come forward, he continues, "Doesn't look as if it scratched into the paint."

"Sheriff, you're right. I don't' think there is any real damage. I saw it earlier when I put some packages in the back."

"Why didn't you report it?"

"What could I say, Sheriff? I see so few people and converse only at the stores where I shop in Dulce. And in this crowd, how would one ever find the individual."

The sheriff turns to the forensic team who are already at work. "Any chance of getting a print from the dust?"

"Not much, we found a partial that we might be able to use. Took pictures, if we had something to compare it to, we could do a handwriting comparison. We'll take all this to the lab and see what we can find out."

"Okay, guys, do the best you can." Turning to Sarah, he states, "We take this kind of threat seriously. Since you are a resident on the Res, this will have to be reported to the council. Your appearance before the council might be necessary?"

"Of course, Sheriff, I would expect no less considering the nature of the graffiti."

"Are you driving home tonight, Ms. O'Hara?"

"No, I have a room at the inn for the night. I plan to return home after the feast ends tomorrow as my animals need care."

Looking out across the sea of cars, deep in thought, he sighs, "Well, I'm going to assign Jake to look after you until we know more about the incident." Walking over to where Jake is standing with the forensic team, he states, "Jake, I want you to keep an eye on Ms. O'Hara until we get this sorted out."

"How close an eye? Do I stay with her or just keep her under surveillance?"

Pondering the question, he answers, "I think it would be wise to stay with her unless she is in her home. If I remember correctly, she has a German shepherd to watch her there. Check with her about her routine and schedule your work accordingly."

Jake keeps his face expressionless, yet inside, a warm glow of delight is spreading through his body. *How lucky can I be!*

"Ms. O'Hara."

"Sheriff. Please call me Sarah. Ms. O'Hara is someone I used to know a long time ago."

Nodding, he says, "Sarah, Jake will be your escort for a while. We don't know who did this and until we find out, I don't want you out alone. Is that understood?"

"Sheriff, I have animals to care for and a horse to exercise on a daily basis. It's a big inconvenience for anyone to babysit an old woman who lives such a quiet, uneventful life."

"Maybe so, but that is his assignment. Don't make it difficult for him. I don't want anything happening to you. And to be honest, I don't want to have to answer to the tribal council for any harm that might come your way. This death threat is going to be hard enough to explain."

"Okay, Sheriff, I will do my part not to be a burden to you or the deputy. I appreciate the concern."

Noting what she had told the sheriff, he spoke, "Sarah, are you ready to go to the inn, or was there something else you wish to do?"

"No, there is nothing else tonight, I'm ready. It's been an interesting evening."

"One other thing, I think we are done with the truck, but you might forgo washing it in case we want another look, then I won't impound it."

Breathing a sigh of relief at getting to keep her truck, she says, "That's not a problem, Sheriff. I just want to relax for the rest of the night." Looking at her watch, she notes that it is just past midnight. *It has been a long day.*

"Sarah, why don't you leave your truck here tonight? I'll drive you to the inn."

"Jake, that's a good idea. I'll post a guard for the night." Reaching for his radio calling dispatch advising, "Mae get hold of Jim and have him meet me at the parking lot behind the arena at Stone Lake. Tell him he'll be on stakeout and send Lee Atepa over to the inn to help Jake."

Sarah, walking beside Jake, feels a myriad of emotions racing through her mind and body. *Who would write such a thing on my truck? Why? What have I done that someone would want me dead?* "Could it be someone's idea of a joke?"

Unaware she spoke aloud, she hears a quiet voice beside her "Joke or not, someone is going to pay for this night's work."

"Oh, I'm sorry I didn't realize I spoke out loud."

They walk in silence to his vehicle; approaching his SUV, suddenly it dawns on Sarah. She *can* be seen with Jake! A smile unbidden slips across her face as Jake opens the door for her to slide into the vehicle.

If one had been paying attention, they would have seen two supposed strangers with countenances beaming brighter than stars in the ebony dome, each unaware of the radiance emitting from their own visage.

The sky becomes a curtain of gray as dawn creeps across the Res. Stretching his tired bones from a night on the sofa, Jake hears a knock at the door. Looking to see that

Sarah's door is still closed, he quietly admits Lee who enters bearing coffee. "Lee, thanks! That sure smells good."

"What's the deal, Jake? Why are we guarding the woman? All I was told last night was to come here and help you. I've been sitting outside the door all night."

"Someone scrawled a death threat on her truck when it was parked at the feast grounds. The sheriff assigned Jim to stakeout just in case someone returned to the vehicle during the night."

"We're not to let her out of our sight until further notice. She plans to go back to the rodeo and attend the dances this afternoon, and we'll be right there."

Neither hears Sarah leave the bedroom until she speaks, "Good morning! I see you already have coffee. Could I interest you gentleman in breakfast before we head out to the grounds?"

Smiling, Jake replies, "You walk as soft as an Indian warrior. And yes, breakfast sounds very good to me, how about you, Lee?"

Like any young man, Lee is ready to eat. "You bet, I thought no one would ever ask." Putting his hat back on his head, he makes for the door as Sarah picks up hers. Reaching the door, he steps to the side, opening it slowly, looking up and down the hall while Jake keeps Sarah behind him. "All clear."

Making their way to the elevator, the officers are alerted to the movement down the hall as a door shuts. Preceding the other two into the restaurant, Lee checks out the patrons dining at the early hour then moves to a booth, giving them a clear view of the entrance, placing their backs to the wall.

Exiting the restaurant an hour later, Jake looks around and sees nothing to rouse his suspicions as he moves toward his SUV. "Lee, you follow us. I'm going to park near the substation. Sarah what would you like to do before the rodeo starts at ten o'clock?"

With a pensive look on her face as though she was undecided, she answers, "Jake, I had thought to visit some of the vendors this morning, but now that depends on you."

"That should be okay. Lee and I will be right with you. Sheriff's orders are to be sure nothing happens to you, and I intend to do just that." Anyone seeing Jake's expression at that moment would have seen a glint of steel emanating from his ebony orbs and his jaw clamped in iron.

Wandering around the different booths with Lee and Jake in tow, Sarah purchases several items of bold turquoise jewelry crafted by well-known artisans. She doesn't need the jewelry, rarely wearing any at all, but she can't resist the craftsmanship of the *diide*.

As time draws near for the start of today's rodeo events, the crowd grows larger, and the noise hovers just slightly below a roar. Everyone is in a festive mood, and Sarah finds herself caught up in the excitement and thrill of the rodeo in spite of the graffiti.

The sun is high in the azure sky as she finds herself looking for the ever-present eagle that is always around when she is outdoors. *Well, guess there is too much noise for him, can't say as I blame him since I to prefer the quiet of my mountain cave.*

Very few words are exchanged between her and the tribal police assigned to keep her safe. Off a ways, she sees Jimmy smiling as he slightly tips his hat. Jake notices the exchange. "Lee, stay with her for a minute, I need to speak to that young man." As he moves toward the lad, he is aware the boy is dressed in native attire watching as he speaks to his parents then races to where Jake is standing.

He's whispering, making it hard to be heard by the old man. "Jake, what happened? Who did this to Sarah? Is she all right?"

Jake leans down where he can hear above the roar of the crowd and so nothing he says can be overheard. "She is fine! And we don't know who. She will be safe. Lee and I have been assigned to stay with her. Now run along, lad. Everything is okay."

"If you say so, Jake," and off he goes.

As the first bronc rider leaves the chutes, Sarah, Lee, and Jake move to the top two tiers of the stadium. The officers sit on the top placing Sarah on the second tier, literally surrounding her on three sides.

She enjoys the rodeo quietly, rooting for the animals. Her attentive concern for the animals does not go unnoticed.

Jake feels a sense of pride as he watches her root for the bull or the bronc, never for the rider. A hint of a smile sparkles in his eyes, but being Apache, it never quite spreads to his countenance.

Neither of them is aware of the two drunken bucks standing in the shadow under the stands. As the last bull leaves his rider in the dust and this year's rodeo comes to a close, the crowd begins to leave the stadium for other areas or back to the inn for gambling and dinner.

When Sarah rises, preparing to leave, Lee places his hand on her shoulder. "Let the crowd disperse before we try to make our way out." She nods without turning to look at him.

"What would you like to eat for lunch, Sarah?"

Grinning, she turns her head to cast an eye at Jake and in a somber voice that holds a hint of laughter says, "Officer, I would like some mutton, fry bread, and black coffee."

The stands are almost empty as he responds, "Well, I think I know just the place to fill the menu. Shall we?"

As the crowd disperses, Pete is standing at the far end of the stadium into his second bottle of whiskey, and in spite of Joe's argument, he is determined to cause trouble for the white woman. He is possessed by an inner demon, driving him harder and harder toward no good. Becoming more and more concerned with each passing hour as to Joe's intent, he keeps hoping he will pass out from all the liquor. *If he doesn't pass out from the liquor, he will probably wind up in jail until he sleeps it off. Ah, hell what is he getting us into?*

As they are waiting on their mutton and fry bread, the sheriff arrives. Moving in close to the three, he states, "We did manage to get a partial fingerprint but, as of yet, have not found a match. The stakeout last night was a bust. Ms. O'Hara, Sarah, you may have your truck when you are ready to return home. There were too many footprints around the area to isolate one. I want you guys to stay with her while she's at Stone Lake. Jake, when she is ready to return home, stay close to her." Turning to her, he asks, "Would it be too much trouble to put Jake up at your place for a few days."

Sarah likes the idea of having Jake around, but she is concerned how other tribal members might see it. "Sheriff, do you really think that is necessary? I'm sure Jake has more important things to do than babysit me."

Watching her face and body language for whatever she might reveal, he answers, "Yes, I do. We take a death threat very seriously." He is surprised to see there is no change in her eyes or her facial expression. *Hm, she is one tough lady.*

Glancing first at Jake and then at the sheriff, she replies, "There's room at the cave, but I feel like I'm a big imposition."

Jake responds, "Not at all, Sarah, I'm retired and only work when the sheriff needs extra hands. I'm sure he can spare me as the feast will be over this evening. Right, Sheriff."

"Thank you, Sarah for complying. I will be meeting with the council tomorrow to report this incident and to receive their prospective on the matter. Jake, if the council wishes to speak with her, I will radio you. How long are you staying today, Sarah?"

"I plan to stay through the Harvest and Good Crops Dance this afternoon. I have animals that need care and thought to be home before the sun sets."

Nodding his approval, the sheriff melts into the crowd as though he was never there.

As the drums ring out across the land the crowd gathers to watch the dancers in their last performance of this year's Go-Jii-Ya. Sarah stands in the shade of a cottonwood where she has an unobstructed view of the dancers; inhaling the faint scent of sagebrush as it drifts on the cool breeze, mingling with the smoke of the pinon used by the food vendors.

Watching from a few feet away, Jake admires this illusive white woman he is supposed to protect from the death threat scrawled on her truck. *Was it really only last evening? The Gods have truly been kind to me. Now I can see her without repercussions at least until the sheriff finds out who made the death threat.*

Lee is near the last row of seats set up for the spectators, making sure he has a good view of Sarah. He scans the crowd for any sign of possible threat. Although he knew a white woman lived on the Res, he had never met her but now marvels at how nice she is, not eccentric at all.

As the two men continue to scan the crowd, their eyes meet both noting with admiration that she is keeping perfect rhythm with the drum beats and the chants of the dancers. Continuing to scan the crowd, they see that most of the tribal council are in seats of honor with the exception of the president who stands slightly apart.

Jake is surprised to see him scanning the spectators, watching the dancers perform the Harvest and Good Crop Dance.

Two men who appear to be drunk are making their way along the back of the seating. Suddenly, an eerie Apache war cry rends the air, causing the drums and the dancers to stop in midstep, puzzled by the commotion. Everyone looks around, trying to determine where the screech originated. Just as the drums start back up, a piercing voice, loud as a ten megaton explosion yells, "Die, white woman!"

Before the echo of these threatening words is carried away on the wind, Sarah is surrounded by five beautiful eagles flapping their huge wings as they perch in the cottonwood she is standing under. The air stirs with the movement of people, but the eagle's piercing scream is so eerie the Apache halt in mid stride as others stampede in the opposite direction away from the huge birds.

As the council stands to see what the commotion is, the drunken Apache stumbles toward her. Just as he gets with in twenty feet of her, a mighty bolt of lightning strikes the ground in front of Sarah, halting all movement in her direction, and with the eagles guarding her on the other three sides, it would be impossible to actually harm her.

The Apache stand frozen, mesmerized by tradition retold time after time as it comes alive before their eyes. As the smoke from the lightning strike dissipates, the eagles still hover over the white woman.

Amid the riotous departure of the spectators, no one sees Pete stumble, disappearing into the retreating crowd; in his drunken state, he teeters toward the small grove of trees. Puzzled by the lightning strike and fearful of the eagles surrounding her, he cowers amid the dark shadows of the trees, unaware that his arms, face, and clothing were singed by the lightning.

Joe, trying to reach Pete in his inebriated state, falls to the ground as people rush past him. Unable to rise, he crawls through the herd, trying to avoid being stepped on as he makes his way into the deepest shadows of a small stand of scrub oak not far from the rodeo arena. Reaching the trees, he comes to an abrupt stop holding his breath; he listens. *Damn! Someone is here. I can hear their breathing.*

While the drunks hide in the grove, unaware the white eyes are fleeing, the tribal elders stand in front of their seats, unmoving except for their eyes following the movement of the eagles.

Sarah stares at the charred ground a few feet in front of her where a pit now exist some two feet deep, singed black by the bolt of lightning. The charred ground spreads across the area some twenty feet. Lying within the blackened area are five perfectly formed eagle feathers untouched by the fiery flames of the lightning.

Looking at the sea of faces in a semicircle some fifteen feet from her seeing only Apache, cautiously she scans the faces mired with shocked disbelief, hair and clothes singed by the blast of heavenly fire. Even Jake stands unmoving, stiff like the wooden Indian outside cigar stores.

Feeling no fear but an unexplained sense of well-being, she knows something extraordinary occurred today. *What just happened? Where did all the visitors go? I didn't see them leave.*

Everything is so still, it's as though a film paused in suspended animation. Slowly the Apache began to move in the opposite direction with the exception of the council and the Respected Elder, who stands unmoving in front of their seats where they were before the war cry, a cry so unfamiliar in today's life on the reservation it was shocking.

The faces of the council members reflect the lingering influence of their ancient beliefs, stoic expressions rigid frozen only the eyes reflecting any emotion. The Respected Elder, wise in the tales heard at the feet of the grandfathers as a child, sees the significance of the eagles and their protection of the white woman. He recalls the eagle dropped one of his feathers at her feet when she first came to the council for permission to live on the Res. Alive with this knowledge, he must speak to the council. *The Gods have chosen her, a white woman. No harm must ever come to her.*

Sarah, without moving, notices a mist drifting toward her; out of that mist, a small voice asks, "Sarah? You okay."

Recognizing the voice housed in the brume, she sees Jimmy standing in front of her yet is unaware that no one else can see him. With a calmness she doesn't understand, she responds, "Yes, Jimmy, I am fine. Should you be talking to me? The council is watching. They won't like you talking to me."

Jimmy looks up at her, his black eyes glistening, "They cannot see me, only the Respected Elder and the Ancient One, who knows of my quest and the path I have chosen. I have been chosen by the Spirits of our Ancestors to protect you. It will all be okay." Jimmy slowly picks up the five eagle feathers with the reverence they deserve, handing them to Sarah. "Take them! No one will ever question your right to have them."

Extending her hands, she takes the precious feathers with the same respect Jimmy shows in picking them from the charred ground; pressing them to her breast, casting her eyes to the clear skies, she sees the five glorious eagles fade, not soaring but dissolving into the clear blue skies. When she looks back, the mist and the lad are also gone.

With only her eyes animated, she watches as the sheriff speaks with the president and the council; concern ripples through her mind wondering what her future holds. After a brief conference, he signals Jake and Lee to approach. After an exchange of words, the three men move in her direction.

Although her future is now in question, she feels a deep sense of peace as they approach.

The sheriff's tone of voice is neutral, not friendly nor angry. "Ms. O'Hara! Jake and Lee will see you home. Their orders are the same to keep you safe. The council will meet tomorrow." Walking away, he pauses and looks back, as if there is more he would like to say, but shakes his head and continues to his patrol car at the edge of the arena.

Across the way, the Respected Elder is talking with Jimmy and his parents. She can't help but be concerned for him. She wonders about his confidence that he will be okay, and that it is all right for her to have the feathers.

Jake is not sure what happened this afternoon; or the significance of the eagles and the lightening. In the legends he was taught as a young warrior, their appearance would mean she is favored by the Gods. *Is she? Is it possible?*

Believing in the old ways where the medicine man explains all the unusual events, Jake knows this is serious. Putting the analysis of the last twenty-four hours aside, he calls, "Sarah, are you ready to leave? When she does not respond, Jake's voice reflects a bit of concern. "Ms. O'Hara! Ms. O'Hara! Sarah! Are you all right?"

Responding to the urgency in his voice, she says, "I'm sorry, Jake, were you speaking to me?"

Looking at her with deep concern showing in his eyes yet his face placid as the lake on a calm day, he answers, "Yes, are you ready to leave for your mountain home?"

Mystified by the events of the past twenty-four hours, Sarah nods her head and cautiously moves toward her truck with Jake and Lee striding beside her. Pausing at the driver's door of her vehicle, she stands holding the key in her hand, not punching it. On her face, there is no expression of emotion, but her eyes seem to be searching the distant horizon.

Jake waits for her to unlock the door, observing the tranquility of her features. "Sarah, is something wrong?"

For the first time since the lightning bolt hit the ground in front of her, she looks at Jake with a smile spreading across her face, a smile that doesn't quite reach the green of her eyes. "What? Oh, Jake, no, nothing's wrong. Sorry, guess I let my mind wander." With that, she unlocks the truck, climbing into the cab.

Speaking to Lee as well as to Sarah, he says, "Lee, do you know where Sarah's home is?" Lee nods in the affirmative. "Take the lead position. Sarah will follow you, and I will fall in behind her. Stay tight."

The three vehicles are observed as they pull out of the fairgrounds heading toward Dulce. Creeping to the edge of the oaks, standing in the shadows, Pete is surprised at the protection detail assigned to the interloper on his reservation. *Now, how the hell am I going to get to her? She has got to die.*

Yet his declaration is tinged with a wee bit of fear as he remembers the eagles surrounding her, and a cold chill creeps down his spine. *Where the hell is Joe! He was right behind me.*

With the sky turning gray as the sun creeps above the horizon, Pete sees that with few exceptions, the area is void of vehicles. After a few minutes of thought, he moves from the shelter of the grove walking toward his old rusty pickup, not giving his longtime friend a thought.

Unaware that just a few feet away covered by the darkness, Joe huddles, afraid to move; too cold and too scared to sleep, he listens to the coyote's howl as it echoes across the prairie. Seeing the ebony night turn to shades of gray, he wonders, *Where is he? Hope the cops arrested him.*

As he sits pondering the fate of his angry friend, he hears a vehicle come to life off in the distance. Sore and aching from the trampling he received when he fell amid the crowd, he wonders how he will get home as he had come with Pete.

The drive is long and lonely as Sarah follows the red glowing taillights of the police SUV, aware of the dimmed headlights of the vehicle carrying Jake reflecting in the mirrors of her truck. Too stunned at the events of the past two days, she concentrates on her driving, aching to be with her animal friends: Mesquite, her trusted roan, and Rusty, her ever faithful German Shepherd—her friends, her companions.

Traveling in caravan since leaving Stone Lake, the vehicles turn off the highway on to the road that is hardly better than a cow trail through the wilderness rutted from the occasional rain and no maintenance. Lee, a dedicated officer, never questioned the wisdom of the council in allowing the white woman to live on the Res, but he was always curious to why she would want to live in isolation. He begins to look at the events of the past twenty-four hours. *Who would want to kill an old lady who lives alone, abides by the council's decree, and bothers no one? It makes no sense*. Following the road to where it ends at a corral built against the mountain, he is shocked that he sees nothing but the face of a mountain staring at him. No house! No barn! *Where the hell does she live?*

As Jake follows the glowing red lights staring him in the face, his questioning nature as a detective begins mentally to alignment the known facts: (1) She has no friends on the Res or off to his knowledge, (2) on her rides through the countryside, she visits with no one, (3) wording of the death threat would indicate an Apache, (4) no discernible footprints at the scene, (4) fingerprint doesn't appear to be in the system so no criminal record. There is simply not enough information to know where to start to find the person responsible—and find them he will!

He keeps going over crime scene information, avoiding the one thing that shocked even an old Apache. *Where did the eagles come from? They did not fly away, I watched. How could they just vanish into nothing? And that lone bolt of lightning out of a cloudless sky leaving a pit two feet deep with the ground charred black everywhere for a twenty-foot distance; even some of the natives standing nearby had hair singed off their arms. Except, not a leaf or dirt or burn touch Sarah. It was like a wall of glass protected her. I thought I saw Jimmy Begay walk onto the burned area, but I did not see where he went. And where did the eagle feathers go that I saw lying on the blackened ground untouched by fire. Oh well, I must have just thought I saw Jimmy walk toward Sarah in the confusion.* The brakes lights of the vehicles ahead broke his train of thought as he realizes they have reached her cave. Pulling up behind Sarah's truck, he shuts off the ignition just as she steps from her truck. Seeing Lee standing beside his vehicle, he motions for him to join them.

Lee cannot contain the curiosity. "Sarah, where is your home? There is nothing but the face of the mountain here?"

Sarah in spite of all the events they have experienced, smiles that knowing smile that only a female can create. "Lee, it is right before your eyes. Wait here and you will see the miracle of Apache engineering." Walking to a natural pinon near the face of the "mountain," she reaches behind it without looking and punches in the code to reveal her private cave.

Lee stands, his eyes glowing with discovery, his mouth gaping open. "No one would know you are here, no one."

Sarah musters a laugh. "That was the whole idea, Lee. I like it that way." She addresses the officers. "There is room in the garage for your vehicles along with mine. I still prefer no one really know where I live."

Still flabbergasted, Lee asks, "You really like no one knowing where you live?"

She ponders his question. "Lee, if I did not like it that way, I would never have agreed to the conditions of the tribal council and abided by them for the past eight years."

Jake steps closer. "Let's get these vehicles under cover. Sarah, you have animals to care for, may we help?"

She looks at Jake with a hint of a smile. "I'll let Mesquite and Rusty decide if you can help."

With her home now open to view, Lee and Jake marvel at the beauty, as they hear a whinny from behind two large sets of double doors. Sarah pushes another pad, opening the garage where there is room for the vehicles. Addressing Jake, she comments, "It's a tight squeeze, but they will all fit.

To the side of that door, she again presses a pad; the door slides open to the indoor corral with a gate connecting the only visible sign of habitation, the corral that Lee saw upon his arrival.

Rusty ducks under the fence bounding forward, racing round and round trying to get her attention. His exuberance is so contagious that soon Sarah is sitting on the ground, wrapping her arms around her joyous friend as he baths her face with his warm, raspy tongue. In his excitement,

Sarah finds herself on her back in the dirt with Rusty lying on top of her, joy radiating from her face as she holds him in her arms. She whispers a quiet command in his ear, and immediately, he is sitting quietly beside her. Giving him one last hug, she rises, moving toward a very patient but indignant horse who has been waiting when he usually gets attention first. She wraps her arms around him, burying her face in his silky mane, cooing softly in his ear.

Jake and Lee stand watching the antics of the trio of friends. In awe, Lee whispers, "Jake, she is one with her animals. How can this be?"

"Lee, they are her only companions and have been for the years she has lived on the Res. Do you really wonder how she can be content living here? I do believe she is one with the land." And barely audible to even Lee who stands so close, he says, "Like an Apache, yes, like the Apache."

Remembering her manners, she says, "Gentleman, we'll enter through the mud room into the kitchen, this way." As they enter, both men are amazed at the simple beauty of a home designed in the character out of the old West but with the modern contraptions of the twenty-first century blending into the rustic décor. "Let me give you a tour of my home. After that, we will have some coffee and decide how this 'babysitting' stint is going to work for all of us."

After having completed the tour, she states "As you can see, it was designed for single occupancy, but I'm sure we can make some comfortable arrangements for the short time you will be here."

Putting coffee to perk, she sits cups in front of the officers who settle themselves at the kitchen table. Standing at the counter, she watches Rusty as he edges toward Jake and is as surprised as Jake when he lays his head in Jake's lap.

Looking first at Lee then at Sarah, he lays his hand on Rusty's head as though he had been doing this for years. *This feels so right! Here with Sarah in her private world.*

"Well, I'll be damn, Jake, he likes you! Ain't that something!" Watching as he nuzzles Jake's hand, Lee asks, "What does he want?"

Sarah can't help but laugh at the antics of her beloved pet; thinking as to how to explain his attraction to Jake, she says, "Lee, I usually sit in that chair, let's see, I bet he wants his treat."

Reaching into the canister on the counter, she pulls out two tinfoil-wrapped pieces of jerky, handing them to Jake. "Try this, he is rather spoiled."

Jake gives her an imperceptible nod, acknowledging that she has handled the situation very well.

"Ain't that something! I thought you weren't to feed dogs salty treats.

Laughing, she says, "That's what they say, Lee, but please don't tell Rusty that he is a canine. He thinks he's human." Pouring each a cup of coffee, placing cookies and chocolate kisses on the table for herself and her guest, she sits down next to Jake with Rusty hoarding in between. "Now, what happens, Jake?"

The conversation takes on a serious tone with her question. "Our orders are to stay with you until we are told differently. The sheriff is meeting with the council tomorrow, where they will discuss the events of the past few hours. You can go about your daily routine. The only difference we will be with you."

"You obviously ride. How often?"

Looking him directly in the eye, she replies, "Lee, I ride out every morning. We are gone several hours riding through the valley and around the tree line. Sometimes we take a picnic lunch and eat out on the prairie. The rest of the time is devoted to caring for my animals or working at my computer." Smiling, she continued, "I live a very simple life."

Lee is surprised at the feeling of respect for this white woman creeping through his whole being. "Sounds like a good life to me."

Casting her eyes down, seemingly looking at the cup she is holding, she quietly replies, "It is! It is a very quiet serene way of life I never want to lose."

Jake feels a sense of protectiveness toward this woman he has known for about a year but is surprised at Lee's response.

"Sarah, we will make sure you never lose the privilege granted by the council. The Respected Elder is a wise man and one who believes in our Apache heritage."

A hint of a smile crosses Jake's face. "It will be okay, Sarah. Lee is right, the Respected Elder does believe in the old ways, and he is gifted by the Spirits of our Ancestors. Wasn't it an eagle feather that influenced him to advise the council of your worthiness and to grant you the ninety-nine-year lease! And what of the eagles this afternoon? I saw five magnificent eagles around you before the bolt of lightning struck the ground in front of you. To those who believe in the old ways, you are protected by the spirits."

Lee pauses in thought. "I thought I saw the lad, Jimmy Begay, walk into the smoldering ground, but when I took a second look, there was only a cloud of mist and the eagle feathers that had been on the ground were gone."

Sarah looks at both of the men sitting in her kitchen, one aged with wisdom and one wise for his years, both showing a tendency toward the old world Apache and both adamant about her future. "You make it all sound so simple. I truly hope it is so." Rising, she says, "Please excuse me, my horse needs grooming, fresh hay, water, and feed." Sitting her cup on the cabinet, she walks out the door, making her way to the barn and corral.

Going to Mesquite, she is aware that both men are behind her. Standing there brushing her horse's coat, an uproarious laughter escapes her mouth. Turning, she looks at Jake sitting on a bale of hay and Lee standing next to him both with puzzled expressions. Gasping to regain her composure, she says, "This is the first time since the workmen finished the house that a man has been anywhere near, let alone inside my private domain. I just find it rather amusing considering I chose solitude and the council demanded it. And yet, by order of the sheriff, you are both here."

The men look at each other, seeing the irony of the situation and burst out laughing. Lee, with eyes dancing, says, "Well, Ms. Lone Wolf, we will stay out of your way as much as possible."

Mesquite who had been restless with the men around his mistress relaxes his muscles as the laughter roars through the cave. Rusty runs from one to the other, wearing down some of the energy built up over the past two days while Sarah was away. Turning back to Mesquite, she puts her arms around his neck, whispering, "Tomorrow, my love, we will ride, but now it's time for your special treat." She walks toward the bin with him pushing her every step of the way, urging her to hurry with his juicy red apple.

Returning to the interior the men trailing behind, she wanders into the main room where she stands looking out the camouflage screen gazing at the velvet sky dotted with millions of brilliant stars, and sighs. Then with resolve, "Gentleman, as you can see the cave was designed for one. I do have quilts and blankets that you can use to bed down here by the fireplace. Jake, the recliner is a fair place to sleep."

Lee speaks with respect and a tinge of laughter. "Sarah, Ms. Lone Wolf, if you don't mind, I would like to sleep in the barn. The smell of sweet hay and Mesquite would be a lot like home, and that is appealing tonight."

Sarah looks at him to see if he is serious. "Well, Lee, it's okay by me, but final approval will come from Mesquite."

"That's okay, I think we'll get along just fine."

Walking back toward the kitchen, she says, "Now that's settled, I'll see what I can scrounge for dinner."

Jake is right on her heels. "Sarah, let me prepare something for us. Just point me in the right direction, and I'll fix a meal fit for any squaw." Pausing in thought, he continues, "Unless you would rather not have me meddling around your kitchen."

Turning around to look at him, she ponders his offer. "It would be a pleasure not to have to cook for myself." Pointing to a door at the left of the fridge, "That's the pantry and the shiny door inside the pantry is a freezer. Good luck!"

Lee stands in the door observing the conversation. "Are you really going to let him cook? I heard he didn't know how." Jake haw haws at his comment and proceeds to conjure up a satisfying meal.

Being young, Lee is more of a conversationalist than Sarah and Jake and amuses them with stories of his youth on the Res and his stint in the army.

Quiet settles through the cave, Lee asleep on a bale of hay found Mesquite most accepting of his presence especially after he bribed him with a juicy treat. Jake stretches out minus his boots on the recliner in the big room; it took him a little while to fall asleep partly because of the strange surroundings and the events of the past two days along with being on duty.

Sarah snuggled into her satin cocoon with Rusty stretched out beside her, having no trouble falling asleep in her own safe world. Although she is usually alone, the presence of Jake and Lee did not seem to bother her; she had Rusty. She trusted Jake, and Lee was okay.

In the shadowy world of slumber, she feels the comfort of the warm buffalo hide wrapped around her and the glow of coals simmering in the darkness. Rising from her warm bed, she invites the ancient medicine woman to enter.

"White woman, the Spirits of our Ancestors honor you with the gift of healing. Come! There is much to learn and only a short time. Trailing the old woman through the pines to the edge of the forest the prairie opening before her, she is amazed at the brilliance of the sun. She points to many plants, telling of their uses for healing and ceremonials. Among those are *ti gah li* (sage) used to smudge their homes to protect from disease and bugs' and to make the home smell good; *ze di kosh* (sumac berries) whose stems are used in making baskets; *tio ya chi de* with a red line running the length of the stem is eaten like spinach and is good for the blood; *shil del bal* is like aspirin, the leaves are chewed, placing the wet leaves on the wart, a cut, or a scrape. As she follows the old woman across the prairie, she continues pointing out various plants that Sarah will need to aid her as a medicine woman. She follows the old woman as the sun makes its way toward the western edge of the horizon where it will find sleep. They return to the teepee hidden deep in the forest, midst an Aspen grove. Entering the tepee, she is instructed to sit on the pile of buffalo hides on the far side of the room as the old woman sits across from her; the embers send flames leaping upward casting shadows dancing on the walls. Opening a small pouch, the old woman drops a pinch of tobacco into the flames, sending a pleasing aroma throughout the room then adds sprigs of sage to sweeten the air. Leaning across the fire, she offers Sarah a small button. "Chew!" Placing one in her wizened mouth, she sits gazing into the glowing embers as she watches Sarah.

As the peyote enters her body, Sarah, whose essence is now a wisp of smoke, travels to the Sacred Mesa trembling as she comes face-to-face the wily Coyote surrounded by five glorious eagles—the same ones who surrounded her at the feast yesterday. *Ah, was it just yesterday?*

In a voice long used to giving orders, the Coyote speaks, "White woman, the spirits of our ancestors choose you to be a healer to the Apache. You are the first in over a hundred years. You will encounter much trouble along the journey. It will not be easy to establish your right as a healer. The eagle is your protector, the Ancient One is your council, and the Respected Elder will aid you in your journey. You are honored for your reverence of the land, your respect and love of the animals that live and grow." Opening her mouth to speak, she sees only the gray smoke of the fire simmering to ashes; she is alone on the Sacred Mountain.

Her spirit returning to the teepee sees the dim flicker of the last ember as the medicine woman, saying not a word, dissolves into a gray mist floating aloft, drifting through hole in the top of the ancient teepee.

Sarah calls, "Wait, please wait." Suddenly overwhelmed by the aroma of sage filling the room, she wakes to Rusty licking her face. Realizing that it was only a dream, she is thunderstruck by its importance and feels the overwhelming burden of the coyote's declaration. *How can I do as he instructs, I'm a "ghost" to the Apache.*

Knowing she will sleep no more this night, she rises tiptoeing into the kitchen to put on a pot of coffee. She didn't get two steps along the hall when Jake calls to her, "Sarah, are you okay?"

"Yes, Jake I woke and have too much running through my mind to get back to sleep, thought a cup would taste good. Would you like one?"

Yawning, Jake joins her in the kitchen. Looking at her face, he sees that something is weighing heavy on her mind. "Want to talk, Sarah?" Standing just inside the door, he waits for her response.

She turns the coffee pot on, and as it starts its *drip*, *drip*, *drip*, she sits down at the table opposite from where Jake is standing. "I doubt if you would believe me. I'm not sure I would believe me if I were an Apache and a white woman told me about my dream. It was so real. I feel a tremendous weight on my shoulders. Oh, Jake, I have been given an impossible task. What will I do?"

Pulling out the chair nearest the door, he turns it around and straddles it facing her. The seriousness showing on her face and the dark shadows hiding in her green eyes gives him concern. "Try me, Sarah, I might surprise you."

Looking at him, a man she has come to care for very much, she wonders if he might understand that her dream is real, or would he chalk it up to the imagination of an eccentric white woman who has experience a traumatic event. *What if I lose the only friend I have, could I live with that loss? I have to talk with someone—who better than an Apache who holds with their native traditions.*

Jake waits; he watches the shadows leave her eyes and resolve replace the tension once seen in the muscles of her face, an indication she's made her decision.

Sitting with her hands in her lap with a calm demeanor, looking Jake in the eye, she relates the events she experienced in her dream, watching for his reaction. When she sees no change in his expression, only a light glistening from his ebony orbs, she concludes her story: "Jake, the last instruction in the dream is for me to council with the Ancient One and the Respected Elder for guidance. The dream was so real I feel the weight of the obligation imposed heavy on my heart. What am I to do?"

While his face is a sea of tranquility, his feelings are mixed: astonished that a white woman is chosen by the ancestral spirits to be a healer, and admiration that this woman is so highly regard. Yet when he pauses to remember her respect for the land, her quiet champion of the animals used in the rodeo, the care of her own critters and her reverence of the *diide*, he smiles at his reaction. Choosing his words carefully, he asks, "Sarah, do you believe, truly believe, what you experienced in your vision?"

Looking at Jake, a lone tear slides down her weathered face, and with a slight nod, she whispers, "Yes, with all my heart. I don't understand why, but, yes, I believe it to be true."

For the first time, Jake's eyes take on a special glow as he reaches across the table, with his index finger, wiping the single tear from her face. Touching it to his lips, he calmly says, "Sarah, you had what the elders call a vision quest. In today's world it is most rare. You will want to council with the Ancient One and Respected Elder who have a strong belief in the tribal traditions. However, I would wait until after the council meets and makes a decision regarding the death threat scrawled on your truck and more importantly the events of yesterday at the dance."

Hearing the door open from the barn, she rises to pour Lee a cup of coffee then turning back toward the table, she continues "I think you are right, Jake; it will be so."

Blasting into the room like the young man he is Lee inquires, "You two are up early. Oh, that coffee smells good, you got an extra cup."

Sarah smiles as she sets a steaming mug in front of him.

As the dawn creeps across the land and the darkness fades to gray with the coming of morning, the president of the council stands at the window of his home watching the sun send its warm yellow rays across the Res. The yellow and gold leaves of the aspen float to the ground spurred by the cool breeze drifting down from the north. He has spent much of the night in thought; the council meets today. His council must be wise as they discuss the death threats against the white woman. More importantly, he must be able to explain the appearance of the five eagles surrounding her, and the bolt of lightning that never singed her striking only a few feet in front of her yet searing those some fifteen to twenty feet from the strike. He stood within the same radius and, like the white woman, was not touched by any of the debris or flames. *There is much to consider. I must be prepared when the council meets this morning.*

Seeing that his wife still sleeps, he walks through the quiet house into the kitchen with its yellow counters that she wanted a few years back. It is bright and inviting, but he would never tell her how much he enjoys her handiwork; it is good for her to wonder. *Yes, coffee is the thing.* He prepares the coffee and sits at the table waiting for it to boil, still preferring coffee the old way. *Never was much for a lot of the new-fangled things; the wife likes them. Guess that's all right, she's a good woman.* Smiling, he returns to the bedroom, dressing quietly so as not to disturb her.

Standing on the porch lighting his pipe, he pays tribute to the four directions, seasons, and colors as he has for most of his life. There are those who would think him foolish, but he will honor the ancient traditions as long as he lives. That is his way.

It is time! He feels the weight of his responsibility as president of the council. Walking to his truck, he unlocks the door, starting the engine, driving toward the meeting house. As always, he is the first to arrive as he prides himself on being early for any meeting; it shows dedication to his responsibility and his preparedness for what is to come. By the time he has the table set with water and glasses, the other members of the council begin arriving.

He stopped earlier to see the sheriff, picking up a preliminary report of the incidents regarding the white woman's death threats. He asks the sheriff to present the report in detail. With all his responsibilities, he is the last to arrive as the council doors are closed for the meeting to begin.

Silence abounds as he stands before the council. "I have asked the sheriff to present the results of his investigation regarding the death threat scrawled on Ms. O'Hara's vehicle, and the same death threat yelled out, interrupting the Spirit Dance at the feast, Sheriff."

"Morning! We were able to get a partial print from the dirt where 'Die, white woman!' was scrawled on the truck. However, we have not found a match in the system at this time. The area around the vehicle was too heavily traveled to pick out a footprint for identification. Because of the nature of the threat, I chose to assign Jake and Lee to stay with her until further notice. Also, I had Ben on stakeout on the off chance that the person or persons making the threat would return—that did not occur." Pausing for any questions, and when there are none, he continues, "As to the events at the Spirit Dance, no one saw the individual yelling the death threat, and we believe he escaped in the melee of the crowd, trying to escape the lightning. You will recall there was not a cloud in the sky, it was crystal clear. You also observed the five eagles surrounding her. There was only one bolt of lightning striking the ground some two feet in front of her, leaving a hole two feet two inches deep at the bottom. The ground was charred outward in a semicircle of up to twenty feet. After close examination, I found no evidence that any of the fire touched her, and there was not one grain of debris on her person." Looking around the room at the council members, he states, "I do recall that several of you had the hair singed from your arms and eyebrows." Pausing he looks out the window. "Should you require Ms. O'Hara to appear here today, I can radio Jake. They can be here within the hour."

"Thank you, Sheriff, I think we have enough information to give consideration to any action we might deem necessary."

As the door closes behind the sheriff, the council sits, quietly pondering the information. What they have heard and seen creates more questions than the report alone can answer. "Mr. President, we would like to hear from you. You are wise in the tradition of the ancients."

"I have given consideration to events of the past two days. The death threat appears to be a vendetta directed at Ms. O'Hara, perhaps because she lives on the reservation. Have any of you been approached regarding her status?" With a negative reply from the council, he continues, "I do believe it is a serious threat, and until we find the person or persons threatening her, she needs the protection of the tribal police. If we cannot solve the problem, we will need to call in the Feds, which I prefer not to do. With your approval, I will direct the sheriff to assign Jake, who is retired and only works part time to stay with her."

"We did say she was off limits to the Apache and to the whites," coming from one of the younger men on the council.

"That is true, and she has abided by the agreement. This council has received no reports of ill favor regarding her actions. In fact, I have heard nothing but good. However, her life is in danger, and it would appear by an Apache, we owe her our protection."

"Gentlemen, you are both correct. What I need to know on this question, does the council approve the action?"

"Mr. President, call for the question."

"All in favor, say I aye." Relieved when he hears "ayes" all around the table, he continues, "I will so instruct the sheriff."

"Now, we have something we need to address, that is the appearance of the eagles. In ancient tradition, this would show the Spirits of our Ancestors place her under their protection." Pausing a moment as he stands before the council he continues, "It is my strong belief that we need to cleanse our minds and bodies before we give voice to this development. I recommend that we adjourn attending a sweat lodge this evening."

An elder speaks, "I have not seen anything like these events, but I do recall stories of the grandfathers telling of a similar event long before we came into being. I do think you are wise to suggest a cleansing in the sweat lodge before we address this serious matter."

The lack of comment from those in attendance signals agreement. "Tom, if you will see to the preparation of the lodge, we will adjourn until sundown."

He requires the assistance of two young boys from the school in preparation of the Sweat Lodge. The volcanic rock is heated to a red hot glow, ready to place in the pit at the center of the lodge shortly before the council arrives. A platter of food is provided for the nourishment of the spirits and placed just outside the door. Water is set inside for the use of the Ancient One who will ladle the water on the glowing rocks.

The brilliant colors of reds and oranges fade to a smoky haze covering the land as the Ancient One arrives, followed by the president and other members of the council, each wearing the traditional loin cloth of the warrior.

Upon entering the lodge in single file, each sits cross-legged around the pit filled with glowing stones. Once seated, the Ancient One sprinkles tobacco over the hot stones and the aroma fills the lodge. His pipe, filled with tobacco, he ladles a dipper of water over the rocks, then lifting his pipe to each direction, offers prayers to the east, south, west, and north, and to the Grandfather, God, and Mother Earth. Again, he ladles water over the glowing stones, and as steam rises, he offers prayers for the universe, the four legged animals, the winged creatures, all the plants of the earth, to the spirits of the water and to all of mankind. Again ladling water over the hot stones, watching the steam rise permeating the lodge, he gives prayers for all the council taking part in the ceremony and their circle. As a haze clouds the lodge, he ladles water on the stones and prays for strength that everyone needs to live each day and for the peace to transcend the world for all.

Adding a piece of a sage to the pipe's bowl, he firsts offers the pipe to the four directions and to the Grandfather/ God and Mother Earth then passes the pipe to each of the participants to pay tribute to the spirits. As the pipe returns to the Ancient One, he passes a small sac from which each participant takes a button of peyote. Then he drops tobacco and a dash of sage on the searing rocks while each Apache chews.

A dream-like atmosphere engulfs the lodge as each participant seeks to cleanse his body and spirit in preparation for the work of the council. Traveling on the mist, drifting through the lodge, the Respected Elder climbs the Sacred Mountain. Reaching the summit hiding in the clouds, he meets the Coyote surrounded by the five beautiful eagles seen guarding the white woman only yesterday. As he stands before the coyote, he hears him say, "President of the council, the white woman has been chosen to be a healer for the Apache. She respects and honors the land, the animals, the plants, and the universe. She is honored by the Spirits of our Ancestors and will be accorded the highest of respect by the council and the tribe. The council's restrictions will the lifted immediately."

Out of the gray haze steps the young boy, Jimmy Begay, the lad she rescued last year. And once again, the Coyote speaks, "The boy has been chosen by the Spirits of our Ancestors to lead the Apache tribe. He is wise in the ancient traditions, and you, Mr. President, will guide him in the ways of today's Apache. He must acquire a balance between the two to guide his people well."

Looking around the Sacred Mountain, he is aware of the shadowy figures to the left of his vision. Puzzled by their presence, he wonders, *Could it be that the others have traveled the same vision quest?*

Once again, the Coyote speaks, "I have seen the evil befallen her it is not over, there will be more. She is protected by the Spirits and the Eagles and no harm must ever come to her. She is Apache."

Standing silent for a moment as the eagles flap their wings in emphasis, the Coyote continues, "Elder, do you understand the importance placed on the white woman?"

Overwhelmed at his words, he hesitates briefly before replying, "I understand, it shall be."

The Coyote turns to the shadowy figures of the other council members, tossing a bit of cosmic dust in their direction. "Go! Heed my words. No harm must come to the white woman." In the blink of an eye, the coyote and eagles fade away into the haze of the mountain.

His mind drifts slowly back to the reality of the sweat lodge. His vision does not come as a surprise; he saw the eagles yesterday and the boy hidden in the mist when he picked up the eagle feathers, handing them to the white] woman. *At last I understand what I saw and what is expected.*

It is near the time when the moon starts its journey toward the western sky as the participants in the sweet lodge gather their things and slowly file out returning to their *kogha*.

Meeting tomorrow, the council will discuss the events on the last day of the feast. As the president returns to his home, he finds that sleep does not come easy. Restlessness dominates the hours until dawn, yet he has no doubts about what he must do. However, he does question if he will be able to persuade the council on the right course of action.

Mr. Sun pokes his head above the mountains, sending his radiant glow across the land much too early. Rising with the first rays, the president prepares in his mind what he must present to the council and trusts the wisdom of the ancestors to give him the right words to convey the importance of protecting the white woman. *How can I tell them that the ancestors consider her an Apache and the importance they place on her welfare?*

He takes time in the early morning hours to visits the *kogha* of the Ancient One, telling him of his vision. "I know of your vision, Respected Elder, your task will be difficult, but you must not lose sight of your goal. Go! You have work to do."

Being tired with the better part of day ahead, he sits calmly in the building, waiting for the other council member's arrival. As they enter the room, he watches each of their faces to see what their expressions might be. To his amazement, most have a serene countenance; only one and possibly two seem troubled. As they each take their seats, he states, "The meeting will come to order. We adjourned yesterday to prepare for this meeting by attending a Sweat Lodge to cleanse our bodies and minds that we might make wise decisions in this very serious matter before us."

"Mr. President, may I speak."

"You have the floor, Jim.

"I can only speak for myself. I do not know what the others experienced last night. In my vision, I was in the presence of the Coyote, five eagles, and a small boy high on the Sacred Mountain. You, Mr. President, were there. The ancestors honor the white woman and call her a healer to be given full privileges of the Apache. She has the protection of the ancestors in the form of five eagles. We are to protect her from any harm. This is a summation of my experience. I would like to hear from others."

Everyone spoke, acknowledging their experience was the same. A couple of the young council members not steeped in the traditions question the sincerity of the vision but could not deny what they experienced.

"Gentleman, I council compliance with the vision quest especially since each of us shared the same vision. Lift the restrictions placed on the white woman and the Apache, allowing those who wish to take advantage of a healer to do so. She is a wise woman. I doubt she would place anyone in danger. You do remember, she defied the council to rescue the boy who would have died had she not done so."

"Mr. President, may I speak?"

"You have the floor, Tom."

Rising to stand in front of his chair, Tom says, "We cannot deny what we have seen with our own eyes. This white woman has been selected by the Gods. Every day we strive to retain our culture and our traditions. If we do not do as requested, then how can we say that our culture or our traditions are important to us? We must act in a positive way to the wision and the words of the coyote."

"Call for the question."

"All in favor of compliance with the God's request, to honor the White Woman, the lifting of all restrictions placed on her and the tribe, and the protection of tribal police until the person or persons threatening her are apprehended." Pausing, he instructs, "Mr. Secretary, we will pole the council."

Going down the list of members, each one responds "aye" with only one expressing reservations yet still voting "yea."

"I will meet with the sheriff. We will drive out to her residence this afternoon and inform her of the changes effective immediately. Mr. Secretary, please transcribe the minutes and bring me a copy by two o'clock, I would like a copy to present to Ms. O'Hara, 'White Woman'." The secretary nods in understanding. "If there is no further business to come before the council at this time, I will entertain a motion to adjourn."

"So move."

"Meeting adjourned."

Saddlebags packed with a picnic lunch for four, and as soon as Jake returns with horses from his place, they will ride out to their favorite stand of trees near the southwest corner of the valley. As Sarah looks out across the prairie, wondering when he will return, she sees dust rising against the horizon and hopes that it is Jake.

Sitting on the corral fence, Lee keeps watch, hoping the dust trail he sees in the distance is Jake returning. He is good at his job but feels more at ease with the older man present; he has experience and much wisdom. "Reckon that is Jake across the way?"

With a pleased sigh, Sarah responds, "Could be, looks like the rider is headed in this direction."

Slipping from the corral fence, Lee says, "Sarah, step inside the enclosure just in case the rider is unfriendly. Jake nor the council will never forgive me if anything happens to you."

Smiling, she does exactly as instructed but keeps close to the entrance so she can observe the rider's approach. Recognizing Jake's silhouette against the golden aspen, she smiles, remembering all the times she watched him ride away after a day on the prairie.

Giving a hoop and a holler Lee yells, "Come on out, Sarah, it's Jake trailing an extra horse."

Taking Mesquite's rein, she leads him out of the corral, followed by Lee who hails Jake. As Lee greets him, Sarah places her cave in obscurity, mounting rides toward her friend, greeting him with a slight nod of her head.

Grinning from ear to ear Lee asks, "Well, Jake, I hope your brought me a tame horse, I ain't into bronc bustin', not any more."

"Well, to hear you tell it, Lee, you're the best bronc rider on the whole Res. Long Tail ain't no kid's pony, so we'll see how you fair." Handing the rein to Lee, he turns to Sarah. "See, you have some grub packed, thought I would add to it. Don't mind, do you?"

The glistening look in her eyes goes unnoticed by Lee as he mounts the pony Jake brought for him to ride. "All contributions welcome." Noticing that Long Tail is being a little frisky, she asks, "Lee, aren't you astride that horse yet?"

Removing his hat then placing it on his head a little firmer, he shouts, "You bet! What are you two 'old folks' waiting on?"

Sarah's laugher rings across the prairie as she leads out with Rusty right on Mesquite's heels. Soon, as he is comfortable with the extra rider, he starts his tour of the arroyos flushing roadrunners as he bounds across the valley.

The two officers keep scanning the glen as well as the tree line as they ride south. "Jake, would we be better riding among the trees instead of out here in the open?"

"Looking around the area, Jake ponders the question. "I think we would be better to stick to her routine. We'll be stopping in a grove of pinon near where she rescued the young lad. We'll be able to take a look around without being observed then."

The trio ride for a little over an hour through the sagebrush, observing tracks of the deadly rattler in areas vacant of vegetation and the ever-present roadrunner scampering ahead of Rusty as he trots across the prairie. It isn't long until they see a stirring of dust off to the south moving in their direction. "Lee, keep your eyes peeled. There's a rider moving toward us."

Glancing into the azure sky, Sarah notices that "her" eagle is soaring high over the stand of cottonwood toward the west. Realizing that the rider to the south is Jimmy, she rides up beside Jake with a degree of concern in her voice and remarks, "It's Jimmy."

Turning in the saddle to look at her, he replies, "I know, we'll wait and see what he does before we take any action. He is a wise boy."

Lee brings his horse up on the other side of Jake. "Do you know the rider approaching us."

"Could be Jimmy Begay, this is near where he fell from the cliff. He rides here often pretending to be a warrior of the old world. He is young but believes in the ancient traditions of the *diide*."

Jimmy reaches the grove a tad ahead of the others and is greeted by Rusty whose enthusiasm at seeing his young friend bubbles over. Dismounting, Sarah and Jake greet the lad as though greeting an old friend. Jimmy speaks first. "Oh, Sarah, you are okay, you really are."

Using the wisdom granted by the Spirits of the Ancestors, Jimmy asks, "Sarah, the eagle watches over you as do I. Have you the five feathers I gave you?"

Sarah stunned by his questions hesitates to respond. "Yes, I do. But I don't think it is something we should talk about in the presence of the officers."

A smile touches his eyes. "Where is the picnic? You never ride without a feast for all whom you meet."

Laughing, she points to her pony where the saddlebags are tied. "Help yourself, lad."

Lee stands, listening to the conversation, unbelieving what he is hearing, a thousand questions running through his mind. Shaking his head, he ties his pony to one of the trees as Jimmy spreads a blanket on the ground, setting the food in place. While he is doing that, Jake retrieves his contribution to the lunch.

As the friends sit down to enjoy their meal, Jake looks across the blanket, asking, "Lee, are you ready to pose the questions I see rattling around in your head?"

"Jake, I really don't know where to begin, but I have seen a lot today that makes me very curious."

Quietly, Jimmy sets his cup down in front of him as Rusty gently lays his head on the boy's legs. "Perhaps it is my story to tell. May I?" Sarah and Jake nod in assent.

He slowly recounts his fall down the cliff, Sarah's rescue, and his desire to thank her even though contact with her is forbidden. "I observed where and when she rode, I made it a point to 'happen' upon her on a Saturday after my recovery. I meant only to say Thank you and never see her again, but after meeting her that one time I was drawn back again and again. I couldn't stay away. As far as we knew no one else knew of our meeting, until one time Rusty discovered Jake in the trees. It was then we became a threesome; met regularly for a while. One Saturday I missed our picnic and never offered a reason for my absence."

Looking at Sarah and Jake, he continues, "The night before that Saturday in a dream, I saw the eagles protect you, Sarah. You were surrounded by a dark cloud of pure evil. Then at my window, I saw two huge glowing yellow eyes peering at me. I heard the Coyote say for me to council with the Ancient One. When I awoke, I was drenched in sweat. Early just as the sun was creeping over the horizon, I went outside to look at the ground outside my window.

There I found two coyote prints in the soft soil. I remember being advised to council with the Ancient One who lives past La Jara Lake. You know, Jake, out past you.

"I asked permission to visit him, and later on that Saturday morning, I set out for his *kogha*. Upon arriving, I explained about my vision and he escorted me to the base of the Sacred Mountain where I was instructed to climb to the very top. On the way, I was pelted with rain, wind, and lightning. Even when I thought I could not reach the top, I kept climbing. When I reached the crest, there waiting for me was Mr. Coyote. On one side of him stood five magnificent eagles and on the other a dark swirling cloud emitting evil. He told me I had a choice to make. In one choice, the white woman would die and the Apache would be destroyed as though they never existed. With the other choice the white woman would live, the tribe would prosper and grow under my leadership. The options were overwhelming and at first I refused, but I knew I must follow in the path of a great warrior. When I made my choice, the dark evil cloud dissolved, and the eagles squawked. The coyote placed his paws on my head, filling it with the wisdom and traditions of the grandfathers."

Finishing his story, he asks, "Lee does that answer any concerns you might have regarding the situation?"

"Jimmy, it's an overpowering story and would be difficult to believe, except I, too, believe in the ancient traditions of our people. Yet I still have one concern. Sarah now has in her possession five illegal eagle feathers and no one but an Apache may possess them and only with a permit."

Quietly Sarah, says, "Six eagle feathers."

Jake smiles at her comment as he ponders the question. "Jimmy, you brought the possession of the feathers up, do you have something in mind?"

Jimmy, wise with the wisdom of the ancients, allows his eyes to gaze first into Jake's black orbs, then Sarah's green ones, and last, he looks long and hard into the dark eyes of Lee whose loyalty he questions. "I have a suggestion, but it will take complete cooperation and a lifetime commitment."

Lee stares back at the young boy whose eyes show wisdom far beyond his twelve years. "You picked up the feathers and gave them to Sarah after the bolt of lightning. How did you do that without being seen?"

Smiling, he answers, "Jake, the Respected Elder and Sarah were the only ones who could see me as I was surrounded by a gray mist that appeared as smoke from the strike. It was then and is now too early for most to know of my quest. Our most important goal for now is to protect Sarah from those who would harm her."

"Okay, I'm with you all the way." Turning to Sarah, Lee continues, "You are an honorable lady and a tribute to the traditions of the Apache. So yes, Lone Wolf! You will have my protection and my secrecy in all matters."

Jake rises, looks out across the prairie, pondering the events of this morning's ride then reaches to assist Sarah in standing; as he does, Jimmy and Lee move from their position on the ground to stand near the two. "Jimmy, how do you propose to protect Sarah's ownership of the eagle feathers?"

He reaches into the pocket of his jeans, withdrawing a well-honed knife, and before the three companions realize what he is doing, he slices across the palm of his hand, handing the knife to Jake. Jake looks into his eyes, slicing his own hand and reaching for Sarah's slices hers. Without hesitation, he passes the knife to Lee, who understanding Jimmy's goal, makes a gash across the palm of his. First Jimmy, then Jake, and then Lee mix their blood, with the blood pooling in Sarah's palm.

Jimmy retrieves his knife, folding and returning it to his pocket; he reaches for Sarah's hand and smears his blood and the blood of the two officers deeper into the open wound. Still holding her hand, the two Apache clasp their hands with hers, mixing her blood with theirs. "Sarah, you are now a blood brother to the Apache, bound by the laws of the Apache tribe."

"Jake, will this allow her to have the feathers without being fined?"

"Probably not with the Feds, but I believe with the testimony of the Respected Elder before the tribal council, they will respect her right to own them."

With hands still clasped, Jimmy continues, "And we are sworn to protect her against all evil."

Pondering whether he should bring up Sarah's dream or not, he looks at her and asks, "Sarah, would you like to share the vision you had last night?"

"No, I don't want to, Jake. I am still trying to come to terms with the magnitude of it all, but it is probably the right thing to do." Sitting down on the blanket, waiting until the men and boy join her, she ponders how to begin.

Well, there is no other way than just to begin. Picking up the cup of cold coffee, she takes a sip and begins. Sarah, relating the events encountered in her dream, watches the faces of the three Apache "blood brothers" sitting with her. All she sees is a glance passing between the three and a slight nod from Jimmy. "And that is what I dreamed last night. While I should have been frightened, I felt only a quiet calm rising from deep within."

Lee gets to his feet, looking out across the prairie before he speaks, "Sarah is not a proper name for an Apache squaw. May I suggest Lone Wolf? After all, is that not what you have been these years on the Res?"

With Jake's assistance, Sarah stands, and with a big grin, spreading across her face she replies, "Lee, I am honored to be an Apache squaw and to accept the name Lone Wolf."

Jimmy looks at the three with the seriousness of his young age quietly reminding, "Lone Wolf is a healer! She will have a hard struggle as indicated in our dreams. The Spirits have decreed." Turning to Sarah, he says, "We, as your blood brothers, will protect you in the many trials you have ahead of you, and you will have the council of the Ancient One and Respected Elder." Turning to his pinto tied nearby, he mounts, riding toward his home. As he reaches the arroyo, he turns, nods his head, and rides away.

Lee brings the other three horses as Jake and Sarah gather residue from their picnic. Taking a kerchief from his pocket, Jake wraps it around her hand to still the flow of blood caused by the activity of packing saddlebags.

In silence, the three riders slowly cross the prairie toward the cave. As they near the place where she always allows Mesquite to run, she lays the reins across the saddle. The minute her body starts to lean forward, he begins his gallop across the half mile stretch as she whispers soft caressing words in his ear. "You're fast as the wind, my pet, fly with the eagles."

Jake, aware of her habit of allowing Mesquite to run, instantly knees his pinto forward, leaving Lee in the dust of flying hoofs, but not for long. He prods his horse and soon matches stride for stride with his two companions as Rusty runs slightly behind the racing riders.

As they race the short distance to the cave, Sarah is aware that a vehicle is parked near the corral as is Lee and Jake.

At her usual distance from the corral, Sarah returns to an upright position, and Mesquite slows his pace to a fanciful step trotting up to the corral with a sense of pride. And why not, he has out run the other two horses by a half-length.

As she nears the corral, she recognizes the president of the tribal council standing beside his SUV. A tingling sensation races through her body, followed by a sense of peace. Dismounting, she greets her visitor. "Good afternoon. What brings you to my home?" Rusty places himself between his mistress and the unexpected visitor.

His action does not go unnoticed by the president. "Ms. O'Hara, could we go somewhere where we can talk? I have just come from the council meeting, and there are things we need to discuss."

"Yes, as soon as I care for my horse, we can go into the cave."

Lee offers to care for the animal. "Thank you, but no! He is my friend and my companion. I will care for him." Keeping her horse between herself and the president, she pushes in the code to open the doors to the second corral and barn, leading her pal inside as Rusty remains on guard.

Lee and Jake unsaddle their mounts and brush them down, both watching the president to see how he is reacting to Sarah's determination to care for her horse before she hears what he has to say.

Taking his head, Mesquite pushes her to the bin where his treats are kept. On his last shove, she wraps her arms around his neck, burying her face in his shiny mane. Reaching into the box, she presents him with the delicious red apple he craves.

Smiling with the joy of his love, she turns. "Mr. President, we can go into the cave now. Jake! Lee! Will you join us?"

PART II

ATTEMPTED MURDER

Months pass and no further attempts are made on Sarah's person, but no one—not the sheriff nor the council, and especially not Jake—believes it is over. Jake has more or less assigned himself to be her permanent protector, spending most of his time with her. He rarely is at his *kogha*, and when he is, Lee watches out for Lone Wolf.

After lifting the restrictions, Sarah's studies with the Ancient One began in earnest with daily visits, learning the Apache ways of healing she will use as the medicine woman. "Lone Wolf, you're an apt student. Soon you will be ready to serve as the medicine woman the ancestors chose for the *diide*." Word spread rapidly among the tribe; the older Apache were pleased with the possibility of a healer with some anxiously waiting for the Ancient One to permit

Lone Wolf to practice the craft. While the young scoffed at such "nonsense," they dared not say anything to their parents. It had been over a hundred years since a healer had been acknowledged among the *diide*. The last one was a woman who came from the Mescalero Reservation, and those steeped in tradition look forward to the many services of a healer.

When Sarah is not studying at the Ancient One's she spends time gathering the plants and herbs she's learning to use. One afternoon in July, as she gathers the *ze di kash* (sumac berries), she is unaware that she is being observed.

Pete had actually been on his way to his parents after hunting when he saw her standing in the field. Now, he stands in the shadow of a huge boulder not far from where she gathers the herbs. "Damn fools! What is the white woman doing gathering *k'ii* [sumac]? Well, we'll just see about this?" Fading into the forest, he rides north; his parents live the other side of Dulce—a fair piece to ride before dark.

After his rampage at the feast last fall, he had gone to Farmington where his drinking got him arrested and sent to San Juan County Detox. Many other nights would find him sleeping on the streets; often spending the night in a jail cell for being drunk and passed out in an alley or behind a dumpster. Between bouts of drunkenness, he had worked construction, mostly to pay for his booze.

Tired of being locked in the pokey more times than not, Pete thought it might be safe to return to the Res. *If anyone had known who scrawled on her truck or interrupted the festivities at the feast last year, or if Joe had squealed, I would be in jail.* Wondering about his friend whom he had not seen since he returned, he had asked at the feed store and was told Joe was following the rodeo circuit and was rarely on the Res. *What the hell! Who needs him, he was always trying to tell me what to do.*

Time slips away as she searches for the different healing plants. Soon, Sarah realizes the sun is on the downward slope toward the western horizon. Rusty and Mesquite have been so patient, but as she glances toward the sky, Rusty bounds to her, licking her face as he pushes her to the ground. Laughter rings out across the valley as she tumbles in the sage with her special friend. Mesquite neighs a warning of an approaching rider; the two friends stop their antics and see Lee loping across the sage-littered valley, waving his hat above his head.

He comes to a sudden stop. "Lone Wolf, what are you doing here alone?"

Smiling up at Lee still sitting in the saddle, she replies, "There have been no threats since the feast last fall, I thought it would be okay. I'm only gathering the healing plants the Ancient One told me to find."

"Where's Jake? He wasn't at his *kogha*. He should be with you."

"Not sure, Lee, after breakfast he said he had something to do and you would be out after lunch. He didn't seem concerned. Is there any reason he should be?"

"I'll see you home and wait with you until Jake returns." As Sarah starts to protest, Lee says. "Don't argue, that's the way of it."

Sarah laughs. "Yes, 'brother.." She puts the sumac in her saddlebags, climbs upon Mesquite, and the friends ride toward home.

At the appointed spot on the trail, she leans forward in the saddle as Mesquite leaps into a gallop, racing toward the corral with Lee on Long Tail, keeping pace. As she returns to an upright position in the saddle, she sees Jake standing at the corral gate.

Jake tips his hat. "Saw your vehicle, Lee. Glad you made it. Did Lone Wolf give you any trouble?"

Smiling a little mischievously, he replies, "Nope, she's a good squaw."

Joining in the game the two are playing. "Okay, you two, where's the proper respect for a healer?"

"Ah, not yet, my white Apache squaw, not until the Ancient One gives his blessing and declares it to be so."

"Okay, Jake! Enough, did you get it?"

Sarah, puzzled by this dialogue, moves into the inner corral, removing the saddle from Mesquite brushing his coat nestling her face into his shining mane. "They think they are so smart, but they haven't been able to keep secrets from me since the feast last fall, I wonder what makes them think they can now, eh boy." Handing him his red apple, she calls Rusty and enters the kitchen.

Jake and Lee, acting like two impish boys, saunter into the room laden with brightly wrapped packages passing through to the big room. "Sarah, would you please join us for a few minutes."

Rusty bounds ahead of her, sniffing each package as though looking for treats slobbering all over the paper. "Rusty! Those are not yours, sit." He immediately obeys his mistress even though he would rather continue his investigation.

"Sarah, sit."

Used to these two giving her orders, she complies sitting on the ottoman before the fireplace. "Okay, now spill it! What mischief are you two up to?"

Lee, barely able to contain his excitement, says, "Jake, being the elder, you tell her. She won't throw things at you."

Sarah grinned at the two mischievous 'boys,' "Okay! That's suspense enough, spill it. What scheme have you two concocted?"

Looking at Lee with eyes that glisten with excitement, Jake says, "Time is approaching when the Ancient One will declare you to be medicine woman, healer to the *diide*, and with the feast only a couple of months away, we thought you should be properly attired to represent the Jicarilla Apache. Lee, start with the big box."

Handling the box as though it would break, Lee lays the box in Sarah's lap, motioning for her to open it. Looking at the nicely wrapped package, she hesitates. "Sarah, open the damn box." As her work-worn fingers touch the delicate lace bow, Rusty moves to her side. Slowly, she lifts the lid as her eyes grow wide in amazement; she gasps with shock at what lays amid the pale lilac tissue paper. Looking at the two men, she sees their dancing black eyes waiting for her to say something. Carefully, she lifts the most beautiful white ceremonial leather dress she has ever seen with many colorful beads sewn into the leather, forming a pattern of wolves and eagles.

Her eyes fill with tears that slide down her sun-browned face as she looks at the two men who have become so much a part of her life. Words fail her, and she just sits looking at them.

Jake reaches her first, taking his snarled fingers, wiping her tears away as Lee picks up her hand, holding it in a gentle caress. "We didn't mean to make you cry."

Her eyes still brimming with tears, she whispers, "It's beautiful!" Rusty lays his head in her lap, whining, trying to understand the tears as she lays her other hand on his head she feels the tension drain from his body.

In the other boxes are white knee-high moccasins to match the beautiful dress, a white strip of rawhide to weave in her hair, and bold rings and bracelets created by masters of the craft. "Sarah, the last box is not traditional but something that we feel must be a part of your attire. Open it."

She takes the round box that Lee hands her; removing the lid, tears cascade down her cheeks, dripping brine on the lilac tissue. Inside is the most gorgeous white felt hat with a Concho band around the brim; attached is an eagle feather. Seeing the feather, her green eyes question the wisdom of its attachment. Lee nods to Jake.

"Sarah, we have permission from the council to place the eagle feather here. Jimmy's contribution is the feather. No Apache will dare question the council." Jake takes her in his arms, holding her close to his heart, whispering endearing words in her ear. "Shush, Sarah, don't cry. We didn't meant to cause you pain."

Sniffling, she says. "Oh, Jake, there's no pain just happiness."

Slipping into the kitchen, Lee smiles saying, "Yup, it's been a perfect day."

The smell of fall is in the air as the temperatures drop lower; the leaves of the statuesque Aspen set the forest a blaze with their brilliant colors of red, orange, gold, and brown, highlighting the dark olive color of the pinon and juniper against the pale blue sky.

Sarah continues her studies with the Ancient One and with a singer who teaches her the songs used in the ceremonies and healings; soon she will be able to practice her skills for the *diide*. On this particular morning, the sky is clear with a hint of winter gliding on the brisk wind as Sarah, Jake, and Lee enjoy their ride through the valley. The three friends seem content to ride with only the natural sound of wind in the trees, the call of the meadow lark, and the rustling of leaves as they drift to the earth below. Off in the distance, a trail of dust rises as a vehicle rambles down the rutted road toward the main highway into Dulce.

Jake pulls his pony to a halt, listening to the stillness and speaking to no one in particular says, "The silence is good!"

Halting Mesquite beside him, Sarah sits quietly in the saddle, turning her head toward Jake; she smiles and nods in agreement as words seem unnecessary on this cool September day. Even Lee is speechless, a state in which he is rarely found, observing his two older friends.

Mesquite becomes restless as they are just a short distance from where he is always allowed to race. Sarah feels the quiver of his body between her legs, smiling mischievously, laying the reins over the saddle horn. She leans forward and Mesquite leaps to action, racing down the home stretch. Instantly, Jake and Lee charge behind her, but her faithful steed noses the other two out, riding through the corral gate a half-length ahead.

After taking care of their mounts, Jake and Sarah sit hand in hand on a bale of hay, watching Lee and Rusty tussle over a tow sack. It is a refreshing sight to see Lee enjoying himself; he is very much a part of her extended family, being blood brother and guardian. With straw stuck in his clothes and Rusty's head resting on his leg, he looks up at the two elders, smiling. He starts to say something, hesitates, downs his head, then asks in a whisper. "Please can I stay the night?"

Jake and Sarah burst out laughing. "Lee, do you even have to ask! Of course. You have a lease on that bale of hay, you know where the extra blankets and pillows are."

Lee is surprised when Jake settles down in the recliner in the big room and Sarah disappears into her room in the back. "Jake, you aren't sleeping with her yet? What's taking you so long? You two were meant for each other."

"Mind your own business, youngster." *I wonder, she is a lone wolf, would she let me share all her world? No, the time is not right, perhaps after she has achieved her status as a healer. Besides, Rusty might not allow anyone to usurp his place.* Jake ponders the questions in his mind as his eyelids close in the quiet respite of sleep.

Sarah stands, looking out across the valley with Jake behind her, his arms wrapped around her waist. The golden rays spread like a fan across the eastern horizon, turning the darkness into a brilliant day; the meadow larks sing, the wind whistles through the pines, and the smell of sagebrush wakes the morning. They hear the kitchen door open as Lee comes stomping into the room. "Do I smell coffee?"

"Yes, help yourself. Breakfast will be ready in a few."

"How about me cooking some bacon and eggs? I'm not a bad cook. You old folks look like you're a little busy!"

Sarah turns in Jake's arms, looking into his ebony orbs. "I do believe a certain young warrior needs to learn better manners toward his elders."

"I agree! Both elders move in Lee's direction with Rusty right on their heels getting into the play. The horses neigh, as they chase Lee out the back door.

As he reaches the inner corral, he comes to an immediate halt, throwing up his hands. "Whoa, how about I fix breakfast, then you can teach me some manners if you still think it's necessary."

The two wiser heads eyeball the culprit, looking at each other. "Sure, that'll work, cook now, discipline later!" All three move back into the kitchen, and Lee goes to work, preparing the meal as Jake and Sarah discuss the ride for the day. "Lee, are you hanging around to day, or are you working?"

"Unless the sheriff calls, I'm off duty. Anything important you want me to do?"

Jake looks at Sarah. "Yes, I have some things I have to attend to in town, would you escort Sarah to the Ancient One's and remain with her until I return."

Grinning, Lee responds, "Just the excuse I was looking for to spend more time with Lone Wolf. I won't let her out of my sight."

Putting her hands on her hips with indignation, she asks in an exasperated voice. "Am I ever going to be on my own?"

Both men answer with a very loud "No!"

After breakfast, Jake takes Lee's truck and heads for town as Sarah and Lee accompanied by the ever-faithful Rusty ride south across the valley. "Lee, where is Jake going?"

"He said he had something to do in town, not what, just ask if he could use my truck. You know how he is, Sarah, he doesn't say much."

Grinning, Sarah says, "Especially, if he doesn't want anyone to know what he's doing."

The two friends ride in silence, enjoying the quiet morning with only a slight breeze rippling through the pines and drifting into the valley, sending the aroma of sage across the glen. Rusty stirs up a couple of prairie chickens and roadrunners, even a rabbit as he lopes into the arroyos darting in and out in playful antics.

Around midmorning, they arrive at the Ancient One's for Lone Wolf's continued education on the services of a healer. "*Da nzho*, Lone Wolf. We begin." He looks at Lee. "Go, be useful. Firewood is needed for the stove."

Lee nods his head in respect. "Yes, Grandfather." With that, Lee moves to the back where he sees a rather large pile of timber, ready for cutting into small logs. His eyes sparkle at the grandfather's method of absenting him from Sarah's lessons and getting his wood cut for the winter. He sets about the task before him, and soon the rhythmic sound of the ax echoes through the quiet of the mountain air.

The sun has slipped past the highest peak of the day when the grandfather calls to him. "Lee, is there wood for the stove?"

"Yes, Grandfather." He walks around to the front of the *kogha* with his arms full of the hewed wood. "Where would you like it, Grandfather?"

"There is a box by the stove for what you hold." Pausing as Lee walks into the *kogha* and returns, the grandfather continues, "Perhaps some would fit by the back door."

"Yes, Grandfather, I see where it has been stacked before. I will give you a nice pile."

"Come! Sit! Have a bowl of mutton stew with me. Lone Wolf, your lessons go well, even the singer says you are progressing."

As the three Apache sit eating their noon meal, Sarah thinks about the importance of the healer's role in securing the help of the Great Spirit to promote the healing of disease, healing of the psyche, and to promote harmony, forming a connection between the natural world and that of the spiritual world. Before she can assume the responsibility of healer, she must be given credence by the community; for Sarah, it will come from the Ancient one, then the Respected Elder and the council. She is overwhelmed by the importance of her role as healer, especially when it finally hits her that she will complement the role of the chief or in the case of the modern Apache the Respected

One, president of the council. A chill creeps down her spine as the magnitude of what she is undertaking seeps into the depth of her psychic. *If I am to succeed in this endeavor, I must call up on the Great Spirit. I will not question the wisdom of the ancestors, but am I really worthy of the trust they have placed in me. Can I earn the respect of the tribe so that I may be effective?*

Upon finishing his mutton stew, Lee shows a deep respect to the elder as all Apache children are taught. "Grandfather, I will finish piling the wood by the back door. Will there be anything else?"

"Dooda [no]." He watches the young "warrior" as he walks behind the house. *He is a good man, a wise officer, and a devoted blood brother to the healer. She will have need of his protection.*

When the wood is stacked, Sarah and Lee take their leave as the Ancient One naps in the shade of his *kogha*. As they round the bend about a quarter of a mile away, the Ancient One peers at their silhouettes, being wise in all matters he knows the questions that Lone Wolf is asking herself and smiles. *The ancestors are never wrong, she is worthy. She will experience many trials, but she will overcome and be a great healer to the Apache.*

The Respected Elder stands on the stoop of his *kogha* watching the trail of dust rising behind the vehicle moving toward him; otherwise, the sky is clear, and the sun shines bright. Jake is expected as he had called from the café in town, asking to speak with him. Pulling up in front of the house, he greets the Elder as he steps from the truck. "*Da nzho.*"

"*Aoo da nzho* [Yes, it is good]. Come sit. Coffee is hot, will you have a cup?"

"It will taste good." The two old Apache sit quietly on the front stoop, sipping coffee. "The smell of winter is in the air. Soon we will have the first snow."

"Yes, Jake, it is past the time for preparation. How is the white woman, or as you call her, Lone Wolf?"

"The Ancient One is pleased with her progress, he believes she will be a great healer. She learns ceremonies and healing. While she has difficulty with the language, she does well with the songs and the chants."

The Respected Elder decides to get to the point of this meeting, "Jake, you did not ask to meet with me to give me a progress report, what troubles you, my friend?"

"I talked with Ben this morning, no person of interest was ever found in last fall's episode. It's as if whoever threatened Sarah just disappeared. The feast is in two weeks. It is just possible the culprit might try again." Jake offers the Respected Elder tobacco then continues, "You mentioned that the announcement of a healer would be officially made at the feast this fall is that still your plan?"

Tamping the tobacco in his pipe, the Elder touches a match to it and takes a puff or two to make sure it is lit.

Looking out across the terrain, he sees a roadrunner dart after a mouse for his meal, and as an Apache who believes in the traditional ways, opines, *That's the way of Mother Earth, it is the natural progression of life.* "Yes, it is time the *diide* had the services of a healer, especially one chosen by the ancestors." Pausing, he hesitates. "Jake, she is important to you!"

Jake looks at the Elder, but as usual his expression is bland. "Lee and I have spent a year in her company. Every day one or both of us has been with her—yes, she is very special. And as you know, she is a blood brother to Jimmy, Lee, and I. Neither of us could ever allow harm to come to her."

He sits, giving thought to Jake's acknowledgment of the time spent in the white woman's company. "Hm, a year. That is good!" Once again pausing. "Your wife has been gone a long time, have you considered taking another wife?"

Jake is taken aback by the question and does not know how to answer the Elder. Taking a cigar from his pocket, poking it in his mouth, chewing on the end, he makes no move to light it as he ponders the Elder's inquiry. "No, I had not thought to."

Changing the uncomfortable subject, he states. "There is one other concern which I voiced to the sheriff, and he suggested I speak with you about the matter. It has been over a hundred years since the Jicarilla had a healer. Is it possible the Feds could object, and what about the white doctors?"

Puffing on his pipe, the Respected Elder searches his mind for the answers. "Jake, I can see where the doctors might object in that the healer has no medical experience. I will meet with the Ancient One and Sarah. We will address the possibility that the situation might arise and devise a plan to handle it. As for the Feds, unless the clinic contacts them, I doubt they will say a word." He sits quietly then. "Jake, part of the Tribal Constitution is to promote the well-being of the members. I believe the addition of a healer chosen by the ancestors will do that."

Jake nods his head in agreement. Pulling out a match, he finally lights the cigar he's been chewing. "Ben wants Lee and me to continue our protection detail, especially with the announcement to be made at the feast. Even if he didn't, we would anyway." Pausing in his speech, Jake continues. "Thank you for meeting with me! There is much to consider."

"Good. You are a wise man, Jake, I trust you to think well on what we have discussed."

Jake starts up the truck, letting it idle for a few minutes before pulling away from the *kogha*. He doesn't look back as he heads toward the road that will take him to his home. His mind is reviewing their discussion; one thing keeps nagging at him. *Why did the elder inquire if I thought to take a wife? The answer is no, it is not something I think about.*

It is late afternoon when Jake arrives back at the cave, finding Sarah and Lee just returning from the Ancient One's. "How did it go, Lee?"

Lee looks at him with a bland expression then smiles. "It went well! At least I think so, I spent the day behind the house while Sarah continued her lessons. The Ancient One is a sly old coyote, he kept me from distracting her and got his wood cut for winter."

"That's why he is called the Ancient One." Glancing into the interior corral, he asks. "Sarah, how did your studies go today?"

Well, the Ancient One says I am an apt pupil, and the singer indicates progress although I know from the look in his ebony eyes that I do not do well with the language. There is a strong hint of a Southern drawl that taints the Apache, as you both know. Shall we retire to the kitchen, and I might be persuaded to fix us an evening meal."

Without another word, Jake and Lee rush toward the door as Sarah burst out laughing at the speed in which they enter the kitchen. I do believe you like the idea of food, gentlemen. Lee, I know you had a noon meal. What about you, Jake?"

"I did, but 'twas some time ago." Sarah is already preparing the roast pork with all the trimmings as coffee perks on the stove. She is curious as to why Jake borrowed Lee's truck but she will not ask. *He will tell me when he is ready*. Only the clatter of dishes can be heard as the friends sit quietly devouring the evening meal. Words between them are highly overrated.

Jake lights his cigar as he sips his coffee. "I visited with the Respected Elder today. I was concerned about a couple of challenges you may face when you are acknowledged as a healer, and I wanted to voice those concerns to him. He has given serious thought to how the clinic will react and the possible interference from the Feds. He feels that a meeting with the administrator and physicians at the clinic will forestall any of their objections and sees no reason for the Feds to be involved." Pausing to look at Sarah, he continues, "He is waiting on the Ancient One to give his approval before a formal announcement."

"Thank you, Jake, for looking after my interest. You, Jimmy, and Lee are wonderful brothers. I am truly blessed by the Great Spirit."

Being summoned by the council, Sarah sits with her hands in her lap, Rusty at her feet, anxiety ravishing her body. Yet her placid face reveals nothing of the inner turmoil as she waits to be called before the council. Jake and Lee entered the sanctuary shortly after their arrival over an hour ago, and no one has left since. Sarah is aware of every sound; the meadowlark's trill outside the open window, the scent of sage sailing on the breeze rustling the cottonwood across the walk; the sound of her own heart echoing the rhythmic beat of the tom-toms used in the traditional dances. She is sure everyone in the building can hear.

Only great discipline prevents her from reacting traumatically as the doors to the chamber suddenly open. Standing beside the entrance, one of the younger members of the council nods. "Ms. O'Hara, please come with me."

As Sarah stands and moves forward, Rusty is on her heels, but she can't believe she is hearing right. "The dog is not permitted." Stopping in mid stride, she hesitates to move when she hears the familiar voice of the Respected Elder. "The dog is welcome. Do come in, Sarah."

Entering the room, she sees Jake and Lee off to the side, standing just inside the door is the sheriff, and sitting with the Elder is the Ancient One. She is directed to a table with three other chairs placed in front of the council and wonders if anyone else will be present.

The Respected Elder acknowledges her then speaks to the sheriff. "Ben, let me know when the Begay's arrive."

"They are here, sir."

"Ask Jimmy to join us." He sips from a glass of water as he waits for Jimmy to enter. "Jake, Lee, Jimmy, join Ms. O'Hara at the table."

Jimmy, grinning, joins the other two men at the table where Sarah sits, all three promptly being seated.

"Ms. O'Hara." As she is addressed, she rises, standing in front of her chair. The Elder is pleased to see she displays respect. "It won't be necessary for you to stand, please be seated."

Nodding her head in acknowledgement, she takes her seat. Jimmy touches her hand under the table, as does Jake. It warms her heart to have her special Apache brothers with her today.

"There are several issues to come before the council today, Sarah, we are going to take them one at a time." Pausing, the Elder continues. "Sheriff, has there been any further development in regard to the threats made on Sarah's life at the feast last year?"

"No. We still have no leads other than the one fingerprint found in the dirt on the truck. However, we do plan to send the print back through the database before the feast in a couple of weeks. Jake or Lee have been with her constantly and have reported no further incidents."

One of the council members asks, "Are you comfortable in removing her protection detail at this time?"

"No, Jim. It was at the feast last year he made his threat. It could be that he will do so again this year. I plan to be prepared." Waiting to see how his statement is received, he continues. "Jake is retired and volunteers his time. Lee volunteers on his own time as well as when I assign him to fill in for Jake. They seem to have worked out a solution between themselves."

"Thanks, Ben." Watching his council nod in approval. he tells the sheriff. "You will continue as you see fit with the councils' okay."

"If there are no other questions, I will return to duty?" Leaving the chamber, he quietly closes the door.

With a twinkle in his eye, the Elder takes up the next item on the agenda. "It appears that one of our young braves contrived a plot to protect the white woman being in possession of the eagle feathers presented to her after the bolt of lightning last year. "Jimmy, please stand and tell the council what you did and identify your partners in this scheme of protection. Which I will say is brilliant."

Standing arrow straight and tall as his twelve years allow, he says, "Respected Elder, Ancient One, and council, the law states that only an Apache may have an eagle feather in his or her possession and must have a federal permit. It seemed to me that since the feathers were a present from our ancestors, Sarah was given permission from a higher source especially since we purport to preserve and respect our traditions. It is prudent that if she were a blood brother, she would meet half of the requirements, and I did trust a lot on the presumption that the council would intercede on the part of a permit." Pulling the knife from his pocket, he continues. "I solicited the help of Jake Tsosie and Lee Atepa. With this knife I sliced my palm and Sarah's, handing the knife to Jake who passed it on to Lee. Then we very carefully mixed the blood from the four of us into each palm, thus in Apache tradition, making us all blood brothers."

"Jimmy, let me see if I understand correctly. You four are blood brothers."

"Yes. That is correct, and we swore to protect her."

"Jake, Lee, do you concur with this young warrior's tale."

The two men stand glance at each other and reply together, "Yes, sir! We are in total agreement."

The expression of the council reveals nothing but the sparkling eyes, especially of the older members, glow with pride at the audacity of the young brave. After conferring with the council, the Elder speaks. "The council will support our Apache brother in her possession of the eagle feathers. However, we will address the question of the permit later."

Sarah feels a sigh escape her and fears everyone in the room heard, yet her face remains expressionless and her eyes directed toward the council.

"Ancient One, the floor is yours."

He raises his hand then says, "The white woman called Sarah Louise O'Hara by the white eyes and who now bears the name of Lone Wolf given her by the officer Lee Atepa was chosen by our ancestors to be a healer, the first in over a hundred years. They chose well. She is an apt student and has shown dedication in her studies. Even the singer says he respects her dedication, although she does have some difficultly with the Apache words." Pausing with his head resting on his chest, he soon continues, "She is ready," then appears to nod off.

"Lone Wolf, you will please stand. Are you ready to assume the duties of a medicine woman to the Jicarilla Apache Nation?"

Sarah doesn't speak for such a long time; everyone, especially her three brothers, are afraid she will not. "Yes, Respected Elder, I am."

"Good, we will make the announcement at the feast later in September at Stone Lake. Now, Sarah, you will face many challenges as a healer. I wish for you to meet with the staff at the clinic and myself. They need to understand you are not practicing medicine and your actions are not to be an alternative to seeking medical help. The welfare of the tribe is paramount to the relationship with the clinic and must be preserved. Is this acceptable?"

Sarah's throat feels very dry as she tries to speak. "Yes! Whatever the council deems important, you have only to ask, and it shall be."

"Once the council has endorsed your status as a healer, you will have very little opposition from the tribe. But there might be some who will take exception because there has not been a healer in over a century. Mostly because they do not follow the traditions as we would like. Therefore Jake or Lee will accompany you on any visitations until we are sure that your acceptance is total." Looking at the clock on the wall over the entrance, he nods his head saying, "We are going to take a break. You, blood brothers, take care of our healer and return in two hours at 3:00 p.m. Meeting is now in recess."

Filing out of the chamber the four brothers gather outside the building and are joined by the Begays. "Sarah, let's get a bite to eat before we have to return. Mr. and Mrs. Begay, please join us."

"That sounds good, Jake. Let's see what the café has to offer. Coffee sounds good." With that, Sarah leads the group across the street to the café. Jimmy crowds in between her and Lee, determined to be next to her. Lee and Sarah's eyes meet over the head of the young lad, and a smile escapes, observed only by Jake. Entering the café, they are greeted by Mary and shown to a group of tables to accommodate the friends. She brings menus and coffee for all but Jimmy, sitting a glass of milk in front him, which garnishes a smirk from his young face.

Chuckling, she walks back to the counter, observing that the patrons across the room are conversing in a loud, augmented tone. She glances at Lee, who nods in acknowledgement of the situation.

Lee moves closer to those in hot debate and listening to the discussion hears. "Stay out of trouble, Pete. Didn't spending time in jail teach you anything?"

Lee realizes that Pete is with his mom and pop who are a little lax when it comes to following rules of the council. Pete has always been trouble, mostly petty stuff on the Res, but nothing to get himself jailed; well, that they could prove.

Lee approaches the rowdy bunch. "Folks, quiet down or take your disagreement outside. You are disturbing the other diners."

Pete jumps to his feet, raising his fist as though to hit Lee when his father shoves him down in the booth. "Sorry, Deputy. We'll be leaving now." He keeps his son close to him as they exit the restaurant.

As Lee returns to the others, Jake asks, "What was that all about?"

"Don't rightly know. Sounds like Pete might have been in some trouble while he was in Farmington." Without sitting down, Lee goes back to the table and picks up the glass Pete had been using with a napkin. He walks back to the table. "Think I'll run his prints and see what comes up. I'm gonna run this over to the office. Will meet you back at the council."

Sarah looks at Jake, smiling. "Lee is as suspicious as you are Jake."

"Comes with being in law enforcement."

The Begays are quiet as they listen to the officers. Jimmy shows concern, asking, "What did Lee hear, Jake?

"Little Warrior, he did not say." Standing up and pushing his chair under the table, he says, "It is time we returned to the council chamber." Leaving the restaurant, Jake is aware that Pete is standing in the shadows of the building across the street, watching. He makes sure Sarah is in front of him as they walk down the sidewalk to the building housing the council. He wonders what Lee overheard that he was unwilling to share with the others.

By the time they reach the council, Lee rejoins them and all enter the chamber as the Respected Elder calls the meeting to order. "We discussed the permit for having eagle feathers in your position, Lone Wolf. We have decided that we will address the issue with the Feds after the announcement at the feast. You have no cause to be concerned. The declaration of your status as a blood brother and a healer makes it our affair."

Sarah nods her head slightly in acknowledgement.

"Jake. Lee." But before he can continue, there is a knock on the council door. "Enter." Looking up, he sees the sheriff enter. "What is it, Ben?"

"Respected Elder, I am sorry for the interruption, but I must see Lee and Jake at once."

"You are excused. Return as soon as you can."

The three men silently acknowledge the Elder and quietly leave the room. Ben leads the two to the end of the hall before he speaks. "Lee, where did you obtain the glass you brought to the lab an hour ago?"

"There was a rowdy group at the restaurant who gave the waitress some concern, so I asked them to take their argument outside. Pete Sosa was with his parents. When I asked them to take the argument outdoors, Pete stood as though to take a swing at me. His father quickly shoved him into the booth and said they were leaving, which they did. I overheard the father say something about him not learning anything while he was in jail. That peeked my interest 'cause we have never been able to prove he was involved in a lot of the illegal activities on the Res. And when someone attempts to take a swing at me even though he is stopped from completing the swing, I wanta know why!"

Jake, listening, asks, "Why all the questions, Ben?"

"The lab is running the prints as we speak and going to run them in the system to see what comes up. If he has been in jail, his prints should show up. Thanks, Lee. Get back to your meeting. I'll get in touch with you both as soon as I hear anything. Stay close to Ms. O'Hara."

As Ben walks off, Lee looks at Jake, asking, "What do you think he means by stay close to Sarah?"

"Don't know, Lee, but I intend to do just that."

As Jake raps on the door, Lee says, "Not without me."

The elder's voice rings clear. "Enter. What did Ben want?"

Lee responds, "Just police business, sir" and resumes his seat at the table where Sarah and Jimmy still sit.

"Gentlemen, I believe we have concluded our business today. Are there any questions from the council? Mr. and Mrs. Begay? Little Warrior? Sarah? When all indicate they have no questions. "Jake, Lee, please remain for a few minutes." Rapping the gavel, the Elder says, "Meeting adjourned."

As the members of the council file out, so do the Begays and Sarah. Jimmy can hardly contain himself. "Oh! Sarah, you are one of us officially." The Begays smile at their son's enthusiasm. They too are pleased.

As the door closes behind the others, the Elder asks, "Jake, what did Ben really want?"

Looking at Lee, Jake says, "Lee, tell the Elder."

As Lee explains the events of the afternoon, the Elder listens intently. "What do you think, Lee? You must have had a reason for your actions?"

"Let's just say it's a gut feeling that I have. We have never found any evidence of who ruined Sarah's truck or who screeched at her at the feast last year. Pete disappeared right after that and has not been seen on the Res until recently."

"Okay, keep me informed."

"Will do." Jake and Lee leave the room. "Sarah, are you ready to go home?"

"That sounds like a wonderful idea, Jake." As they walk out to Sarah's truck, Jake asks, "Lee, are you joining us?"

Grinning, he replies, "You bet, what's for dinner?"

Laughing as Lee is always hungry, Jake and Sarah climb in her truck and, with Jake behind the wheel, leave town.

The morning dawns clear with a brisk cool breeze rustling the pines and aspens high in the mountains. When Sarah enters the big room, Jake is standing with his back to her, looking at the vastness of the valley, sipping a cup of coffee. Without turning around, he says, "This is really a beautiful view."

A contented sigh escapes Sarah as she walks up beside Jake. "Yes it is! I never tire of the panoramic vista. It's so peaceful." Slipping her arm around his waist, she lays her head on his shoulder. Glancing down, he kisses the top of her head.

The serenity is shattered as Lee bounds in from the barn. "I smell coffee. Are you two up?"

Laughing, Sarah turns, walking into the kitchen, pouring two cups of coffee, handing one to Lee. "Okay, who's cooking breakfast? It's not me, I'm on holiday."

"Squaw, you go too far. Jake, aren't you going to say anything?'

With black orbs aglow with mischief, Jake replies, "Not me, youngster! I like the arrangement I have with Lone Wolf." Laughing, he adds, "Besides you're the one with a smart mouth."

Sarah sits down at the table, props her feet in the chair across from her, and asks, "Jake, I did hear Lee volunteer to cook breakfast, did I not?"

"Sounded like that to me."

Throwing his hands up in the air, Lee surrenders. "Okay! Okay!

The three enjoy a quiet breakfast. Lee leaves for town to check on the results at the lab, hoping to find Pete's fingerprints in the system.

As Jake and Sarah leave for the Ancient One's, they pass through the terrain of a winding rutted road with arroyos on one side and tall cottonwoods on the other interspersed with aspen and juniper. As they near a particularly deep rutted section of road, Jake hears the crack of a rifle and feels the truck swerve, one wheel slipping into a deep rut. He fights to gain control of the careening vehicle but fails as the truck flips on the passenger side finally skidding to a stop against a huge cottonwood.

Blood pours from a cut on his head as he looks to see Sarah laying on her side, unconscious, still held in place by the seatbelt and the airbag. Reaching for the knife in his pocket, he slashes his airbag to deflate it; grabbing hold of the door, he releases the seatbelt. Pushing the door open, he climbs out then crawls back into the vehicle headfirst to try and reach Sarah. He touches his finger to her neck and is relieved when he feels a pulse, weak but there. Taking his phone out of his pocket, he checks to see if he has service in their location; the signal is weak, but maybe it's enough. Dialing 911 relief spreads though his body when the operator picks up. He hastily reports the situation, adding, "Please notify the sheriff and Deputy Lee. Tell them this is no accident." He hears moans coming from inside the truck. "I'm going to hang up now and attend to Ms. O'Hara." Jake clicks off before the operator can protest.

Jake crawls back into the truck. "Sarah, don't move. Wait until the paramedics arrive." He struggles to hear what she is saying and, in spite of the situation, smiles when he realizes she is chanting the song of healing. *Yes, she is truly a healer. Our ancestors have been good to the diide.*

Pain is beginning to ravage Jake's body until it is hard for him to hang over the edge of the truck, yet his concern is for Sarah. It will take a good hour to reach them in the remote area of the Ancient One's *kogha*. He keeps his voice low as he whispers to Sarah, "Stay still, my little squaw. Help is on the way."

He keeps up his monologue until he hears her very weak voice. "Jake, shut up, and get me the hell out of here."

Against his better judgment, Jake punctures the airbag, reaches in, and unhooks her seatbelt. "Easy, girl. Can you move?"

"Yes, I can move. My right arm feels like it might be broken. Can you pull me up by my left arm?"

Jake takes hold of her free arm, slowly pulling as Sarah tries to get her feet under her to stand in what was the window. She winces with pain as she realizes her right foot is extremely painful. Jake stops. "What's wrong?"

"My right foot is hurt. Jake, just pull me to an upright position and get me the hell out of here. Then we can assess the damages. "Jake hesitates. "Do it, Jake, now!" Sarah clamps her jaws tight to ward off the pain as Jake pulls her to where she is leaning against the seat.

As she opens her eyes, not realizing she had shut them, she sees the blood flowing down his face. "Jake, how bad are you hurt?"

"Just a bump on the head. Let's get you out of there." Being only five feet three inches tall, the truck is slightly wider than she is. Jake doesn't have much leverage since she can't help him. "Sarah, this may hurt. Let's see if we can slide you out past the steering wheel. If you can stand, it that will be easier than trying to lift you over the seat."

Gritting her teeth for another moment of agony, she says, "Do it." As Jake lifts her, he is glad he was driving because the gap between the seat and the steering wheel is wider, offering a better opportunity of success since her arm is useless and her foot won't take her weight.

In spite of determination, tears of pain slide down her dirt-ridden face as she loses consciousness. Gently lifting her limp body, he places her in the shade of a nearby cottonwood to wait for the ambulance.

It has been a little over an hour when he hears the ambulance's siren still some distance away. Then he hears the police siren as well and notices that the vehicles are leaving a dust trail rising into the clear blue sky.

In a voice strong for one in so much pain, she asks, "Jake, do I hear the ambulance?"

"Yes, Lone Wolf, they will soon be here." As he looks down at Sarah and the pain showing in her face, his heart leaps into his throat, making speech impossible. *How did she get to be so important to me?* Brushing her hair from her brow, his touch becomes a tender caress.

With the arrival of the officers and the ambulance, Jake shuns their attention, demanding they attend to Sarah first. He chats with Ben and Lee. "Look at the flat tire, I think you will find a hole, and I'll bet you will find a bullet in the tire. I heard a rifle fire, and the truck careened out of control."

Ben looks at him. "Jake, are you sure? If there is a bullet hole..." And he let the sentence hang. Jake doesn't bother to answer. Ben knows him; if he said he heard rifle fire, he did.

Jake walks over to where they are attending Sarah. "How is she?"

Her right arm is broken, her right foot appears to be sprained, but we won't know for sure until we do X-rays. She has a nasty bump on her head and is bruised from the seatbelt." He turns to the other two. "Let's get her loaded and to the clinic in Dulce." Turning to Jake, "Okay, it's your turn."

"Nope, you can look at me while you transport Sarah. I'm going with her." The EMT looks at the sheriff.

Ben smiles. "You heard him. Move it."

As the ambulances pulls away from the scene of the accident, Ben calls for a tow truck. Taking his binoculars, he scans the tree line but fails to see the figure hidden behind a large cottonwood.

Pete sees the sheriff scanning the area and slips behind the large tree, keeping the gun with him. He smirks with satisfaction as he watches the ambulance roar down the road, siren wailing.

We'll see what the council thinks about the white woman now, she's no magician, just an interloper where she doesn't belong.

Moving further back into the forest where he left his horse tied to a pinon, he mounts, holding the rifle pointed into the air and rides deeper into the trees. As he rides away, he is confident that he was not seen by the nosy sheriff. The terrain rises toward the crest of the mountain as he moves toward his truck and horse trailer some ten miles from the "accident."

What Pete doesn't see is the lone eagle soaring above him as he moves higher up the mountain. He rides for a couple of hours, reaching the crest where he rests his horse in the open glen full of yellow mountain flowers sipping from his canteen. On quiet wings, the eagle swoops down and with his claws grabs the strap on the canteen, leaving a deep scratch across the back of Pete's hand; the eagle rises into the sky, circling as he comes ever closer to the rider, he screeches, causing the horse to rear, dumping Pete on his ass in a bed of cactus. He sits there stunned with the spines puncturing his backside. "Damn you, worthless piece of horse flesh. I'll teach you to dump me." But when he tries to get up, the spines of cactus puncture his butt, hands and arms even deeper, causing agonizing pain. "Now, how the hell am I going to get out of here?" Slowly he manages to work his way out of the bed of cactus; as the punctures began to ooze blood, he tries to pull them out, only succeeding in breaking them off at the juncture of his hide. Through the frustration and pain, he glances up to see his horse hell-bent for leather galloping across the small mesa silhouetted against the sky and the eagle still soaring high in the blue sky directly overhead. *What the hell is that eagle doing still hanging around?*

Standing in the lengthening shadows, he has no choice but to walk back to his truck. As he trudges on, each step is pure agony; growing weary from the pain, he stops to rest. Realizing he can't sit or lay down, he continues to stomp through the trees, every other word a cuss word, ranting at his horse then railing at the white woman's evil, the council's stupidity, and finally, Joe, who abandoned him. As the hour moves toward evening, exhaustion and pain leave him spent with only a hundred yards to go to reach his waiting truck, a distance that feels impossible. In his pain-fogged mind, he remembers he left his cell phone in the truck and tries desperately to quicken his pace. Jerking the door open and wincing with the pain, he grabs the cell phone lying in the seat, flips it open, dialing his brother's number. Nothing happens! "What the hell?" Shock spreads across his face as he realizes the battery is dead. In a rage, he flings the phone as far as his pain-riddled body can muster.

At that instance, the eagle swoops down, grabbing the extended arm as it flings the phone into the night. As Pete struggles to free himself from the grip of the eagle, he feels the sharp claws digging into the flesh just below his elbow. A hot glow surrounds the talons as they clamp tighter on the pain-ridden arm, leaving charred flesh wrenching a bloodcurdling scream from deep in the man's gut. Pete drops to the ground unconscious.

Regaining awareness sometime after the radiant sunset turns to gray, Pete crawls under the truck pain, gnawing him every inch of his torturous journey. He quickly collapses on his stomach from the agony of motion. No water, no food, no help! A lone coyote's howl echoes through the ebony night as he passes out from the pain.

Not far from where he lays, the eagle sits on the limb of a tree overlooking his truck, keeping vigil as the stars above sparkle in triumph and the man in the moon winks in the darkness.

Delirious with fever caused by infection from the cactus spines embedded in his body and the charred arm, Pete's screams ravage the quiet morning hours, screams with only the wild creatures to hear. In his delirious state, he rails against all white eyes spurred by the hate passed down through the years. The grandfather's lore telling of the forced confinement on the reservation and how his ancestors were slaughtered by greedy white's hunger who killed the buffalo and stole their land. He rants at his father who has forgotten the white eyes greed. Toward nightfall of the second day, he loses all consciousness drifting toward death.

Just a few miles across the mountains in Dulce, the doctors have stabilized Sarah, and she is being transferred to San Juan Regional Medical Center in Farmington for more extensive care.

The nurse enters intensive care. "Ms. O'Hara, we're going to prep you for transport."

Weak but aware of her surroundings, she asks, "Why am I being sent to Farmington?"

"The doctor will be in soon to explain."

Agitated, Sarah asks, "Nurse, where is Jake Tsosie? Lee?"

The nurse, walking over to the bed, trying to calm her, replies, "Jake was here until a few minutes ago. He went to change clothes and get some breakfast. He has been here ever since you were brought in."

"How long have I been here?"

"They brought you in thirty-six hours ago. You were injured in a truck wreck." Looking up as the doctor enters, she says, "Good morning, Doctor."

"Ms. O'Hara, you had a bad spill. How are you feeling?"

"I'm sore. Why am I being transferred to Farmington? What if I don't' want to go?"

We have a small clinic here as you know. Your arm is broken, and your foot is badly sprained, and we are concerned about broken bones. Then we have to consider your age. You're lucky, there is no internal bleeding, but you will be bruised and sore for a while."

Sarah knows she cannot tell them she will be announced as a healer at the feast in September. The council must do that. *I must show I trust the doctors at the clinic if I am to be accepted.* "Doctor, I do not wish to be transferred. I wish to remain here under your care."

"Do you know what you are saying? We have splinted your arm, and it will heal. You will need physical therapy for a complete recover. But if there are broken bones in your foot, you will need surgery."

"What do the X-rays show?"

Just as Jake walks back into the room, he hears the doctor say, "You are a stubborn woman."

Jake starts laughing. "That squaw is about as stubborn as they come. Whatever it is she wants, you just might as well give it to her 'cause you can't win."

"Mr. Tsosie, she refuses to be transferred to Farmington, and it is not in her best interest."

Jake looks at Sarah with complete understanding of her motives. "Doc, I'd just let her be if I were you. If she says she wants you to treat her, do it." Grinning, he sits down in the chair by the bed, picking up Sarah's hand, giving it a squeeze.

Later in the day, as Lee wanders in, they are just getting ready to take Sarah to a private room. "I thought you were going to the big city."

"Not me, Lee. This is my home, and I will stay here. Got good doctors and good friends that's all I need to heal." Looking at Jake, she says, "Okay, big boy, what did they say about your tumble?"

"Lots of bruises from the seatbelt and airbag, a slight concussion, but nothing to slow me down. Lee kept a watch on me for twenty four hours like the doc said. I'm fine."

Looking at Lee, he says, "Now, squaw, let's get to business. We'll be taking care of your horse while you are here. So don't think you have to hurry, just take your time and mend well." Turning to Lee he asks, "What did you find out?"

"We found a 30-06 slug captured in the tire where it went through and hit the wheel. The wreck was no accident. I'm going out today to ride around the area to see if I can find where the shooter hid."

"Think you'll find anything?"

"Jake, there's been no rain and no high winds. It's possible, the shooter had to be where he could not be seen, probably in a sheltered location. Dammit! I gotta try. Oh yes, the prints off the water glass at the restaurant showed up in the files in Farmington. Pete was in jail for drunkenness and petty theft. He did six months in the county lockup."

"Okay, you two, get outta here. We're taking Ms. O'Hara to her room. It'll take a few minutes to get her settled in."

"Okay, Sadie! Sarah, we'll be back in about an hour. Can I bring you anything?"

Smiling mischievously, she says, "Yeah, feed my addiction, you know my favorite soda and bring at least a six pack."

The two "warriors" wave to Sarah as they leave the hospital room. Hearing her laughter as they walk down the busy hall, a smile spreads across their faces and their eyes meet in acknowledgment she is going to be okay.

"Okay, Ms. O'Hara, let's get your things together and we'll get you settled"

Finding Sarah propped up in bed when they return with the requested drinks, Lee checks with the nurse to see what her status is. Hearing that she will be there for a few days, he returns to the room. “Okay, I’m outta here. Now, you do what you are told Lone Wolf. And, I’m leaving Jake here to make sure you do.”

“Lee, that’s not necessary. I’m perfectly safe, it was only an accident.”

“Jake, you better tell our strong-willed squaw the reality of this ‘accident’ while I check out the area around the incident.”

Jake nods at Lee as he leaves closing the door behind himself. Turning, he moves to sit down in a chair near the bed where she lays. “Sarah, you need to know what’s going on.”

Sarah’s eyes turn dark with concern at the serious tone of his voice. “What do I need to know?”

“The wreck was no accident. Someone deliberately caused the truck to flip by shooting out the tire. The forensic team found a 30-06 slug trapped inside what was left of the tire, probably because the rutted road caused the truck to flip almost on impact.”

Jake watches Sarah as her eyes flash fire. “Who the hell would do such a thing?”

“That’s what Ben and Lee are trying to find out. Lee has gone out to the crash site, looking for evidence of anyone being in the area. So I’m here to stay, a fact not up for discussion. Do you understand?”

Sarah leans back on the pillows propped behind her and closing her eyes she nods.

Lee stops by Sarah's, picking up his horse and making sure Mustang has feed and water. Rusty jumps all over his playful companion, not wanting to stay in the barn. "Old friend, if anything happened to you, I would not like to be the one to tell Lone Wolf, so it's best you stay with Mustang here. I'll be back soon." Rusty cocks his ears, listening to Lee then goes over and sits by the door. "You are a smart boy, Rusty. Take care of the place, your mistress will be home in a few days."

Lee rides in the direction of the incident; as he draws near, he searches the ground for signs of any recent rider. Leaving the site, he broadens his search in ever-widening circles, keeping alert to broken branches, hoof prints, or anything else left by a human. As he nears the cottonwood at the edge of the small glen moving into the woods, he sees the hoof prints of a single rider along with boot prints. *Hm, looks like they are about two or three days old. That would put it about the time the truck flipped.* Seeing the tracks move deeper into the woods, he follows, staying to the side of the trail itself; not only is the trail moving deeper into the forest, it is steadily climbing. As Lee nears the crest, he becomes more cautious, checking his holstered revolver and the one clipped to his belt at the back of his waist. Unhooking the strap and removing the safety, he moves into the small clearing, noticing the field of yellow flowers against the backdrop of olive green pines. Checking the perimeter, he moves slowly across the open area until he spots a section where the sea of yellow has been interrupted. He smiles as he sees the cactus flattened by the impact of something falling on top of it. Stepping down from his horse, he notices what appears to be blood. Reaching into his saddlebag, he takes out a small evidence bag, placing a piece of cactus with the blood on it inside and labeling it with time, date, and location, placing his initials on the pouch.

That done, he mounts, moving in the direction of the erratic footprints in the soft earth. *Who the hell are you, and where are you going? You have got to be in a great deal of pain, probably full of cactus spines.* Crossing the rest of the glen, he starts the descent down the opposite side of the mountain. He wonders, *Is this the shooter or some misfortunate rider who had the luck of being thrown by his horse? Startled by what?* As he moves down the mountain, the trail becomes more erratic and much easier to follow. Several times he sees tiny drops of what he believes to be blood on foliage lying on the ground. Once again, he gathers a leaf with what appears to be spots of blood, placing it in an evidence bag for analysis.

It is nearing late afternoon as he descends lower into the valley. He sees a flash of light through the trees. Still on alert, he stays in the shadows of the pines riding toward what appears to be sun glinting off a mirror. Soon he spots a truck with a horse trailer behind parked at the foot of the mountain. Peering through his binoculars, he doesn't see anyone but in a tree near the truck sits a beautiful eagle, and he is reminded that eagles are always near Lone Wolf. *Hm! Interesting.*

Riding slowly toward the vehicle, he approaches through the trees coming up on the passenger side of the truck. As he steps down from the saddle, he hears low moans. Looking in the trailer, he finds it empty and moves toward the other side of the vehicle, still hearing sounds of pain. Kneeling on one knee with pistol in hand, he lowers his head to look under the truck. What he sees is the bloated body of a man with dark spots randomly spaced across his backside. There is slight movement of the corpse. "Shit." Lee stands erect, pulling his phone out, calling the paramedics and police, giving them his location. Getting back down on the ground near the truck, he asks, "Mister, can you hear me?" Getting no response, he gets to his feet and begins to check out the area for evidence of anyone else in the vicinity. Marks on the ground shows where the man crawled up under the truck, but he sees nothing else. Yet he makes a wide circle of the area; finding a rifle some three hundred yards back in the woods, he takes a picture with his phone, then picks it up, proceeding until he comes full circle. When he arrives back at the parked vehicle, he looks in the truck to check the vehicle registration. "Hm, it is registered Pete Sosa." Hearing no more sounds from the victim, he moves back to the shade of a scrub oak, lighting a smoke then waits for the emergency vehicles to arrive. Close to an hour passes before he hears the wail of the siren coming down the dirt road and sees the dust swirling above the trees.

As the ambulance comes to a halt, he sees Ben's patrol car only a hundred yards behind along with another deputy. He tells the EMTs, "The victim is under the truck. He was still alive when I arrive."

"Okay, Lee, we'll take it from here." Moving toward the truck, the EMT lays down on the ground to assess the condition of the man while his partner brings up the equipment.

As the EMTs go to work, Lee approaches the sheriff. "Ben, the vehicle is registered to Pete Sosa. The body is lying face down, and I was unable to identify the man without moving him, which I chose not to do."

"Good move, Lee. What else can you tell me?"

Lee briefed the sheriff on his ride over the mountain following the hoof tracks found behind a tree near the edge of the glen where the wreck occurred. Showing the picture he had taken, he says, "Found this rifle about three hundred yards out from the passenger side of the truck with boot tracks leading up to the vehicle."

"Hey, Sheriff, W're ready to transport. He is alive, but barely. He has numerous spines from the cactus. He's bloated with infection and delirious with fever. Damn if I know what this is, but a small portion of his arm is charred. Come take a look."

Looking at the burned arm, Ben is puzzled. “Well, that is a strange-looking shape. Interesting. Lee was the vehicle warm when you arrived?”

“No, Sheriff, the hood was cold. Like it had been here for a while.”

“Okay! Lee, go with the ambulance. I’ll see that your horse gets home.”

He smiles as he looks up at the sheriff. “Ben, my truck is out at Ms. O’Hara’s where I keep my horse.”

“Okay, I’ll call the crime scene crew to come out here and have them bring a trailer to haul him to Ms. O’Hara’s and pick up your SUV. If Mr. Sosa comes around, find out what you can.”

Lee hops in the back as the driver hits the gas and the ambulance speeds down the dirt road; the lonely wail of its siren echoes across the hills with dust flying into the atmosphere. He watches as the EMTs work to stabilize Pete. It doesn’t look good. It is nip and tuck with the crew working to keep him alive. Arriving at the Jicarilla Emergency Medical SVC, he is rushed into the ER for an evaluation. After taking pictures on his phone of the seared portion of the victim’s arm, Lee stands guard just out of the way of medical personnel.

As the doctor arrives in the alcove, he asks, “Lee, what are you doing here? Is the patient involved in a crime? Who is he?”

"Doc, he was found under a truck registered to Pete Sosa, but none of us could identify him in this condition. For now, let's say he is a person of interest in an attempted murder case we're investigating."

The doctor frowns; it's a small community, and he only knows of one such incident. "You don't mean Ms. O'Hara, do you?" He continues to stare at Lee until the nurse calls him. As he moves toward the patient, he is aware that Lee did not answer him. Upon examination, he orders X-rays to see what caused the small puncture wounds all over his back side. A couple of hours later, he approaches Lee who is still standing by. "The puncture wounds are cactus spines broken off. The fever is from infection, and he is dehydrated. We will be transporting him within the hour to San Juan Regional Medical Center in Farmington."

Just as he dials the sheriff, he steps into the room, motioning for Lee to join him as Ray takes over for him at the bedside of the patient. "Lee, what's the doctor say?" As he brings Ben up to date on Pete's condition they are finalizing the preparation for transport. "Okay, Lee, I'll send Ray to accompany the ambulance. I want you and Jake to stay with Sarah."

Lee's face is grim as he listens to his words. "Lee, the prints on the rifle are those of Sosa, and we're waiting to see if the slug matches the one found in the tire of Jake's truck. Do we know yet if this is Sosa?"

Looking intently at the sheriff, he *states,* "Ben, if we hurry, we can take his fingerprints for confirmation."

"Don't let that ambulance pull out until I get the crew here. They can be here in a few minutes as they just returned with the truck and trailer." Ben dials the lab as Lee heads to the ER to halt the ambulance's departure."The crew isn't happy, insisting time is of the essence. However, within twenty minutes, the forensic team has the prints and the EMTs are on the road.

It is around midnight when Lee returns to the clinic, expecting to find Sarah and Jake asleep; tiptoeing into the room, he is surprised to see them awake. "What are you two old timers doing? Don't you know it's time for sleeping?" Grinning, he stands at the foot of Sarah's bed. "Hey, squaw, how you gonna take care of me if you don't get out of here?"

In spite of her soreness, Sarah burst out laughing at the antics of her friend. "Where have you been all day, you whippersnapper?"

"Out doing police work, like any good lawman." Sitting on the edge of her bed, he briefs them on the events of the day. "Okay, I'm gonna pick up my SUV and drive out to your place, Sarah. I did promise to take care of the animals. I'll see you two in the morning." With that, Lee leaves the two alone, his steps echoing down the empty hall; reaching the nurses' station, he nods to her and exits the building. Stepping out into the star-studded night, he takes a deep breath of the fresh air as he looks around to see where the deputy parked his vehicle. Spotting it, he walks in that direction, more aware of his surroundings than usual; the accident that was not one has his cop senses working overtime. He scoots into the driver's seat, closing the door; he sits there looking out into the darkness. His thoughts wander over the evidence he found around the crime scene and the injured man he discovered. *How are they connected? Is the man Pete Sosa? Well, by morning, we should know since his fingerprints are already in the system.* With that thought, he starts the engine, pulling out on to the highway; he has a long drive to Lone Wolf's and his permanent bale of hay reserved just for him. Lee smiles, the night is no longer lonely; he is headed to the place he has come to regard as home.

Released from the clinic with only a few days to ready for the feast, Sarah is excited at the upcoming announcement. Her meeting with the clinic's personnel while she was at the clinic had been all she had hoped. As she looks out across her valley, strong arms encircle her waist and a gentle kiss whispers in her ear. Smiling, she says, "Jake, good morning. You slipped out early, where have you been?"

"Squaw, Lee, and I had some things to discuss. Police stuff. How about fixing us some breakfast?"

Bursting in the door with Rusty right on his heels yelling, "Hey, Sarah, are you going to feed me today or not?"

Laughing, she replies, "Jake, does that answer your question? I believe I better feed this hungry 'boy.'"

"Well, he does get rather testy when he hasn't eaten. So go ahead while I check with the sheriff. Then we'll ride out a short ways, we all need some fresh air." Turning back as he reaches the door, he remarks, "Lee save me something to eat, I want be long."

Lee picks up a towel, throwing it at Jake as he ducks, closing the door just in time for the soft missile to slide down the wooden frame, his laughter roaring from the other side.

By the time the food is on the table, Jake stomps in the door, a grim look on his visage.

"Jake, what did the sheriff say?"

Shaking his head, he says, "Lee. Sarah. The forensics confirm the fingerprint taken off Sarah's truck this time last year matches the ones of Pete Sosa. Pete is still in critical condition in Farmington. Ben talked to his parents. As far as they are saying, he was not here for the feast last year. He had a friend he hung around with by the name of Joe. Right after the feast, he started riding the rodeo circuit and has not been back in the area. The police department is trying to locate him, but right now they don't have a last name." Looking at Sarah to gauge her reaction, he continues, "Lee, the sheriff wants the two of us with Sarah at all times. We don't know if Pete acted alone, and we are to be ready for anything."

Eating had ceased during Jake's report; gradually, the three friends move the food around on their plates, consuming very little. Sarah picks up her plate, placing it in the sink as Jake meets her eyes; he hands his to her also. They are surprised to see even Lee has stopped eating and is just sitting there, sipping his coffee deep in thought. Looking at his two friends, he says, "Okay, let's go for our ride. We need a diversion."

The morning dawns bright and sunny with a cool breeze, rustling the leaves of the pines and aspen scattered across the valley. As she walks into the front room, Lee hands her a cup of steaming coffee. "Thought I would wait on you today, Lone Wolf, healer of the Jicarilla Apache Nation."

"Youngster, you are a little premature. The announcement has not been made and will not be made until the rodeo this afternoon." But as she makes the comment, she can't help but smile.

Standing near the window with his usual cigar in his mouth, Rusty at his side, Jake turns to see the two exchanging barbs. "Lee, I could use a cup of that coffee you're so generously passing around."

Moving toward the kitchen, Lee responds respectfully, "Yes, Grandfather." Shortly he returns with the steaming cup, handing it to Jake. "Sarah, you better get dressed. We will need to leave soon."

"What about you two? Don't you need to dress for the feast?"

Lee nods at Jake and moves toward the door to the barn. As he exits the door, he hears Jake. "Sarah, Lee and I will be in uniform. You are not to make a move, not even an inch without the both of us. Do I make myself clear?"

"Jake, are you all that concerned? Isn't Pete Sosa still in the San Juan Regional Hospital in Farmington?"

Moving to Sarah, he wraps his arms around her, pulling her to him, "We still don't know if he is working alone or not. We are taking all possible precautions."

Looking into his dark eyes, she sees the intensity glistening from them, then she briefly leans her head on his chest, feeling the beat of his heart and smiles. "I won't be but a few minutes." Jake loosens his hold on her, and she walks toward the back of the cave to her room. She has already laid out the native dress the brothers had brought her not long ago. She felt a sense of pride, not as a healer but as a blood brother to Jimmy, Lee, and Jake. Quickly dressing, she places the Western hat with the eagle feather on her head, peaks in the mirror at the vision smiles and returns to the living room where the two officers, properly dressed, are waiting.

Lee steps forward as Jake takes her arm. "Mesquite and the other horses are loaded in the two trailers. We're ready to pull out if you are ready, Lone Wolf. Jake, you and Sarah take the lead and I'll be right on your bumper."

As the vehicles follow the barely visible road the trail of dust can be seen rising into the atmosphere soaring through the trees. Peering into the blue sky, Jake sees the ever-present eagles soaring along the valley floor and smiles. *Yes, Lone Wolf was chosen by the ancestors. Whoever dares to oppose their decision will answer to the ancient ones.*

The trip to Stone Lake is smooth and enjoyable arriving about mid-morning. Lee and Jake are constantly alert as they park the vehicles in an area reserved near the rodeo grounds. It was agreed that Lone Wolf would stay out of sight until time to enter the arena with the dignitaries before the competitions begin. As they enter the room assigned to them, they are greeted by the Respected Elder, the Ancient One, and the sheriff. The Respected Elder steps forward. "Lone Wolf, welcome! It is good to see you have recovered well."

He is interrupted as the door slams back against the wall. Immediately, Lee and Jake, pistols drawn, grab Jimmy Begay as he dashes in the door. As Lee's hand grips his arm, Jimmy glances around, "*Oops!* Did I do something wrong?"

Jake holsters his gun and picks up Jimmy, holding him tight as his parents step into the room, calling for him to mind his manners. Lee laughs. "It's a little too late, our young brother shocked everyone one with his excited entrance."

Jimmy is twisting in Jake's arms. "Put me down, Jake, and tell me what this is all about." Jake sets him down but still holds his arm as he feels a quiver in the youthful body.

Looking at the Begays, his eyes askance, Mr. Begay gives a slight nod and Jake pulls Jimmy to a seat in the corner telling him about the attempt on Sarah's life.

In the meantime, Lee moves to stand by the door to prevent any further such incidents when the sheriff says, "Lee, no one else is expected here. Stay alert."

Time passes with idle conversation after the Respected Elder explains to Lone Wolf what he wants her to do as riders enter the arena. About an hour later, he says, "It's time. Are your mounts ready?" Pausing, he looks at the Begays and smiles. "Jimmy, is your pony saddled?"

Jimmy looks puzzled. "Yes, Grandfather."

"Then you will ride between Jake and Lee behind Lone Wolf." Jimmy cannot believe his ears; he peers at Jake mouthing one word. "Really?"

Laughing, Jake responds, "We're ready. Lone Wolf, Lee, Jimmy, let's go." The four blood brothers move to the corral where their horses are saddle and waiting; mounting, they wait until the Ancient one, the Respected Elder, and the council reaches the announcer's box where they will be seated for the afternoon's competitions. The sheriff stations his officers in various locations around the arena with a couple of officers mounted and patrolling the outer edge of the grounds.

The Dulce High School Band waits for a motion from the council to begin playing. Seeing the nod, the band director strikes up the music. As the riders enter the arena, hush falls over the crowd as they see the white woman leading the parade in full native dress, followed by two deputies and the young man she rescued over a year ago. They circle the arena several times until all the participants have paraded before the cheering spectators. Then Lone Wolf pauses, turning Mesquite to face the viewing stand with her blood brothers directly behind her. As the Respected Elder, the Ancient One, and the council moves to form a semicircle round the microphone, the announcer calls for quiet, waiting until the noise subsides. "Ladies and gentlemen, it is my pleasure to welcome you to the Go-Jii-Yah Feast. Before we begin the competition this afternoon, the Respected Elder and the Ancient One have an announcement they wish to make."

As the president of the tribal council stands before the microphone, waiting for the applause to subside; he feels the eerie silence echoing across the wind. "Thank you! For years, we have existed without the benefits of a healer in our midst. It was over a hundred years ago when a healer traveled from the Mescalero Res to offer her services. The ancestors have chosen well for us. After many council meetings, the cleansing of the Sweat Lodge, and consulting the Ancient One, we are confident that the Jicarilla will find great value in the benefits of a healer." Pausing for the rumble of curiosity to subside, he continues, "We are honored today to present to you, Lone Wolf, blood brother to Jimmy Begay, Jake Tsosie, and Lee Atepa, who has been approved by the ancestors, the Ancient One, and the tribal council." There is an eerie silence, then a roar of applause.

At this moment, Lone Wolf and her guardians circle the arena as five beautiful eagles swoop down, hovering over her head. A gasp escapes from the spectators as a rumble of whispers drifts across the land on the cool September breeze. As Lone Wolf, accompanied by her guardians, return to the announcer's box in one swift motion, the crowd comes to their feet, the silence is deafening. Seeing a nod from the Respected Elder, she lifts the white hat with the eagle feather from her head, waving it in the air in salute. Her movement breaks the spell cast over the land as *thump, thump* of stamping feet, resounding applause, and war hoops echoes through the forest, announcing the history making proclamation.

Looking at her three companions, she turns Mesquite toward the exit, followed by three grinning blood brothers and the ever-present eagles.

As they exit the arena, they are unaware that Pete's parents are standing in the shadows behind the horse barn. They are modern Apache not prone to honor the traditions passed down through the ages by the grandfathers. Pete's father shakes his head. "I didn't believe the council would really accept this white eyes as a medicine woman. I knew she was studying with the Ancient One, but this is going too far. Maybe Pete was right to be angry."

Dismounting behind the arena Jake, Lee, and Jimmy surround Lone Wolf with hugs. "Squaw, it is official, you are now a medicine woman to the Jicarilla Apache."

"Oh, Lee, it is a daunting task that lays before me, and I welcome the challenge." Leaning against Jake, she looks up into his eyes as Jimmy wraps his arms around her waist.

As his parents approach the group, Jimmy squeezes her. "Lone Wolf, I am proud to call you, "Blood Brother."

"It is a good day to celebrate the feast.

Some seventy miles to the west in the intensive care of San Juan Regional Medical Center in Farmington, Pete has regained consciousness after three weeks. The swelling has left his body, and the infection is slowly clearing where he was punctured with hundreds of cactus spines.

However, the burn doctor is mystified by the seared mark on his arm. And if Pete remembers he is not talking. He is unaware that a Farmington police officer sits outside his ICU room. The staff wasn't too pleased with the idea, but when they were told he was under arrest for attempted murder, they cease to argue.

The officer had notified the detectives when Pete awakened from his trauma. The doctor had reluctantly given his permission to ask the patient questions and the officers were expected within the hour. Arriving promptly, they immediately sought the doctor, "Doctor, what is the condition of Mr. Sosa?"

"He is awake, cognizant of where he is. Most of the infection is gone. His right arm was charred almost to the bone and will have a deep scar unless he has extensive surgeries and skin grafts."

"Can he be moved?"

Picking up the chart at the desk, he states, "I'm just beginning my rounds, let's take a look." Walking into the room with the two detectives right behind him, he says, "Good evening, Mr. Sosa, how are you feeling today?"

"What are they doing here?"

Turning to the two detectives, he asks, "Please step outside while I talk to Mr. Sosa."

Reluctantly, the officers step just outside the door, managing to leave it open an inch or two. Listening to the surly voice of Pete, they smile, aware that he has no idea he is charged with attempted murder.

Stepping into the hall, the doctor says, "Officers, he will need to be here a few more days, maybe a week before he is well enough to be move to a private room. After that, his progress will determine when he can be discharged. Where will he be taken from here?"

"He will be picked up by the Jicarilla Apache Police and transported to Tierra Amarilla, Rio Arriba County Jail to await trial. There will be an officer here at all times until he is discharged." Pausing, he asks, "Has any one asked after the prisoner?"

Shaking his head, the doctor makes a few notes on the chart and excuses himself. As he walks around the corner, the officers enter the room.

Pete looks. "What the hell are you doing here?"

"Pete Sosa, you are under arrest for vandalism, public disturbance, and attempted murder."

"You have the right to remain silent. Anything you say can and will be used against you in a court of law. You have the right to speak to an attorney, and you have the right to have an attorney present during any questioning. If you cannot afford a lawyer, one will be provided for you at government expense. Do you understand these rights?"

When he finishes the Miranda, he hands Pete a copy of the arrest warrant. "There will be a guard outside this door at all times, any attempt to leave will be thwarted and further charges will be added."

Once again, the officer asks, "Do you understand?"

"Yes." Pete snarls at the officers, turning his head in the opposite direction. He has been in jail before he knows the scenario. *They gotta get me back to the Res then the county seat. I don't intent to make it easy for them.*

Exiting the room, they speak to the guard. "Be on the alert, I don't think he is going to go quietly. I do expect him to run."

"You got it, Joe. Sam should be here in an hour to relieve me. I'll brief him. Good night, Detectives."

The two San Juan County detectives stroll down the hall toward the exit. "Ryan, think I'll alert Dulce PD that Mr.

Sosa is uncooperative and should be ready to travel in about a week."

"Think our Farmington PD will be the one to transport him to Rio Arriba County Jail, Joe?"

"Don't know, partner, could be."

As they walk out the door, a young man enters Pete's hospital room. "Mr. Sosa, my name is Daren, and I'm here to discuss your physical therapy, which will begin tomorrow." He is aware that he is being ignored. "Sir, the therapy will help strengthen your muscles. You have spent almost thirty days in bed, and your muscles are going to be weak. This will help in the preparation for discharged where you can return to your home."

Erupting in evil laughter, Pete snarls, "You saw the cop sitting outside. Do you think I'm going home? Hell no! I'm going to jail, and who is in a hurry for that!"

Just as the nurse enters the room, she hears Daren ask, "Am I to understand you are refusing physical therapy?"

"Damn right! Get out!"

Daren turns to leave and sees the nurse standing just inside the door. "Sue, I'll write this up on his chart." Looking back at Pete, "I'll be back."

As he steps through the door, the officer stands, "What was the ruckus about?"

Shaking his head, Daren responds, "Mr. Sosa is refusing physical therapy. Said he was in no hurry to go to jail."

"Well, I'm sure that's true, but he is going to jail either way." Sam dials Joe's cell. "Sam here, Mr. Sosa is refusing physical therapy to delay his going to jail."

"Well, now, Sam, that is real interesting. I'll bet we can do something about that little problem. I'll get back to you." Turning to Ryan, he says, "Pete is stalling to prolong his stay in the hospital. Let's go talk to the captain."

As night descends across the county, Pete lies awake, pondering his situation. He has no intention of going to jail, but it dawns on him that his refusal to even discuss physical therapy was not in his best interest. *Come morning I'll be a meek agreeable patient. Then my time will come. Yes! That's the way of it.* With that thought uppermost, Pete sleeps quietly though the night.

Making his rounds, the doctor is prepared to confront Mr. Sosa with his actions of yesterday. But when he enters the room, he sees a jovial patient talking nicely to the nurse as she takes his vitals. "Good morning, Mr. Sosa, and how are you today?"

"Doc, I'm doing better."

"I see you refused physical therapy yesterday when Daren can to visit with you." Looking at the chart, he keeps an eye on the patient's expression. What he sees puzzles him as much as the words he hears.

"Ah, Doc, that was just a misunderstanding. I'm ready any time."

Dubious of the statement, he says, "Well, then I'll see that Daren returns and you can get started. It will certainly help with your recovery and speed up your discharge."

With the morning, Joe returns for guard duty. Jerking a finger toward the prisoner's room, he asks, "Doc, did I hear him right?"

Smiling, he replies, "Yes, he agreed to the therapy, Officer. I feel there is an ulterior motive."

"Doctor, you can count on it. We expect him to try to run either from the hospital or during transport." Looking toward the room, he asks, "When do you think he will be released?"

"I'll be able to set a date when I get a report from Daren on how the therapy is progressing."

"Thanks, Doctor. Would you please let me know his release date before you tell him?"

"Sure."

Ten days later, Pete Sosa is discharged from San Juan Regional Medical Center with Officer Sam Henson and Joe Roth transporting him to Rio Arriba County Jail in Tierra Amarilla. The day dawns bright, not a cloud across the blue sky with a slight breeze stirring the pines and rustling the aspen. By the time all the paperwork is complete at the hospital, it is just after noon as they turn on to US 64. Lee Atepa from Dulce will meet them at the county lockup to handle the transfer. Having sat outside the prisoner's door for about four weeks, these two are ready to turn him over to someone else. He had been such a cantankerous patient for the first few weeks that when he became almost docile, the officers began to worry. As they look at each other, their eyes show their concern as to what he might do before they arrive in Tierra Amarilla.

As the afternoon wears on, he tries to make conversation with the two officers, but they are not inclined to talk. Pete finally gives up and stares out the window. *Okay, if that is the way they want it, I'm just waiting for the right time to make a break anyway.*

Stretching in the seat beside Joe, Sam says, "We should be nearing Monero, wanta stop for coffee."

He glances at his watch before answering, "Let's keep going, I would like to get home to my family tonight. It's my son's fourth birthday. I missed his third last year, and I was sure hoping to make this one tonight."

"Sure thing, Joe. I didn't know. How come you never said anything?"

Thinking before he replies, "Not much to say. With this job they call we go. It's that simple. My family…"

The big semi plows through the intersection of US 64 and US 84, hitting the unmarked police car broadside, shoving it so hard it flipped several times before coming to rest in the pasture a couple hundred feet off the blacktop, the semi laying on its side, the contents spilling all over the roadway. Joe is pinned under the steering wheel and the airbag; Ryan slumped forward with a big gash in his head.

Both officers are unconscious. They didn't hear the moans from their prisoner as he struggles to release his seatbelt, scrambling to escape the patrol car before anyone arrives at the scene. With the car upside down, Pete fell to the floor, opening the cut on his head further. Dizzy from the crash, he desperately searches the officer's pockets, looking for the key to the handcuffs, fearing they might awaken any minute. Finding the key in Ryan's pocket, he unlocks the cuffs, letting them drop to the floor. He starts to crawl out the window then stops and reaches back in taking both officers pistols. Then with as much haste as he can manage, he disappears across the terrain. The further from the wreck, the more pain he experiences. Looking down, he sees blood oozing down his leg. When he pulls back his torn pants, there's a piece of glass stuck in his thigh. Moving to a small thicket of scrub oak, he sat in the shade, debating whether he should pull the glass out or not. *What the hell am I going to do, now? If I leave it in, the pain will stay. If I pull it out, I could bleed to death.*

The truck driver had banged his head on the steering wheel and was unconscious while Pete made his escape. After a short period of time, he regains consciousness. Stepping out of the cab, he staggers his way to the upside-down car tossed like a twig in the wind some distance from where the truck came to rest.

As he approaches the vehicle, he can see the occupants are in serious condition. Returning to the truck, he gets on the CB, calling for assistance. Off in the distance, he hears the sirens, their wail echoing through the cool air seeping through the late afternoon shadows. By the time the police and EMTs out of Dulce arrive, he has managed to staunch the blood flowing from his head wound.

Bailing out of their trucks, they ask, "Mister, are you all right?"

"Yes, I'm fine. You better see to the ones in the car. I think they are in bad shape." He watches the officer approaching as the paramedics went to the overturned auto.

"Sir, may I see your driver's license?" Looking at the license, he asks, "Mr. Tyler, can you tell me what happened?"

Shaking his head, he replies, "Yes! And I wish to hell I couldn't."

The officer immediately becomes concerned by Mr. Tyler's statement. "Why is that?"

"Officer, the brakes on the truck failed, and I barreled through the intersection, hitting the car broadside. I was driving about sixty miles per hour, but with the slight incline to the intersection, the truck picked up speed. The governor should give you the exact speed on impact."

One of the paramedics approaches the officer. "Could I speak with you, sir?" As he steps away, the officers follow him.

"What's up?"

"The men in the car are police officers. The driver, Joe Tarkin, is dead. The other one is Ryan Bennett, he's unconscious. We're going to transport immediately. There's blood in the back seat, could have been third person in the car."

"Thanks!" Getting on his radio, he calls for the forensic team.

Lee is sitting at the county jail in Rio Arriba, waiting for the officers from Farmington to arrive when the call comes through. "Shit." He radios to the officer on the scene. "What about the prisoner they were transporting?"

"Lee, there was only the two officers in the vehicle. Your prisoner is on the loose." He stands silent waiting for Lee to continue.

"Radio the sheriff. I'm on my way."

"Will do." As he disconnects, he sees the forensic team arriving. Greeting them, he says, "Guys, I need everything you can give me. These guys were transporting a prisoner to Rio Arriba. Lee Atepa is on his way here."

Calling into the sheriff's office, he reports the accident, the dead officer, and the escaped prisoner. "Lee is on his way to the scene from Rio Arriba. He should be here in about thirty minutes." Pausing, he continues with a somberness to his voice, "The EMTs are leaving now with Ryan Bennett, whose condition is not good. The other ambulance will transport the body of Officer Joe Tarkin to the hospital for death certification." Looking up at the sound of a car engine, he states, "Lee's here now, Sheriff."

"Okay. Tell him to call in when he can tell me anything more."

"Will do."

Lee approaches the first officer on the scene. "What can you tell me?"

Bringing him up to date on what they found, he then adds, "Both of the officers guns are missing."

Making a wide sweep of the area, he spots footprints, moving off to the west. Looking closer, he sees drops of blood sporadically spaced. As he follows the trail, he sees a small pool of blood where the prisoner stopped. Realizing he is moving in a westerly direction, he ponders, *Hm! Looks like he's head for the back country. I doubt he will go home, at least not right now.*

With the blazing reds and gold of the western sunset, Lee returns to the accident. As he approaches, he sees the sheriff standing by his car. "Hi, Ben. Looks like he is going into hiding. I don't think he'll go home, at least not for a while, he's good at living off the land."

"Okay, Lee. Find Jake and make sure he knows that Pete has escaped. You two stay with Lone Wolf. Don't let her out of your sight." Looking toward the horizon, he emphasizes, "No matter what! Keep her safe."

He sees the serious demeanor of the sheriff's face and hardness in his eyes. "Yes, sir. We will do just that." Lee crawls in his car and heads out to Sarah's cave.

He doesn't look back as he hears the sirens coming closer. *What a break that truck barreling through the intersection.*

Running as fast as his legs will go, he slides down an embankment, landing near a cactus. *Hell, this is what got me in trouble in the first place.* Sitting back against the wall of the arroyo, Pete takes time to ponder his situation. *I can't go home, that will be the first place the cops with go. Not much choice, but to hide out in the mountains and try to get word to my folks. Dammit! Where is Joe when I need him?* As the sun sinks behind the tree, Pete moves further down the arroyo until he finds a slight indenture sliding as far under the overhang as he can, he settles in for the night. *It's going to get cold; snow covers the grown in the higher elevations. Hell! Man, that's where I gotta go.*

Pete shivers from cold as the winds drift down from the high mountains. When he fled from the wreck, he was ill clothed for hiding in the mountains. Toward the midnight hour, the cold became so intense he couldn't decide whether to try to travel in the pitch darkness or hover in the alcove until the morning. Having been raised in these mountains, he knew the coldest part of the night was near dawn. Off in the distance, he heard the lonesome howl of a single coyote. *Damn! Stay the hell away.* Remembering the Apache lore of the mischievous coyote, he removes the gun from his pocket and sits; fear driving images of the evil coyote eating him alive.

No sleep came to the escapee through the night of frigid temperatures. As the sun peaks over the mountains, spreading its warming rays across the snowcapped peaks,

Pete is slow to stand, stretching his muscles to get his body moving. As he glances out across the land, he sees a shadow gliding across the ground. Looking up into the clear blue sky, he sees a magnificent eagle. Shouting "Go away! You're evil" he moves quickly out of the arroyo, heading for the trees at the edge of the prairie.

The eagle follows him as he makes his way toward Horse Lake some ten miles from the junction of US 64 and US 84 where he made his escape. Thirsty and tired, he uses his knife and a stick to break open a cactus to get some moisture for his parched lips and throat. With the sun directly overhead beating down on him with a warmth that does nothing to relieve the chill from the icy winds. Pete notices the shadows of two eagles now soaring above him. He becomes even more uneasy as he rubs the deep scar seared into his arm from his last encounter with an eagle.

Slipping into the stand of aspen about sundown as the night air turns to freezing temperatures, Pete huddles against the trunk of a tree, shivering as the cold seeps into his body. The night deepens, turning the shadows to ebony, and with the frosty sheen settling across the land, his teeth begin to chatter. Rising to his feet, he stomps around, trying to get circulation back into his legs, but the cold persists.

Once again, the sky turns to gray as the sun peaks through the trees, hugging the sky line spreading its golden glow across the frost bitten land. Yet no warmth heats the forest as Pete stands quivering in the pale brightness.

Moving higher up the mountain, traveling in a westerly direction, he becomes even more rattled as he sees not two eagles, but three! In spite of the frigid weather, sweat saturates his clothes, turning the fabric stiff as the moisture freezes. His nerves taut with fear, he loses all rational thought, traveling in a more erratic pattern, stumbling, even falling to the ground in his haste to escape the eagles.

The snow deepens as the terrain becomes steeper, and with the setting of the sun, the temperature dips near zero. Pete looks for a place to get out of the cold, but none is to be found as he grows groggy from the cold seeping into his innermost core. Even as tired as he has become, he knows he must keep moving if he is to stay alive. The stars, glowing like diamonds in the velvet sky, guide his journey westward, as he seeks any kind of shelter from the frigid temperatures. By the time the sky turns gray, heralding the morn, Pete is totally exhausted. Entering a small clearing deep in the pines, he drops to the ground in a patch of sagebrush. Sage hens scatter in all directions, voicing their disgust at the displacement by the human sitting near their nest.

In spite of the cold, Pete dozes off, sleeping until he hears a ruckus. He opens his eyes and manages to get shakily to his feet; looking around, trying to locate the noise he sees five eagles surrounding him. Each time he moves they seem to close the circle.

"Pete, you have harmed an Apache, a member of your tribe. That is forbidden! You damaged their truck, you screeched angry words, disturbing the feast a year ago, you attempted to kill one chosen by the ancestors to aid the Apache, one protected by the Gods. You fled to avoid punishment for your crimes. Now it is time to answer for your transgressions."

As the eagle speaks, Pete tries to dart through the gap he perceives to exist between the eagles, only to find it is protected by an invisible shield. Shock spreads across his face, and fear grips his soul as he realizes there is no escape. Standing erect in the middle of the five magnificent eagles, perspiration running down his face, his body shivers from an icy chill as he hears the death chant.

"You will never harm the Apache Lone Wolf again." As the echo of the eagle's words fade from Pete's mind, out of a clear blue sky, a powerful bolt of lightning strikes the exact spot, leaving a charred hole in the prairie floor. Not a cinder, a piece of hair or shred of clothing remains to tell that Pete Sosa ever existed. As the last wisp of smoke clears the sky, five eagles lift from the ground and soar through the sky toward the valley where Lone Wolf resides.

The horses are in the corral, groomed and fed from an early ride through the countryside. Lee arrives just before dinner with the news that Pete Sosa has escaped. He is saddened to report that Joe Tarkin from the Farmington

Police was killed in the accident and Ryan Bennett is in serious condition.

Sitting at the kitchen table over dessert and coffee, she asks. "How could he have escaped unhurt?"

"Sarah, we don't know. He was able to release the seatbelt, get the key, and remove the handcuffs. What's worse, he took both the officers' guns and fled the scene." Hesitating, he continues, "He is considered armed and dangerous."

"What about the truck driver, Lee?"

"Jake, I don't know if there will be any charges. The brakes on the truck failed, and the company mechanic showed where they were serviced just two months ago. I'm sure there will be further investigation, but right now, that's all we have."

"What is the sheriff's orders?"

Smiling in spite of the seriousness of the situation, Lee replies, "You and I are not to let Lone Wolf out of our sight. I don't think that will be a hardship for either of us. Do you, old man?"

"You, young whippersnapper, watch your tongue. Don't you think we can take him down to size, Sarah?"

Laughing, she says, "I'll just bet we can. I think extra chores would be perfect to take some of the starch out of him. The Ancient One had him cutting wood and stacking it neatly. You think that wood splitting would work, Jake?"

The pleasantness surrounding the kitchen table continues into the wee hours of the night. "Gentleman, I shall call it a night. Tomorrow, let's plan a ride to the old rendezvous and have a picnic."

"You're on, Sarah. Good night."

As she quietly retires to her room, Lee and Jake plan their protection detail. "Jake, it's time I found my bale of hay." Picking up his shotgun, he enters the barn where he continues to sleep in spite of Sarah's efforts to get him to move in by the fireplace.

Jake cleans up the dishes from their coffee. Removing his boots, holster, and gun, he moves to the recliner where he has spent almost every night for over a year. *Why the hell can't I get up enough nerve to ask Sarah to allow me in her bed? I want to feel her body next to mine, hold her, and protect her. She has stolen my heart, this white healer of the Apache.* With almost a whisper, he says, "Ah hell."

Leaving his boots where they are, he picks up his pistol and starts down the hall to Sarah's room. In the dark, he doesn't see her coming toward him until she reaches for his hand, drawing him toward her personal sanctuary. "Don't you think it's about time, Jake?"

Standing a little straighter for his eighty-five years, he follows her down the dark corridor to where he never dared hope to be invited. Slipping out of his jeans and shirt, he lay down beside the lady of his dreams, wrapping his arms around her. As sleep claims her, he lays there, wondering how he is going to keep her safe.

Somewhere in the wee hours of the night, Jake finds himself high on the mountain, face-to-face with the five guardian eagles. The one in the center steps forward. "Jake, the enemy of Lone Wolf will never harm her again. There is not a trace of his existence to be found, only a charred hole in the ground high in mountains near Horse Lake. Rest easy. Lone Wolf is safe. No harm will come to her again. The Gods have spoken."

The vision fades into the night as Jake wakes with a start. There on his chest is the most beautiful eagle feather he has ever seen. He smiles, drawing Sarah closer to him as a peaceful sleep creeps through his body. He gets his first night of restful sleep since Rusty first revealed his location in the trees where she and Jimmy Begay had their first purlieu.

Part III

Apache Medicine Woman

Jimmy had grown into a handsome young man. His graduation from high school is highlighted by his speech as valedictorian of the Dulce High School. The award and speech come as no surprise to his blood brothers. Jimmy, a traditional Apache, speaks of the great legends passed down through the centuries by the grandfathers, the changes that have come to the reservation, and the opportunities available to the youngsters of the tribe.

As he exits the auditorium with his classmates, he is hailed by his parents. Jake, Lee, and Sarah, who says, "Jimmy, you will soon be joining your friends for the evening. We did want to congratulate you at this special milestone in your life."

He looks at his parents with a frown. "Did you not tell Lone Wolf and the others?"

Smiling, his mother replies, "We thought perhaps you should be the one." His dad nods his agreement with Mrs. Begay.

Jimmy can't resist giving the antiquated Apache war cry! "Blood brothers, will you do me the honor of having dinner with me and my family?" Then turning to Sarah, standing straight as an arrow, he says. "Lone Wolf, I have reached the age of eighteen. It would pleasure me if you would invite me to your cave for the night. I understand there might be a bale of hay in the barn that would accommodate my large frame."

Sarah is taken aback by his invitation. "Jimmy, would you not rather spend your last night with your classmates?"

Locking his eyes on her glistening green orbs, he replies, "It is not the last night. It is the beginning, and I wish to spend it with my blood brothers."

Jake moves beside Sarah, slipping his arm around her as Lee steps up on the other side. Grinning, Jake responds, "Jimmy, we would be honored."

Sarah looks at both gentlemen then at the Begays. "Jimmy, may I make a suggestion?" If you truly want to spend your graduation night with us, will you and your family join us at the cave?" Glancing at Lee, she asks, "Do we have a bale of hay long enough for this warrior?"

Trying to be stern, Lee fails miserably. "If we do not, I do believe I can find a solution. Of course, he understands the barn is my bedroom, so he will have to share."

Jimmy shifts his eyes aglow with desire to his parents and sees a smile cross his mother's face. Nodding to her son, she replies quietly to the question posed in his black eyes. "Sarah, we would be honored."

For the second time in the aftermath of the ceremonies, an Apache war cry splits the air. As the sun dips past midday, the caravan heads down NM 537 toward the home of the white woman hidden in the mountains on the Jicarilla.

Sarah and Jake lead out in her SUV. Jimmy opts to ride with Lee and the Begays follow behind his jeep. "Sarah, Jimmy has grown into a fine young man, has he not?"

Smiling as she watches the road ahead, she replies, "Yes, Jake, he has become a great warrior. He will be a fine engineer…four years college then his apprenticeship." A dark shadow crosses her face. "I will miss him."

Silence reins as they traverse the bumpy trail after leaving the pavement. Anyone observing would see a long trail of dust rising into the air as the caravan moves across the valley floor. The sky is crystal clear with only the shadow of the ever-present eagle reflecting on the ground below. The afternoon sun warms the land as the hearts of the "blood brothers" swell with pride at the accomplishment of the youngest.

Everyone piles out of the autos as Jake punches in the code to the entrance of the inner sanctum. Sarah smiles as Mesquite and the other horses neigh their welcome.

His excitement barely contained, Jimmy asks, "Ah, Lee, this is to be our bedroom. Where is my bale?"

"Where is your Apache restraint, my brother? The horses have to be tended, and Rusty will demand his treats. All before we indulge our own desires."

Sarah and Mary are laughing at the antics of the two. "Mary, will you join me in the kitchen while these brothers sort out the chain of events?"

Walking through the inner corral and opening the barn door, Sarah is struck by the silence. *Why is Rusty not here to greet me?* She leaves Mary in the kitchen as she goes in search of her faithful canine. Reaching the bedroom, she sees he is resting on her bed. A dark shadow engulfs her as a cold chill runs down her spine. With dread, she approaches the bed. Kneeling down beside it, she lays her head on her companion of some twenty-plus years. Instead of warmth and a rhythmic heartbeat, she hears the eerie silence. Placing her hand in front of his nose, she feels not a whisper of breath. As the icy chill seeps to her very core, Sarah crawls up on the bed, pulling her beloved friend into her lap. She sits with tears streaming down her face, dropping on the bundle of fur now stilled in death.

In almost a whisper, she begins to chant the death song. Her voice rising in tempo draws the blood brothers to the back of the cave. Reaching the door first, Jake, taking in the scene before him, goes immediately to Sarah; and he maneuvers behind her, wrapping his arms around both her and Rusty.

Not a word is uttered—there is nothing to say. They all join her in the death song. When the song is almost over, Lee and Jimmy slip from the room; they know what to do. Lee takes two poles from the barn, making a travois, placing a blanket from his bed on it. Then he gathers Rusty's favorite toys and jerky from the cupboard, placing these items on the edge of the blanket. Jimmy and Lee agree they will take the canine to the grove of trees near where they held their rendezvous where Jake first joined them. Saddling the horses, Jimmy attaches the travois to his horse, which has pulled one many times. The Begays return to the kitchen. "Jimmy, what will you do?"

Jimmy explains the plan to them. Then he and Lee return to the bedroom. As they stand in the entrance. Jake softly speaks, "Lone Wolf, it is time." She lifts her eyes to Lee as Jimmy moves to the bed, gently picking up the corpse. Jake supports her until they reach the great room where she shakes off his arm and straightens her spine, striding like the great woman she is.

The sun is on the downward side of its highest peak as the mourners ride across the valley—

the two Begays on Lee's horse, Lee and Jimmy on his horse with the travois, Jake and Sarah on their individual mounts. Sarah's eyes are dry but a deep sadness shadows their usual brilliance.

No word is been spoken, but as they near the rendezvous point, a small gasp escapes from her tense mouth. Jimmy halts his mount, allowing her to come up beside him. "Lone Wolf, it seemed appropriate to bring him here where we pledged our loyalty as blood brothers."

Sarah nods her head in ascent.

Dismounting, Jake and Tom prepare the grave while Sarah sits beside her companion. When it is ready, the four warriors lower the shrouded corpse into the grave, covering it with stones to keep the predators from digging up the body.

The ride back to the cave is a silent one, even the ponies sense the solemnity of the occasion.

Shadows are creeping across the valley as the setting golden orb drops below the western horizon, bathing the mountain, housing her cave in shades of purple and lilac. Dismounting as the sky turns to ebony, Lee motions for Jimmy and the Begays to follow him into the kitchen, leaving Sarah and Jake with the horses. They remove the saddles and curry the animals. Placing her arms around Mesquite, she nestles her head in his long mane just standing there. Jake moves up behind her and wraps his arms around her. Slowly, she turns laying her head on his chest his steady heartbeat a soothing comfort.

Aware of activity in the kitchen, she steps out of Jake's arms. Entering the room, she is accosted by the aroma of steak and frying potatoes; and sees her 'brothers' at the stove with the table set. Sarah smiles at the warmth of the room now filled with food and family. Her family, her home. *It is good to be alive.*

The meal over the men are relaxing with a beer and their cigars. Mary and Sarah sit quietly in front of the glowing fire each lost in their own thoughts as flames dance around the electric logs.

Rousing from her world of sorrow, Sarah looks across the room at the men, but her eyes rest on the young warrior she rescued some years back. "Jimmy, when do you leave for the University?"

Lifting his eyes toward her, he answers, "I will be leaving the tenth of August for the fall term." *How can I leave Lone Wolf? She is the reason I chose to attend UNM. I must be near if she needs m*e.

Glancing at Jake who nods that it is time, she rises from her chair. Walking to her desk, she pulls open the center drawer, withdrawing a legal-size envelope. She returns to stand beside Jake and in front of the boy. "Jimmy, before I was honored with the privilege of serving the tribe, I was a writer of fiction. My books have done well. You and all those in this room are my family and the tribe my extended family." Pausing for this revelation to sink in to his awareness, she continues, "You have an academic scholarship that will cover tuition for four years but that still leaves books, housing, and transportation." Jake takes her hand in his as she hands Jimmy the envelope. "This will cover most of those expenses. The S10 sitting in the garage is yours, compliments of Lee and Jake."

Jimmy and his parents are shocked by the generosity of the three blood brothers. But when he opens the envelope and draws out the cashier's check for ten thousand dollars, he is overwhelmed. His eyes cloud, but not a tear escapes. When he hears his mother gasp, covering her face as the tears pour down her face, he takes her in his arms, holding her close to his heart.

His father chokes on the coffee he is drinking. When the coughing subsides, he stands and with a firm grip takes the hand of Jake then Lee, in acknowledgment of the gift to his son. Trying to control his emotions, he turns to Sarah, finding his voice barely audible. "Lone Wolf, you do us honor."

Moving to where his wife sits. "Squaw, let's leave these blood brothers to enjoy the camaraderie of true warriors."

As they say their farewells, Jake closes down the screen hiding the white woman's cave and all retire to the great room. Lee stands in front of the fireplace. "Jimmy, it is time for us to retire to the barn and our bales of hay. These old folk need their rest."

Jake takes Sarah's hand. "You young pups better watch it as we can still outwit you." Turning the two lovers, aged in years but young at heart, retire to the quiet of the bedroom. Sarah smiles as she hears the two youngsters chatting as they exit the kitchen moving toward the barn.

Night settles over the mountains and stars glitter in the velvet sky as a soft breeze sweeps through the trees; and the lonesome howl of a coyote echoes across the ebony expanse. The soft flutter of wings whisper in the silence of the night as an old hoot owl on his nocturnal hunt searches for rodents to appease his hunger. All is quiet inside the white woman's cave—eerily quiet in the absence of her canine companion.

For the last few years, Lone Wolf has been conducting various activities as the healer. The medicine dance planned for the middle of June will be held in La Jara Canyon where the last ritual was held in 1898 by the old Apache woman, Sotl, who made the journey of nearly a hundred miles on a burro. The medicine lodge built within a fence made of pine brush is under construction supervised by the Ancient One. Mary Begay, mother of Jimmy Begay, is arranging the food necessary for the ceremony, which would last five days. The Ancient One selects men with the talent capable of outlining the dry paintings in the lodge; at the back of the lodge, a space of about six feet is cleared and covered with a thin layer of sand in preparation for the paintings. The first day, pictures of snakes with their heads facing the west are created.

The sun symbol drawn around a shallow hole six or eight inches in diameter in the center of the painting and is indicated by a ring of white sand, next a circle of black, and a ring of red with white rays.

Mary, aunt of Jimmy Begay, was bitten on the shin as she walked through the brush by a rattlesnake. While she had undergone treatment at the clinic in Dulce, she asked for the healing ceremony with Lone Wolf. Over the years, she established a good working relationship with the staff; the physician's assistance at the clinic is an Apache and attends all healing ceremonies.

When the preparation is complete, Mary, dressed in simple attire, walks through the pine brush fence, lays her shawl on the ground, and enters the lodge. There are four bear tracks leading to the dry painting.

As she moves toward the sand painting at the back of the lodge, she steps on the prints; reaching the painting, she spreads *kat-u-tin* (pollen) from the flag of the cattail and then she sprinkles sacred meal. Then Mary sits on the painting, facing the east.

Songs sail on the breeze, and prayers echo across the prairie, heralding the sun. When the last refrains of the prayers fade, the women of the tribe enter the enclosure with food. Those seated around the outer wall of the lodge are served by the doorkeeper. Jake, an elder and grandfather, carries the food from left to right, serving each Apache inside the lodge. When everyone is served, he gathers a morsel from each one, tossing it out the door as a sacrifice to the sun. While Jake joins those in the medicine lodge eating, as does Mary, those outside dine within the pine brush barrier. The leftover food is placed in the enclosure by the men and will be removed later by the women.

As shadows spreads across the land, turning the gray of evening into darkness, a fire warms the interior as the men again paint snakes in the medicine lodge. A small pine tree is set to the left and right of the sand painting. Then the children are sent from the enclosure of pine bushes.

The offerings of *kat-u-tin* and meal upon the painting represent the snakes. And the bear is called on to drive the disease from her body. Mary once again enters the lodge, offering *kat-u-tin* [pollen] and meal seating herself on the painting.

Rushing into the shadowy lodge, a horrid figure of a man lunges toward Mary, not quite reaching her. Even knowing it is one of the men painted black and covered with pine branches who wears no mask, it is still frightening to her.

The singing men yell as loud as they can to scare the bear from the building. Mary fell to the ground, trembling with fear. Lone Wolf waves an eagle feather to and fro over her head while she rises, falls, shakes, and cries. She appears to be dying in the frantic state she is experiencing.

Placing a live coal in a dish of blue corn, Lone Wolf lets Mary inhale the smoke rising from the dish. Soon, her crying and gyrations stop as she sits up, staring blankly as though she were intoxicated. After smoking the pipe filled with "Mexican" tobacco handed to her by Lone Wolf, Mary is more alert to her surroundings. The serious part of the day's events is concluded by the singing of three songs. Mary now moves to the north side of the lodge where she remains for the rest of the evening.

Placing an old buffalo hide over the sand painting, the sacred basket—a white basket decorated with the approved red butterflies presented to Lone Wolf—is inverted with the hide over the hole in the center of the painted area. The hide is then doubled over the basket. The men sitting around the outer edge of the lodge place their feet on the edge of the hide to hold it in place.

Removing her moccasins from the bundle, Mary, using them as drumsticks, strikes the basket drum four times, a signal for the whole tribe to come inside the enclosure to dance. Two notched sticks, one black on the east side while one white on the west side, are placed against the basket with one end on the drum and the other end on the ground. Young girls begin the dance when Lone Wolf rubs the tarsal bone from a deer across the notches.

The southern portion of the enclosure is occupied by the women of the tribe while the men arranged themselves on the opposite wall. A circle of fires situated around the inside wall of the lodge brightly illuminates it giving a translucent glow. The dance ceases just as it began—four strokes upon the basket.

Soon, the drum sounds again, signaling those with ailments of any kind to place their hands on the area of concern and symbolically cast out the disease by taking their hands, tossing the ailment away from their bodies.

With the scraping of the sticks, the women select a partner from the men and boys; dancing and merriment replace the serious aspect of the ceremony—the atoning to the Gods, the awed inspiration by the healer, and the deity represented by the bear. Their revelry continues until the drum ceases its cadence near midnight as the voice of the Ancient One announces the dissipation of the festivities.

As the clans leave the enclosure, Lone Wolf, Jake, Lee, along with Jimmy and the Ancient One, retire to a grove of trees a short distance away, Lone Wolf tired but exhilarated.

"Jake, we have until noon tomorrow. Let's all spend the night at the cave." Looking at the Ancient One, she asks, "Will you go with us? I must see to my animals, and you will be able to have a nice rest."

His eyes twinkle at the invitation. He nods, moving toward the SUV. It is early morning when they arrive at the cave; all are curious what the old grandfather will do or say when he sees the white woman's cave.

The Ancient One, his expression never changing, realizes that if one did not know where the medicine woman's *kogha* was they would never see it. A snicker of amusement escapes from Jake as he observes the ancient ones' nonresponse. When Lee opens the screen, the inner corrals with the horses, the barn, and the garage are revealed. Parking the SUV in its usual place, they all traipse into the barn where Sarah greets Mesquite, checking on his water, hay, and oats. As he nuzzles her, she reaches into the special bin and retrieves his juicy red treat.

The three blood brothers care for their own mounts as the Ancient One sits on a bale of hay watching. Finishing with the horses, Lee and Jimmy bring out the bedding, setting up their usual beds on bales of hay they claimed for their own some time back.

Sarah, opening the door to the kitchen, says, "Ancient One, please join us in the house."

Looking at the two youngsters, he asks, "This is where you sleep?"

Lee and Jimmy laugh a deep belly laugh. "For many years, Grandfather, we have slept here. This is our private room, which we are pleased to share with the ponies. There is only one bedroom, it belongs to Lone Wolf. For years, when we protected her, Jake slept in a recliner in the big room. After the truck wreck where she was injured, Jake never left her side. It was then she invited him into her bed."

Then Jimmy takes up the story. "We thought it was a special day, so we celebrated behind her back 'cause we thought she took much too long." Looking at the faces of Jake and Sarah, a smile spreads across his face. "You two were meant for each other, but we thought you would never realize it."

The Ancient One listens then moves to the bale of hay Jimmy had claimed for his own several years ago now covered with his chosen blankets. "This will be mine, find another."

Laughter erupts from Sarah. "Come on, Jimmy, there are other blankets for you to use. Set up another couple of bales." Seeing the look on his face, she responds to the unasked question. "Because you are the youngest and most adaptable. That is the grandfather's way."

The gray dawn slowly turns to pale yellow as the sun creeps above the mountains, lighting the valley filled with the chirp of wrens, the caw of the crows and the sweet aroma of sagebrush wafting in the breeze, singing through the pines.

The boys wake to find the Ancient One sitting cross-legged on his bale of hay, smoking his pipe. The aroma of bacon frying and coffee perking permeates the air. Grinning, the boys stretch as they rise from their beds. As Lee tries desperately to get his attention, Jimmy respectfully says, "You are up early, Grandfather."

Only the eyes move in his placid face. "It would do you well to rise early, young warrior. The eagle watches as the coyote goes to his lair. He sleeps by day you do not."

Glancing at Lee who is trying not to laugh, Jimmy replies, "You are right, Grandfather. Would you like a cup of coffee and breakfast?" Waiting for the grandfather's reply, he moves toward the door.

With a twinkle in his aged eyes, he replies, "Lone Wolf has seen to my needs." He continues to enjoy his pipe as he watches the two young warriors move into the kitchen. The smell of hay and the snorts of the horses bring back memories of when he was a young man riding free across this very valley, paying tribute to the wisdom of the ancestors. *You have chosen well for the Apache. Lone Wolf is a true blood brother to the tribe and a dedicated medicine woman.* Puffing on his pipe, he thought, *My time is near. I am ready.*

Preparations for the day are well underway when Lone Wolf and the others arrive at La Jara Canyon. On the second day, the ceremonies are similar to the first. The figures drawn on the sand are bears, foxes, and other animals with an occasional snake. A man from the tribe enters the lodge spreading *kat-u-tin* and sacred meal on the painting. Sitting up on the sand painting, he faces the east. After the songs are sung and prayers offered to the sun, the women as before bring food into the enclosure. Jake, again the doorkeeper, serves the food left to right. Once everyone has been served, he gathers a morsel of food from each one in the lodge, tossing it into the enclosure as a sacrifice to the sun. Then he offers prayers to the sun. While Jake and those in the lodge consume their food, the others dine in the enclosure. The men carry the food from the lodge, placing it in the enclosure. It will be removed later by the women.

As the ceremony continues once again, the signal is given and the dancing begins first with the women and then the men. Soon the signal is given, and the women choose partners among the men and boys. The dancing continues until the moon starts its westerly descent and the Ancient One directs the assembly to retire.

As she watches the crowd disperse she ponders. *I know I should be exhausted, but I am exhilarated by the activities. My feeling of kinship to the diide defies description. My life is rich beyond imagination. I have been blessed by the Gods, or more to the truth—the ancestors.*

As the Apache leave the area either by motorized vehicles or by horse, Lone Wolf notices the Ancient One sitting by the wheel of her SUV. She smiles, nodding to Jake. "Ancient One, your bed of hay is waiting."

As he starts to rise, he hesitates, but like the wise woman she has become, Lone Wolf offers no assistance. However, Jimmy has no such compulsion; he takes the old man by the arm, allowing him to pull himself up. Then without a word, he allows Jimmy to help him into the vehicle.

Jake and Lee's eyes meet in the dark as they watch the Ancient One and the Young One. By letting Jimmy help him, he has shown great respect for the boy. At once, the two remember the quest the young man went on when he was just a tadpole. And the silence that passes between them speaks louder than the many voices raised in song just a few short hours ago. As the realization hits them, they glance in Lone Wolf's direction and sees awareness reflected in her green orbs.

Arriving at the cave, the sleeping arrangements are the same. Everyone is tired, and as soon as the horses are tended, the weary natives retire to their respective bales of hay. When Jake and Sarah are alone, she asks, "Jake, the Ancient One is not well. What can we do to help him?"

"Nothing, he will choose the way of the ancestors. When he is sure his time is near, he will go into the hills to a location he has chosen, and there he will join the ancestors, or he will stay in his *kogha*." Seeing the look or her face, he says, "Will you interfere, Sarah?"

Understanding his question, she hesitates only a moment. "Lone Wolf will not interfere. She will respect the Ancient One's wishes."

Jake wraps his arms around her pulls her to him. "You are truly an Apache squaw and a true healer to the *diide*." As she lays with her head on his chest, the steady beat of his heart a soothing cadence, steals her consciousness as sleep over takes her.

The sun is just creeping over the trees, the shadows still lingering when they are aroused by chatter from the kitchen area. Sarah and Jake, half-dressed move rapidly toward the sounds and discover the three barn sleepers busy in the kitchen. The Ancient One sits, smoking his pipe and sipping coffee as Lee and Jimmy prepare burritos.

Lee burst out laughing as he sees the two standing in the door. "Grandfather said we should be up with the sun if we did not wish to be considered lazy. We respect his declaration, as we should."

Grabbing a cup of coffee, the two return to the bedroom to finish dressing for the third day of the healing ceremony.

The activities began at noon with the change of the animals used in the sand paintings, but there is no representation of the horse or the elk, having been forbidden when Sotli conducted the healing ceremony in the fall of 1898.

As the ceremonies continued through the day and into the night, Lone Wolf notices the demeanor of the Ancient One who appears to be tiring. Yet at the midnight hour, when he instructs the Apache to leave the enclosure, his voice is strong and forceful.

The reminder of the night is quiet as the blood brothers and the grandfather return to the cave. The night chill reaches its lowest peak, and the wind howls through the pines as off in the distance a coyote howls, his loneliness echoing on the wind.

The Grandfather is slow in rising at midmorning. Lee and Jimmy feel some concern but know that it is best not to mention their feelings to the Ancient One. They hand him a cup of coffee and his pipe as he sits on the bale of hay where he spent the night. He acknowledges their courtesy then pays tribute to the Gods as he has every morning of his life.

Sarah brings him a warm breakfast burrito but isn't surprised to learn later that he ate only a few bites.

As they arrive back at La Jara Canyon, the chosen men have drawn two deities in the painting, adding several animals; outside the painting is a black circle that represents the ocean. As the evening draws near, men divided into two groups are painted and dressed in the tradition of the Jicarillas for the rites—one group of six, the clowns, their bodies and limbs painted white with horizontal black rings. Their clothing consists of loincloths made from the rags of old blankets. The accouterments are made of bread baked in unusual shapes. Four are adorned with buffalo skin caps having the appearance of horns pointing upward and to the side of the head with an eagle feather and a turkey feather attached to two of the horns. The hair of the other two is twisted to look like horns.

A second group of twelve are painted white with black stripes radiating form the corner of their eyes downward; necklaces adorned their bodies with an eagle feather woven into their hair and are wearing bands of pine brush circling their waist, arms and ankles.

With the passing of the hours, the women, as with each evening, begins the dance, then the women select a partner from the assembled warriors.

Soon entering the enclosure are two deities marching directly to the medicine lodge, circling it four times in an easterly direction. Those in black and white line the pathway on the south side from the entrance of the pine brush enclosure to the lodge.

The clowns are entertaining for everyone as the dance continues 'til the sun creeps over the high mountains, lighting the canyon. With the appearance of the golden disc, every Apache present joins in the dancing. As the golden rays wipe the shadows of night, a seriousness returns as the band of Jicarilla-Apache march out of the enclosure toward the sun.

Lone wolf leads the parade, carrying the two young pines from their resting place at the ends of the sand painting and the sacred basket holding the meal. As the Apache pass by the healer, a pinch of meal is lifted from the basket and tossed on the pine trees. Again, the line is formed and the Respected Elder steps forward, shaking his blanket four times. With this gesture, all shake their blankets to drive the diseases away then race from the enclosure.

With the ceremonies over, every tepee or temporary shelter must be moved at once. Mary is cured. By tradition, Lone Wolf must warn her not to sleep on a rope or string; no one is to sing the bear songs for some time or the bear with kill them. And the twelve were not to sleep with their heads toward a clay vessel in fear of a severe illness. There was ample food, excluding the forbidden bread baked in ashes for the tribe during the five days and no one went hungry.

Every Apache in attendance at the healing ceremony understands that Mary had seen the doctor at the clinic, but by participating, they help to preserve the traditions of the Jicarilla. Even the young with the educational opportunities of the century and the wealth of the Jicarilla Apache, it is an honor to perpetuate centuries of Apache lore housed in tradition.

Mary listens to her directive. “Lone Wolf, it was good, the healing ritual, yes.”

Smiling at Mary, eyes glowing with delight, she says, “Yes, Mary, it was good. I am glad you requested it. Such is the traditions that the Apache strive to preserve. I am pleased to be a small part of their ancient rituals.

As the crowd disperses, Jake, Lee, and Jimmy see to the comfort of the Ancient One. As Jake bends over to assist him, he whispers to Jake, “It is a good day to die.”

With the solemnity of the moment, Jake asks, “Grandfather, do you have a special place you would like to be?”

He nods. “My *kogha*,” as he slumps in Jake’s arms. Rousing and in a faint voice, he says, “I must speak to Lone Wolf.”

“Sarah, Grandfather would like a word with you, Lone Wolf.”

At his words, Sarah moves toward her mentor, and seeing the seriousness of Jake’s face, she knows the grandfather’s time is very near. “Yes, Grandfather, what do you wish?”

Opening his eyes and raising his head slightly, he whispers, "You are a true Apache and a great healer. The Gods chose well. Grant me one wish."

"What is it you would ask of me, Grandfather?"

"Take me to my *kogha*, walk away, leave to me die. When there is no smoke from the fire for one full moon, return, burying me in the traditional way."

Had it not been for many years of discipline and the training she had received by this great Apache, she would have dissolved in tears. Choking back the emotion she felt, she says, "It will be so, Grandfather. We, as blood brothers, vow to honor you wish."

Lee and Jimmy lift the Ancient One, placing him in the SUV, wrapping a blanket around his withered body. It is a very solemn group that travels the rode to the grandfather's *kogha*, a place where all had been many times.

Reaching the *kogha*, they place him on an old bear rug in front of the fireplace as he requests. Jimmy starts a small fire to ward off the chill griping the old man. Then he places water and food near him, knowing he will not partake. He lays back, closing his eyes, his breathing even but labored as the Apache brothers leave, closing the door behind them.

The four sit in the SUV for a few minutes, silence permeating the enclosure. What can they say? The Ancient One said it all when he said, "It's a good day to die."

PART IV

GOZHISH [TIME PASSES]

Sarah's work as the Jicarilla Apache medicine woman placed her in position of honor and respect. And she has been able to encourage and inspire the older members of the tribe to combine the ancestors healing with the modern techniques of the clinic. The Respected Elder, council president at the time she was chosen by the ancestors to serve as a healer, had been wise in his requirement that she work with the doctors. Their work relationship had been complimenting, thus aiding both in their respective areas of expertise. He retired from the counsel and enjoys sitting on his front porch, smoking his pipe and visiting with those who drop by to seek his wisdom. This pleases the grandfather.

Jake and Sarah have been together since the attempt on her life, but neither felt it necessary to marry. He passed his home to a young Apache working for the Wild Horse Casino in Dulce, who at present is a bingo attendant, but hopes to advance with the casino. With a degree in business management, he wants to find something on the Res. Pete Tsosie comes from a traditional family and is comfortable staying close to his family who still tends a small herd of sheep.

Sarah has stopped writing her books but lives comfortably on the royalties from previous publications, even having one on the best-seller list. When she turned eighty, she changed her will, making Jimmy Begay and Lee Atepa her sole heirs.

She and Jake hardly ever leave the reservation; their trips into Dulce became fewer. Lee always makes sure they have what they need. He visits with them at least on the weekend unless he was on duty.

This happens to be a Saturday when he is off. After making a couple of stops he arrives at the cave after sunup with a flatbed full of hay for the horses, a bushel of apples for their snacks, and a big bag of jerky for Tacky. He finds the two elders sitting at the kitchen table drinking coffee. Tacky, a full-blood German shepherd, Jimmy had brought to Sarah on his last day before leaving for the university sitting at Sarah's feet, begging for his treat. Tacky, almost three years old, is as devoted to Sarah as Rusty had been.

Since the cave had not been opened, Lee went to the secret box and punched in the code. As the cave opens to the outside world, Lee takes time to look across the valley, listening to the wind rustling the aspen as it rolls down the mountainside, rippling across the sagebrush. As he goes through the barn, he smiles as he sees his bale of hay covered in the blankets just as he left it last week.

"Jake, I do believe Lee has arrived. Betcha he hasn't eaten." With that, Sarah goes to the fridge, grabs a package of bacon, and sets four eggs on the counter. Reaching down in the lower cabinet, she takes out a cast iron skillet.

His ebony eyes twinkling as he hears Lee greeting the horses, Jake replies, "That's not a bet, that's a guarantee."

As Lee bursts into the kitchen, his firsts words are the same ones he always utters. "What's for breakfast?" Putting the bag of jerky on the counter, he squats down, getting his face washed by a rough canine tongue. Standing, he says, "Be right back."

Jake and Sarah's eyes speak volumes—no words are necessary—as she continues her preparation of Lee's breakfast.

When Lee returns, his arms are laden with two huge bags of groceries. Setting them on the counter, he begins to put things away. Lee has never left Sarah to put things away and always seem to know just what they need in the pantry and freezer.

Smiling, Sarah sits his plate of bacon and eggs on the table with a cup of coffee just as he puts the last item away and folds the bags. She would never insult him by offering to pay for the things he brings to them.

As he straddles the chair, Tacky is right at his knee. Lee thinks he is unnoticed as he slips the canine a piece of bacon.

Jake smiles at Sarah as they remember the first time he fed Tacky from his plate. *Oh, it always surprises me how these youngsters still think they can outwit their elders. Guess he has never figured out why I place extra bacon on his dish.*

Lee sighs with contentment as he finishes the last bite of egg. "Are you two old folks up for a ride this morning?"

Mischief sparkling in his ebony orbs, Jake says, "Sarah, this young'un has no respect for his elders. Should we teach him a lesson or two?"

Putting her hands on her hips, she replies, "I think that's a very good idea. Saddle Mesquite for me, I'll be right out." Returning to the bedroom, she steps out of her flats, slipping into her boots, grabbing her old hat and heads out the door. "Lee, you proposed this ride, do you have a picnic for us?"

His laughter echoing across the valley, he answers, "Of course, Lone Wolf, we always have a picnic."

The morning air is crisp, snow in the higher elevations and a dusting sprinkled across the valley. *The Gods have been good to the Apache and especially to me; to have blood brothers who are not only my friends but family is unbelievable and truly a gift.* He watches the horizon looking for the surprise he has planned. *Ah! Yes, there just to the edge of the old oak.*

At the instance, Tacky darts ahead, running full bore. Sarah and Jake notice the rider by the tree near their special spot. Sarah yells, "Jimmy." Spurring Mesquite with her knees, they dash after Tacky. He, too, knows who waits.

Without hesitation, Jake gives a war hoop, racing to keep up with Sarah, knowing that his mount will not keep pace with Mesquite who has a slight lead.

As soon as Mesquite comes to a halt at the tree, Jimmy helps Sarah to dismount, wrapping his arms around her, touching his lips to her leathery cheek. "I have missed you, Lone Wolf."

Jake and Lee dismount, taking Mesquite's reins, tying all three horses to limbs of the scrub oak so they will be in the shade. Lee takes his saddlebags to the quilt Jimmy has already placed in the usual spot. He notices that Jimmy has brought a thermos of coffee, jerky and apples—a must to all their picnics. Lee has brought burritos with fresh roasted green chili, which he had learned a long time ago was one of Sarah's favorite foods.

The four blood brothers enjoy a Thanksgiving dinner. As they sit quietly in the shade of the tree, Jake asks, "Jimmy, how are your studies going?"

"Jake, because of the scholarships and the money Sarah gave me, I have not had to work, so I have been taking extra classes. I currently have 4.25 GPA and will graduate in three years instead of four. Following with a four-year internship, also eight-hour fundamentals test, an eight-hour principles and practice test, I can be licensed."

Sarah's heart swells with pride as her eyes glow with unshed tears at the accomplishment of the young "warrior" she rescued some ten years ago.

Jake reaches for her hand, giving it a gentle squeeze of understanding. He feels the same pride of this "blood brother." Tacky lays his head in his mistress's lap, reminding her that he is a part of this celebration and it is time for jerky.

Smiling at his gentle push, she reaches for his favorite treat, unwrapping one piece. Then as had become the custom among the four, she handed each one a piece.

Without a word, Jimmy picks up the juicy red apples, taking one to each of the ponies. There is comfort in tradition, and these brothers had formed their own.

"Jimmy, when do you return to the university?"

"Lee, I will leave Sunday about midmorning, so I can be in the dorm before dark. I still have a few things I want to go over before class on Monday."

Jimmy nods, hoping he will follow him as he moves to the edge of the cliff where he had fallen as a young man. He is pleased that Lee is right behind him.

The expression on his face serious as he asks, "Jimmy, what is on your mind?"

Looking toward his two mentors with concern in his voice, he asks, "Lee, are the grandmother and grandfather all right?"

He glances in the direction of the hills before replying. "They are beginning to show their age. They rarely go into Dulce anymore and seem content to spend time with each other, Tacky and their ponies. Most of the time, I bring feed and hay for the horses and always bring several bags of food. I make sure they are never in need, and when I'm not on duty, I still spend my nights with them."

"Lee, why have you never married? Am I being too personal?"

Shaking his head with a barely audible sigh, he said, "From anyone else, I would take offense, Jim. However, to answer you, I strongly believe in our pledge to take care of those two. They are beginning to show their age, but don't dare let them hear me say so. I would probably get my ears boxed."

Pondering what Lee has said, Jim asks, "You will let me know what is going on with them, wont' you?"

"That won't be a problem since you have an e-mail account. I will give you weekly reports on them. Now, before we get quizzed, we better return to those wise old birds. Looking up into the clear blue sky, he asks, "Jim did you notice the eagle soaring overhead? Isn't it amazing how the most beautiful eagles are always wherever Sarah is?"

"Yep, they have protected her from the time she first approached the tribal council some years ago. I believe it was an eagle and one of his feathers that convinced the respected elder to permit her to live on the Res and imposed the restrictions."

Sarah observes the two as they return to the shade of the oak. "What are you two youngsters up to?"

As their eyes meet, Jimmy replies, "Just reminiscing Lone Wolf. A lot has happened since you rescued me." Gazing toward the mountain peaks, he continues, "I need to be going." He shakes hands with Jake and Lee then wraps his arms around Sarah. "Lone Wolf, take care of the grandfather."

PART V

IT'S A GOOD DAY TO DIE

The brothers, friends, lovers sit by the fire, Jake puffing on his pipe and Sarah with her eyes closed listening to Braun's. "Squaw, we have had a good life and the Gods have smiled on us. I am growing weaker each day."

She opens her green orbs, gazing at the weathered face she has come to love. "Yes, my warrior, I too feel the time is near." She pauses. "Jimmy will be home for the holidays soon. It will be so nice to see him. He has only two years left on his internship, I do not believe we will be able to celebrate with him."

His eyes tender with the love, he feels for this white squaw who is more Apache than a lot of the young full blood of the tribe. "You are a wise medicine woman. The Ancient One taught you well." Looking out across their valley, he asks, "Have you noticed that our five guardians have been here for some time?"

"Yes, Jake. Usually, we have only one on duty, but when they are all present, there is a serious event on the horizon." Smiling at the memories of her years on the reservation, she quietly continues. "My brave warrior, they have come to bid us farewell and guide our journey to the spirit world."

"Shall we put our house in order, squaw?" Slowly rising from his chair zaps most of his strength. He takes her hand, leading her to the barn where together that lay out extra hay for the horses. She wraps her arms around her beloved Mesquite, snuggling her face in his mane as she has so many times over the years. Reaching in to the special bin, she gives him what she knows will be his final sweet red treat from her hand. With Tacky on their heels, she and Jake return to the kitchen where they put everything in order. They stop at her desk where she wrote all her stories. Turning the computer on, they wait patiently while it boots up. When it is ready, she types one simple sentence, duplicating it below then prints it out. Cutting it in two pieces, she unplugs the computer. Their eyes afire with love, hand in hand, they retire to the bedroom, dressing in their Apache finery. Lying on the nightstand on the side where Jake sleeps, a small button of peyote awaits. Jake weaves the lone eagle feather into her once-auburn hair now turned gray with age, touches her cheek with his lips, and carefully places the other five eagle feathers as a tribute to their guardians. When she is ready, he lies down beside her.

The preparation drains both of all the strength they had left in their aged bodies. "Are you ready, squaw?"

Smiling into the darkness of the room, she says, "It is time, my warrior."

Reaching for the buttons, he places one in his mouth, and as he begins to chew, he places the other on the lips of the medicine woman. She lets it slip into her mouth and savors the taste as they begin their final quest—a journey into the spirit world. Slowly, the life slips away and all is quiet in the cave of the once-forbidden white woman who became a revered medicine woman of the Jicarilla Apache.

PART VI

THE REQUEST

Jimmy into his second year of apprenticeship returns home for the Christmas holidays. The last two nights at his parents' home sleeping in his old room he has seen the haunting yellow eyes of the coyote glowing through the window pane. The same one where he saw the coyote when he was ten years old. *This is troubling, I'll go into town and visit with Lee.*

As he approaches the police station, Lee is just stepping outside. Approaching him, Lee hails. "*Yaa` ta` sai`*. What brings you into town so early?"

Disturbed by the dream and knowing that Lee is a traditional Apache sworn to protect Sarah and Jake, he asks, "How are Jake and Lone Wolf?"

"About the same as I e-mailed you last week. Their spirit is good." Pausing. "Why do you ask?"

Without answering his query, he says, "What time does your shift end? Could we meet later?"

Seeing the seriousness reflected in his eyes, Lee responds, "At 4:00 p.m., let's meet at the café."

Jim acknowledges. "See ya then." Standing in the shade of the building, he watches Lee enter his SUV and drive off on his rounds.

Picking up the mic, he calls dispatch as he leaves town. "Kate, anything going on around the area?" Hearing that there is not, he proceeds to make his rounds. Stopping by the Respected Elder's place to see if he needs anything from the town, he then proceeds across the acreage where he's assigned today. Everything is routine; he finds Fred's old truck in the ditch with Fred walking across the prairie. Before he gets too far away, Lee gives three blasts on the horn. The old Indian turns, waves his hat, and turns back toward his old truck. Fred doesn't see too well but his hearing is sharp, and he knows the sound of Lee's horn. He should, since pulling him out of one ditch or another is a weekly thing. *Hell, I like being on the Res. I never intend to leave. Helping the elders brightens my day.* Without being asked, he follows behind Fred's dust trail until he is sure he has reached his home some ten miles off the dirt road from where he found him. Then he turns toward Dulce and home.

Jim moves to the mercantile, picking up a few things his mother wanted and tobacco for his dad. Stopping by the feed store to chat with a schoolmate, he moves on to the post office. The old postmistress has been there since he was a young boy. They visit about school and the weather. Picking up his mail, he saunters past the other businesses, thinking, *This is home.* As he enters the restaurant, he makes his way to the back, selecting a table in the corner.

"*Yaa`ta`sai`*, Jimmy, it's good to see you. Visiting your folks for the holidays? How are they?"

"They are doing well, Mary. Glad to have me home."

"What can I get you?"

"Just coffee for now." He notices that Mary's hair is turning gray. *Have I been gone that long, or am I just becoming aware of the aging process?*

While Mary is getting his coffee, he sorts through the mail, most of which is catalogs, advertising all sorts of products. One is the seed catalog where his mother orders her garden seeds. He notices a large brown envelope with his name on it. Looking at the return, he sees that it is from a lawyer he never heard of and notices the postmark stamped on it reflects Texas as the origin. He sits there, looking and wondering what it contains. As Mary sits his coffee on the table, Jim removes the small knife from his jeans and slits the top open, spreading the contents on the table. Picking up the letter lying on top, he reads.

> Mr. Begay,
>
> One does not usually receive a missive of this nature until the subject of the information is deceased.

However, it is the desire of Ms. Sarah Louise O'Hara that this request be conveyed to you prior to her demise.

The name is surprising to him; she has been known as the white woman, Sarah, and Lone Wolf; but he doesn't remember ever hearing her last name, but then he must have when they all appeared before the council for her acceptance as a healer. He continues reading....

You and Lee Apeta are her sole heirs. However, the extent of her estate will not be revealed until a death certificate is submitted to this office. Find enclosed a sealed envelope with specific instructions that is for you alone and is to be opened upon receipt; she was very emphatic about this.

If you have any questions, please contact the law office.

Sincerely,
Jack Green
Attorney
Cc: filed
Encl: sealed envelope

Jim picks up the sealed envelope with only his name printed on the front. He sips his coffee, hesitant to open it yet curious about the content, considering the attorney's cover letter. Gazing up as the door opens, but seeing it is a tourist, returns to what he was doing. Taking his knife, he slits the top and withdraws a single page. At the top of the page he sees…

Instructions upon the Demise
of
Lone Wolf, Apache Medicine Woman

As he reads down the list of instructions, his jaw tightens, and his eyes turn even darker than their usual inky hue. He reads the page in awe at what he is asked to do, knowing that he will do anything Lone Wolf asks of him. When the time comes, and he hopes it is a long time off, he will carry out these instructions.

He is so intent with the contents of the single sheet he is not aware that Lee has entered the restaurant until he hears the scrape of a chair as he sits down across the table from him. As Mary sits a cup of coffee in front of Lee, Jim is staring out the window at the buildings across the street, seeing nothing, not even the blue sky above with the soft billowy clouds drifting on the breeze.

Noticing the blankness emanating from the ebony orbs, the tense face, and the clinched fist, Lee wonders what is troubling the young Apache. "Jim, you look like you have seen a ghost."

The boy, who is no longer a boy but a man, continues his trance-like stare out the window, where he sees a lone eagle soaring in the azure sky near where the cave is hidden. He remembers the significance of the eagle in her life—how the eagle and one lone feather was the deciding factor in her being granted residence on the Res so long ago. The eagles who always seemed to be near her and who protected her from that vile Sosa who tried to kill her. *What is the meaning of him hovering over the cave?* Turning from the window, he says. "Lee, glad you could make it. How was your day?"

"It was good. You seem a little disturbed. What is going on with you?"

Jim turns the envelope around where Lee can see the return address, saying nothing.

"Yeah, I got one yesterday. We are to inherit from Sarah's estate. You can't be distressed over that."

Again staring out the window, seeing nothing, he thinks, *Lee is a blood brother, her friend, her protector, but he is also a cop and must abide by the law. How would he react to what she is asking of me?* Shaking his head as his mind returns to the present, he says, "Lee, I have instructions from her attorney on the performance of certain responsibilities upon her demise. I am honor bound as a chosen leader of the Jicarilla Apache to do as she asks."

When he does not continue, Lee states, "Then I don't see the problem you seem to be wrestling with, Jim."

"The problem is one of legality more than it is anything else. I can't refuse to execute her wishes, but it could put me crossways with the law and you. I might add that the same thing that she is asking of me applies to Jake as well." Picking up his cup, he sips coffee that has long since cooled then raises his cup to Mary.

She refreshes the men's coffee and returns to the counter where she waits on other customers. She knows her nephew well, he is troubled by something. She will not interfere; it is not her way.

After a few sips of the hot liquid, his decision is made. He turns the single sheet toward Lee without saying a word. He just sits watching his eyes as he reads the missive.

Lee gives a low whistle. "I see what you mean, Jim. But let's clear the air right now. Where Lone Wolf is concerned, I am her blood brother first and law officer second. You intend to carry out Sarah's and Jake's request, do you not?"

Jim looks Lee in the eyes, neither flinching. "You can count on it." Breaking eye contact, he says, "I certainly hope it is a long time to come.

Lee shakes his head as a burst of cold air enters the café, laughter echoing across the room as teenage boys come charging in. Their laughter and antics seem incongruous to the somber air around the pair of "brothers."

"It may not be as long as we would like. Those two seem too content with themselves." Smiling…not an ounce of sadness, he states, "It reminds me a lot of when we took the Ancient One to his home and following his instructions went back in one full moon.

"Lee, there is more." He does not continue; he just stares at nothing and everything at the same time. "Remember back when we began our secret meetings I related a dream that I had about the fiery eyes of the coyote glaring through my window? My trip to the Ancient One and the quest he took me on."

Frowning, he said, "Yes, Jim, I do. But what does that have to do with this letter?"

A dark cloud settles over the table where they sit in conversation. "The past two nights since I have been home, the same golden eyes appeared in the window, and again, only two prints were on the ground under the window—none coming to or going from the house." Pausing to give Lee time to understand what he is saying, he continues, "I feel their time is very near. I keep hearing one phrase in my head. 'It's a good day to die.'"

Looking around the café then glancing out the window as the sun sinks behind the horizon, he asks, "Do they know you are home?"

"They knew it was my intent to be here for the holidays, but no, they do not know I have arrived."

Signaling to Mary, he says, "Then let's get a burger and drive out there. They will be glad to see you, and it will be a sneaky way of checking on them."

"What can I get you, boys?"

"Burger and fries for me, Mary."

Lee chimes in. "The same for me."

The boys devour their food, pay the tab, and walk out into the crisp December air. "I'll follow you, Lee."

Raising his hand in acknowledgment, he climbs in his SUV, pulling out onto NM 537 with Jim in his S10 right behind him.

The drive out to the cave never seemed so long as it does this night. Jim usually has his radio on full blast on the western channel, but tonight, there is a pall hanging in the cab. A feeling of sadness closes in around him in spite of his training. *How can I explain being closer to Lone Wolf and Jake than to my parents? As a foretold leader of the Jicarilla, I must be a strong warrior; I must never disappoint my two mentors.* Wondering what is going through Lee's mind, he glances ahead and sees the glow of a match as Lee lights a cigar. A small chuckle escapes. *Yup, he picked up the habit from Jake.*

As Lee puts out the match, he glances in the rearview mirror. *Jim is like Lone Wolf; he has the wisdom of the ancestors and the gift of conversing with the Gods. He will one day be considered an ancient one. His insight gives me reason to be uneasy about what we will find at the cave.* As he watches the road ahead, he sees that the moon is in the last phase and the sky is unusually dark—even the stars seem to have lost their luster.

Arriving at the cave, the boys park outside the corral. Lee, seeing the cave is obscure, walks to the hidden switches and punches in the code, allowing them entrance to the inner corral and barn. As they enter the barn, Lee notices that there is very little hay and grain for the stock. Opening the kitchen door, they find no sound, no fire, and no coffee aroma. Everything else is in order—not a dirty dish in the sink, nothing out of order. All the vehicles were in the garage, so there should be something. Lee and Jim's black orbs meet and the two blood brothers head back to the bedroom Jake and Sarah have shared for the past few years.

Stopping in the doorway, they are not surprised at what they see. Jake in his best Apache dress and Sarah in the white leather dress with the beautiful beaded eagles presented for her to wear at the announcement of her acceptance as medicine woman of the Jicarilla Apache. Woven into her hair is the one eagle feather that determined her residence on the Res. The five feathers Jim had picked up and presented to her at the first Go-Jii-Yah Feast when someone yelled "Die, white woman" lay across her breast. How well they remember the bolt of lightning singing the onlookers yet never touching her. In the mist hovering around Sarah, Jim as a small boy walked unseen, picking up five feathers left by the most regal eagles ever seen on the Res, handing them to Sarah.

Tacky, the German shepherd puppy that Jim had given to her after Rusty died, lay between the two his eyes, watching carefully the friends standing in the door.

Without approaching the bed, the boys know that their mentors are dead. Clasped in Jake's hand was a note reading. "It's a good day to die." And upon examination, Sarah held a duplicate.

Returning to the kitchen, Lee went to the stove, putting on a pot of coffee. It was automatic; it is what he had done many times over the years. Jim followed with Tacky in his arms.

Almost choking, Lee asked in a gruff voice. "What do you need to carry out their request?"

Jim stands with his face buried in Tacky's furry neck, remaining silent until he has the composure worthy of an Apache warrior. "To honor their wish, I think it would be better to use C4 with timers set to implode the structure. That should close the mountain down on itself."

"Jim, is there a way that would seem it was an act of nature."

"Well, Lee, we could use a nice earthquake like we had back in '66. It would cover the implosion with a rock slide, but there has been no recent activity. So we can't count on nature."

"Let's see if I've learned enough to create a cave in then a landslide to cover the explosion." Pausing as he thinks how he can achieve the task successfully. "Lee, let's say we accomplish the task, how do we keep them from attempting a recovery effort?"

"Let's try a little Apache lore—perhaps the eagles will protect them from intruders who would desecrate a burial site. We, as blood brothers, should be able to stay the authorities, neither one has any kin other than us." Winking, he says, "We do have an inside track to the tribal police, don't we! And, Jimmy, you have a creative mind, devious at times but always in a positive way."

Lee pours two cups of the fresh brewed coffee. "Now, you're the engineer, Jim. How do we go about our mission?"

Sipping from the familiar cup with a picture of a bridge under construction on it, one he has used many times sitting exactly where he sits now. Tonight, he turns the chair around and sits straddle it, a habit he had acquired during his internship. "Well, the best explosive would be C4 with small detonators set to explode at various intervals like imploding a building. Since the beams and studs are steel placement, it is crucial to cause the whole cave to buckle. Then we will need to set charges above the roof of the cave in the side of the mountain."

"How do we acquire the C4, and how long will it take?"

Pondering the question over in his mind, Jim snaps his fingers. "I might have an idea on that. One of the engineers I am studying under might let me have some to blast stumps out where my parents can plant a small area of silage for our sheep. I'll admit it's a long shot. I'll have to return to Albuquerque, might take a day or two. "

"Do we have that much time?"

"Yeah, Lee, if you can keep anyone from coming out here. It just might work."

Standing to put his cup away, he says, "I'll take care of that. When would you leave?"

"Let me get a couple hours of sleep. I'll leave about midnight. That way I could possibly be back late Sunday or early Monday morning. That's assuming I can get the C4, detonators, and timer."

"Jim, what about Tacky? We can't leave him here."

Standing at the sink, washing out his cup, Jim turns. "I'll take Tacky with me if you will see to their horses. Wow! That brings up another problem, what about the horses?"

Putting his hands in his hip pockets looking down at the floor, he says, "Been thinking about that. Our blood brothers were both traditional Apache. The old way was to slaughter the horse so they would have a way to travel to the happy hunting ground. I think the horses should be left where they are."

"Lee, what about your own mare?"

"She stays."

Jim nods in response. With that, the two young Apache men retire to their bales of hay where they have slept many years. As they settle down, Tacky snuggles next to Jim his cold nose resting against Jim's cheek. Off in the distance, the howl of a lonesome coyote echoes across the valley, adding to the somber aura permeating the barn.

Part VII

The Angelic Flight

To keep visitors from the cave, Lee spends Sunday afternoon in Dulce where he is glad that few questions are asked about Jake and Sarah. When they are, he always responds that they are well. Returning to the cave late in the evening, he is becoming anxious as he has not heard from Jim. It is nearing sunup on Monday, and he still has not heard anything.

He is outside sitting on the corral fence when he sees headlights off in the distance. When he recognizes Jim's S10 relief swells through his body and the tension in his jaw relaxes. He remains sitting on the fence until Jim turns the truck's ignition off then hops down and goes to meet him. "How did it go?"

Jim breathes a sigh of relief. "I have all we need to blow out tree stumps." Opening the camper shell, he asks, "Are you on duty today?"

"No, I believed in your success and took the next two days off."

"You wouldn't happen to have some hot coffee, would you?"

Pushing the keypad to allow them to enter, he replies, "Not only do I have hot coffee but how about some bacon and eggs to go with it."

"Sounds good! You cookin'."

Over the next eighteen hours, the charges are set inside the structure. The sun is at its highest peak as the last charge is placed on the side of the mountain high enough to create a landslide to cover the destruction of the cave.

Gazing up at the crystal clear blue sky, there is not a cloud in sight. "When do we detonate the charges?"

"There is no point in waiting, we might as well do it."

"Jim, do you have any special words you would like to say?'

Shaking his head, he replies, "No, they said it all." As he reaches for the detonator switch, a monstrous bolt of lightning descends, blanking out the clear sky with its brilliance strikes the cave setting off the charges—*boom, boom, boom!*

Standing in awe, the two modern-day' warriors are amazed at the natural phenomenon of the Gods burying the white medicine woman. The awed warriors stand gaping at the implosion of the cave; the roar deadening as boulders, dirt, and pines cascade down the mountainside, filling the cavity, obliterating what once was the home of their healer.

As the roar of the landslide ebbs, the cloud of dust drifts high on the breeze, obliterating visibility. Lee and Jim feel the movement of air surrounding them as the five guardian eagles settle, forming a half circle with them at the center, smiling, not at all surprised that the guardians have come to send the healer on her way to the happy hunting grounds. A shiver of excitement and astonishment rifles through their bodies as they watch rising from the dusty cloud hanging over the cave poised against the sky the most beautiful eagle ever seen on the Jicarilla. The sun glistening off her magnificent feathers gives an angelic glow as she tips her wings and soars into the brilliant blue sky. The five guardian eagles escorting the first medicine woman in over one hundred years toward the ancestral home of the Gods who found this white woman a worthy Apache.

EPILOGUE

It seems only yesterday when Jake and Lone Wolf traveled to the place of our ancestors. But in reality, it has been some twenty years ago. Time spent building bridges, roads, airfields and other types of construction in some pretty exotic, interesting, and dangerous places in this world of ours. There was an oil refinery and pipeline in Kenya, a hydropower plant in Ethiopia, subways in Rio de Janerio, and other places around the world too numerous to mention. Most of my time was spent off the reservation and out of the United States of America.

There was one night when we were moving from one construction site to another in a remote area of the Arctic Circle. The desolation and cold engulfed me, giving me a feeling of emptiness to the point I felt a chill more severe than the frigid arctic air that ravished my body.

That night, sitting in our hut, soothed by warmth emanating from the oil stove in the corner of the room and the hum of the generator, my eyes slowly close in slumber.

Then once again I find myself standing on the Sacred Mountain. There in the mist I see the piercing golden eyes of the coyote before me. As the haze slowly dissipates, I found my self surrounded by the five guardian eagles circling the trickster who in a commanding voice speaks. "It is time to return to fulfill the commitment you made as a young warrior."

I woke with a start, sweat pouring from my body surrounded by ice and frigid temperatures. As I sat there, I remembered another vision I had some thirty five years ago when I was a young warrior of ten summers and the bravery it took to seek the vision quest that had been given to me. *Yes! It was time for me to return home.*

Within a month, I was winging my way home to fulfill my destiny foretold by the Ancient Ones the ancestors in my first vision quest. I wasn't sure how I would I feel reurning home after all these years. But I knew I would soon find out as the pilot landed at the airport in Farmington, New Mexico. As we taxied to the terminal, I had a bad case of anxiety not knowing what to expect, but that was soon replaced by a serenity that came over me as we slowed to a stop. Stepping down the ladder on to the tarmac, I was surprised to see a herd of Apache come running across the tarmac with Lee in the lead and my parents following. *I was shocked to see how old they had gotten in my absence as I gallivanted around the world with my job.*

Lee came slamming into me, wrapped his arms around me and gave me a bear hug I won't soon forget. Then he stepped back and let my parents' have a go at me. It was a welcome I shall never forget.

Once we claimed my luggage we left the terminal. I found they had a bus with Jicarilla Apache Reservation printed on the side. Lee, with a gleam in his eye said. "We all wanted to come and give you a proper welcome home."

It was at that moment an Apache war cry cut through the air reminding me of the many times I had heard that tone used on me. "Come here, James."

A young warrior steps out of the crowd, bubbling with excitement. "Yes, Grandfather! Is this your blood brother?"

Looking at the young man, my eyes glowing with a memory of a time I was filled with such exuberance and I had to ask, "Lee, where is this young warrior's Apache restraint?" From those gathered around came resounding laughter.

With that the, president of the council, Rance Valarde stepped forward. "*Da nzho.*"

"*Aoo da nzho.*"

"Jim, when you get settled in, come see me. We are in need of a traditional leader."

With his words, I felt the weight of the burden I had assumed so many years ago. Then as I looked into the cloudless azure sky there sitting in a pinon not far from the bus, a beautiful guardian eagle watches over me. I knew then and there my journey had begun.

REFERENCE MATERIALS

Foods the Jicarilla Apache consider taboo: https://www.aanativearts.com

Apache Healing Ritual-Medicine Dance: http://www.mpurplehawk.com/apdance.htm

"Apache" by Alan Wilson with Rita Vigil Martine

Site of the Jicarilla Apache Nation: www.Jicarillaonline.com\Home

Glossary of Jicarilla Apache Terms

Da nzho.	It is good.
Aoo da nzho.	Yes, it is good.
lii	horse
ligai isdzani	white woman
ha annsi shiitsooyee	grandfather
doo ansj	I am fine.
keesda	feast
kogha	home
Go-Jii-Yah	feast held in September since forced to live on the reservation
diide	people
ti gah li	sage
ze di dosh	sumac berries
k ii	sumac
tio gah li	like spinach with a red line running the length of the stem

shil del bal	like aspirin
DoodA	No
kat u tin	pollen
sitl'ideen	coyote
gwii bitseeghalee	rattlesnake
itsa	eagle
gozhish	time passes

LosiiDulce, New Mexico